Praise for A REAL SHOT IN THE ARM:

'A terrific début for a wholly sympathetic, wryly witty sleuthess'

The Times

'Whoops of delight for a clever and refreshing newcomer'

The Observer

'Outstanding ... a brilliant début'

The Independent

'Fast moving and funny with a totally credible heroine'

The Sunday Times

'A REAL SHOT IN THE ARM is a terrific read, and I can't wait for Annette Roome's next novel'

Simon Brett

and for A SECOND SHOT IN THE DARK:

'With its spirited heroine, its narrative drive and its splendid intracacy, this novel should put Annette Roome at the forefront of detective writing'

The Times Literary Supplement

'More Chris Martin, please'

The Observer

'Zestful mix of criminal and domestic comedy with droll, dyspeptic editor and flashy live-in lover. Home counties ambience is sharply observed. Encore! Encore!

The Guardian

About the author

Annette Roome won the Crime Writers Association John Creasey Award for best First Crime Novel with A REAL SHOT IN THE ARM in 1989. Its sequel, A SECOND SHOT IN THE DARK, which continues the story of Chris Martin, was published to wonderful critical acclaim in Hodder & Stoughton hardcover.

Annette Roome lives in Guildford. Her hobbies are the usual: gardening, filling her living-room with jungle plants and subjecting her family to cruel culinary experiments.

A Second Shot in the Dark

Annette Roome

NEW ENGLISH LIBRARY
Hodder and Stoughton

First published in Great Britain in
1990 by Hodder & Stoughton Ltd

*New English Library paperback
edition 1992*

*The characters and situations in this
book are entirely imaginary and bear
no relation to any real person or actual
happenings.*

British Library C.I.P.

Roome, Annette *1946–*
  A second shot in the dark.
  I. Title
  823.914[F]

ISBN 0-450-55343-4

Printed and bound in Great Britain for
Hodder and Stoughton Paperbacks, a
division of Hodder and Stoughton
Ltd., Mill Road, Dunton Green,
Sevenoaks, Kent TN13 2YA (Editorial
Office: 47 Bedford Square, London
WC1B 3DP) by Clays Ltd., St Ives plc.

For Liz,
with thanks for just being there
– and much, much more.

1

It was at three thirty on a Friday afternoon in mid-November
that I made the startling discovery that according to my diary
I didn't actually exist. I'd turned to the Personal Reminder
page to fill in my new address, and found that every single
entry – from Name to National Insurance Number – was as
blank as the screen of an unprogrammed Amstrad. All this
past year I had been a non-person. All this past year I had
had untyped blood coursing through a network of veins that
didn't apparently warrant any form of medical insurance. Of
course, the reason for this was simple. Keith had always kept
records of our National Health numbers and credit cards in a
locked, fireproof box to which he kept the key. It had been
Keith who filled in any kind of form which dropped through
our letter box, and Keith who worked out how much my
veins and their future were worth insuring for. Keith had
always taken care of me. I gritted my teeth and stared at
the blank spaces. Keith wouldn't be taking care of any part
of me any longer. I picked up my pen and wrote my new
address into the diary in bold blue capitals. Then I sat back
and stared at it, trying to get used to it.

Mr Heslop emerged from the Editor's office. I expected
him to give me one of his "it's not knocking off time yet"
looks. Instead he strolled towards me with a friendly grin,
and perched on the edge of my desk.

"Well, then," he began, sucking his stomach in slowly, in
the hope that I wouldn't notice this manoeuvre. "So today's
the big day, is it?"

I smiled as brightly as I could. "Yes. It all went as smooth
as clockwork. Even the removal men turned up on time."

"Good, good," he said. "So you've burnt all your bridges
now, have you? Well, well." He hesitated. "Just one thing,
Chris. A word of warning. I suppose you do realise that

someone who's spent half his life drinking and womanising isn't going to change overnight?"

I smiled sweetly. It wasn't the first time he'd given me this lecture. "Of course I do," I said.

But I didn't really. Not then.

"Good," said Mr Heslop.

Gillian, the latest in his line of secretaries, was approaching diffidently with a cup of tea and a tube of Sweetex.

"Awfully sorry if it's cold," she said, offering it to him. "I put it on top of my filing tray and forgot about it. Sorry."

"Not to worry," said Mr Heslop, forcing a smile. He took the tea reluctantly and watched Gillian's ungainly departure. She couldn't type properly or take shorthand, but she had a Sloane Ranger accent and was awfully thrilled to be working in journalism. I imagine her parents were awfully thrilled she'd found something to do to fill in her time between Ascot weeks.

"Nice girl," he remarked. "Not quite got the hang of things yet. Where was I?"

"What's that?" I interrupted, pointing at his saucer. "There's a letter stuck to the bottom of your tea."

"Oh, so there is." Using thumb and forefinger, he prised the envelope away from the saucer. It was marked by several brown caffeine rings and puckered from water staining. He pulled a letter from inside the envelope and handed it to me, still folded. "Have a look, will you? My eyes are playing up."

I spread the letter out on my desk. Using words cut from newspapers, somebody had written the message, "I have information of wrongdoings by a Hudderston businessman. All I ask is peace of mind. Ring Hudderston 23572, eight thirty p.m. Wednesday 4th". I stared at it. My immediate reaction was that it must be someone's idea of a joke, but I didn't want the very first anonymous letter I encountered to be a joke.

"Look at this!" I exclaimed. "Do you think it's genuine?"

Mr Heslop took it and peered at it. "Whatever it is, we're two weeks too late – *Gillian*." He frowned after her. "You know, if that girl's father wasn't Chairman of the Golf Club – "

"So what shall we do then? Send it to the police?"

"What, and make ourselves look like idiots? No. There's probably not much to it anyway – some small shopkeeper's been keeping two sets of books and his ex-mistress wants to tell someone about it. If the person who sent that letter really had something worth saying they'd've written again, wouldn't they? I'll bet it's a hoax anyway."

I studied the glue splotches on the blue notepaper. The letter had been put together by someone with an unsteady, troubled hand. It didn't look to me like a hoax.

Mr Heslop rose from the corner of my desk, which gave a groan of relief.

"Can I keep this?" I asked. "I could ring the number anyway."

"Go ahead. And then you might as well knock off early – I'm sure you've got some unpacking to do."

"Thank you," I said, surprised.

When he'd gone, I lifted my receiver and dialled Hudderston 23572. At the other end, the phone rang and rang. Finally the ringing stopped, and a breathless female voice enquired, "Tim. Is that you? I was just about to go!"

"Er, who is this?" I asked.

"Oh – Is that Tim's Mum?" responded the voice, sounding stronger now, and rather young. "Where is he? I've remembered to bring the maggots and everything."

"I'm afraid I don't know anyone called Tim," I said. "Can you tell me where this phone is, please?"

"It's outside the office," replied the voice, indignantly. "The payphone outside the office – you know."

"No, I'm afraid I *don't* know. Could you tell me what office you're talking about?"

"Oh *God*!" said the voice, in exasperation. "The office at Burymead County School, *dummy*!"

My receiver emitted an angry dialling tone. I replaced it and looked again at the note. "Kids," I muttered, thinking of my two. So the phone number given in the letter belonged to a payphone at a school – what did that mean? Well, most probably it meant that Mr Heslop was right, and the letter was a hoax. Rather a pointless one, too; surely even a juvenile hoaxer could have come up with somewhere more embarrassing for us to ring – like a VD clinic, or one of those advice lines where they give you recorded advice about incontinence, and so forth.

I screwed up the letter, tossed it at the wastepaper basket, and began collecting up my things for a quick getaway. I might have made it too, if the lamb chops in my shopping bag hadn't thawed and leaked blood on to our new office carpet. I was scrubbing frantically at the stain when Mr Heslop put a hand on my shoulder. "Glad I caught you," he said. "I've just heard. Someone's found a body in Cottis Wood."

"A body?" I placed my foot over the bloodstain and stood up. "Oh, how awful."

He rubbed his hands. "It's just what we need, actually. Our circulation figures are down five per cent this month, and our advertising revenue is *thirteen per cent* below last year's – Cross your fingers and pray for a murder."

I was only mildly shocked. I'd worked for Mr Heslop for a year.

"Well, don't just stand there! Find out where this wretched place is and get over there," he said, urgently. "There's already a TV crew on their way down – This could be the big story we're looking for to get our figures back up!"

I pulled a face and reached for my notebook.

"You can go straight home afterwards," offered Mr Heslop, generously.

Cottis Wood is halfway between Tipping and Hudderston, located amid that no-man's-land of ploughed fields, clustered copses and electricity pylons that passes for the open countryside. It got darker as I headed out along the dual carriageway. Flocks of starlings swirled against the night sky and melted into the blackness of the fields. I slowed, almost missing my turn-off. "Manning Green, 3, Institute for the Rehabilitation of the Chronically Mentally Ill, 4", said the sign, and I had this silly thought about there being nothing ahead except madness and death. Something like that. I shivered, switching my headlamps to full beam, and the lights bounced back at me from the hedgerows bordering the narrow road. If only I hadn't been taken in by that hoax letter I could've been halfway home now, instead of

– Suddenly, just beyond a sharp bend, I had to brake to avoid a large vehicle with its brake lights glaring. It was a BBC outside broadcast van. Beyond it, the rotating blue lamps of three police cars sent splinters of light zigzagging among the trees. I wound down my window and the chatter and squeak of police radios came in with a drift of cold, damp air. The BBC van was apparently parked as close as a sheet of wallpaper to the front window of one of a pair of cottages overlooking the entrance to the wood. I manoeuvred the Mini as close to it as I could.

"Christ, are you parking there?" came a shout from behind.

I looked in my rear view mirror. A white Fiesta had almost piled into my bumper, and because I recognised the driver as a reporter from the *Hudderston Advertiser* (a paper which could boast a larger circulation and fewer printing errors than the *Tipping Herald*), and because in any case I was no more of an obstruction than the van, I ignored him. He got out of his car, leaving the door open, and strode towards the policeman on duty at the gate into Cottis Wood. I leaned out of my window to listen.

The *Advertiser* reporter flashed his Press card.

"What's all this about?" he asked, briskly.

The sergeant gave him a cagey look. "We'll have to see, won't we, sir? All I know is it's a woman and she's got gunshot wounds."

"All right. When will we be getting a statement?"

The sergeant pulled the sort of face builders go in for when they inspect a fault in your damp proof course. "Couldn't say, sir. DI Carver's in charge. You'll have to wait for him to finish back there." He inclined his head towards the wood.

"Well, I hope it won't be long! It's gone four now – and it's *Friday*, you know."

The sergeant, who probably had a long shift ahead of him, grinned maliciously. If there's one thing I've learned about crime scenes, it's that nobody really wants to be there – starting with the victim but excluding bystanders.

The *Advertiser* reporter returned to his car, muttering, and began making notes. Beyond the sergeant three police officers with torches were picking things up from the track and depositing them in plastic bags. Two men in anoraks leaned against what was left of a rusty wire fence, poring over a newspaper in the light from the blue lamps. I guessed they were BBC technicians. They looked up as I opened the car door and got out, and smirked as my high heels sank into the soft chocolate mud at the side of the road.

"You're as bad as Shona, love," one of them said. "You don't dress for the occasion."

I smiled, and didn't bother to explain that I'd dressed like this to report a Council meeting earlier in the day.

"What are they doing?" I asked, pointing to the policemen with the plastic bags.

"Collecting evidence, love." He pulled a clingfilm wrapped sandwich from his pocket, then glanced at his watch. "Where the hell's bloody Shona?" he demanded, of his companion. "We'll never make the six o'clock news at this rate."

I was awed. "This is going to be on the six o'clock news?" I asked, realising that the Shona they'd mentioned was a well-known TV reporter.

He nodded, then leaned forward conspiratorially. "The word we had – although monkey-mouth over there won't confirm it – is that this is another Face Murder. Number Five, isn't it, Ken?"

Ken looked up from the sports page of the *Mirror*, but said nothing.

"A *Face Murder*?" I repeated.

"Yes." He bit into the sandwich, then continued talking through masticated ham and bread. "Didn't you see that Beeb Two documentary on serial killers last week? It was good stuff. They did Peter Sutcliffe and that Nielson chap as well. This Face Murderer, what he does is sneak up on women from behind and then bash 'em over the head. He did the first two with a brick, but now he's moved on to lengths of pipe, apparently. Anyway, then he picks 'em up and takes 'em to the woods and shoots their faces off with a shotgun."

Ken looked up. "You know what makes me sick," he said. "They paid this bloody expert from an American university to come on the programme and tell us that the guy does it

12

because he doesn't like women. Christ, I could've told them that. You just wouldn't want to know where your licence fee goes, love."

The man with the ham sandwich finished the last morsel and wiped his hands on his anorak. "It's something to do with the face being a person's identity. This nutcase wants to destroy women completely, so he's got to knock off the face." He shrugged. "They don't know if he gets a sexual kick out of it or not." He looked at his watch again. "That's it! We've *had* the six o'clock! They must've sent Shona out on the BBC bike."

"Don't be stupid," said Ken. "Shona *is* the BBC bike!"

They both laughed uproariously.

There was a sudden flurry of activity at the gate into Cottis Wood. A man in a dark blue suit had appeared and was conferring with the sergeant. The *Advertiser* reporter emerged from his car and we all clustered expectantly round the gate.

"Right, gentlemen," said the man in the suit, appearing to do a quick head count of those in attendance. "I'm DI Carver, and I'll be in charge of this investigation. Would you all like to follow me, please? And keep to the path, if you wouldn't mind."

The sergeant opened the gate and we trooped through. I managed to hang back. I didn't want to have to look at the body. We followed the Inspector's muddied trousers along a pot-holed, tarmacked track to a point where limp fluorescent tape barred our way.

"If you look along there," said the Inspector, pointing into the woods, "you'll be able to see the body."

A pathway of trampled long grass led between trees to a small clearing, in the centre of which glaring white floodlights illuminated a long, low mound covered by a green tarpaulin. After a moment, I identified the small pale object protruding from the edge of the tarpaulin as a foot. Around the mound, white marker pegs threw long shadows.

"Right," said the Inspector. "The victim is a woman. She's obviously been dead for several days, and though I can't of course give you exact cause of death at the moment, initial examination leads me to believe she may have been the latest victim of the killer you people call the 'Face Murderer'."

We all made notes. The Inspector was smiling, and rubbing his hands as though cold in his thin suit. He waited until we'd finished writing, and then said. "We've had a stroke of luck on this one. We've already found a witness whose information may lead to the identification of the killer."

There was a murmur of surprise. The Inspector rubbed his hands again. "Yes, gentlemen," he said. "Our investigations have turned up three local residents who can pinpoint the time of the shotgun blast as nine p.m. last Tuesday evening. They all saw a vehicle, a – maroon – Ford – Granada – " He enunciated the words separately and carefully. " – parked in the layby at the entrance to the wood. And one of these witnesses had the presence of mind to make a note of the vehicle registration number."

"Jesus!" exclaimed one of the BBC men.

"Does that mean we can expect the murderer to be arrested and brought to Hudderston within the next few days?" asked the *Advertiser* reporter.

"I think that's a very strong possibility, yes," agreed the Inspector, happily.

"Have you ID'd the victim yet?"

The Inspector shook his head.

"A handbag was found close to the body, but it did not contain any obvious means of identification," he said, pronouncing the first "a" in the phrase "a handbag" so as to rhyme it with the "a" in "hay". I think there must be a police training manual somewhere that instructs officers, when addressing the Press and public, to pronounce the indefinite article as the "a" in "hay", and to refer to cars as vehicles. "And so far no one fitting her description has been reported missing. She's approximately 5'4" tall, aged between twenty and thirty, slim build, short fair hair – Clothing includes a tailored red jacket, grey skirt, white blouse and black shoes."

"Had she been sexually assaulted?" asked the *Advertiser* reporter.

"We don't know yet."

"Don't you think it's odd no one's reported her missing?" I asked. "Was she wearing a wedding ring?"

14

He consulted his notes. "She was indeed, yes."

"And who found the body?" I asked.

"The body was found," began DI Carver pedantically, "by a Miss Corby from Hound House, which is just up the road from here. She was walking her dog, so rather an appropriate house name in the circumstances."

Someone tittered obligingly at this little joke.

My eyes became fixed on a small black object at the side of the path, half hidden by bedraggled fronds of bracken. A gleam of light reflected from it. It was a patent stiletto heeled shoe with a bow at the ankle.

"Is that the victim's shoe?" I asked, pointing to it.

DI Carver referred to his notes again. "Yes, it's been matched with the one on her foot. Presumably it fell off while the murderer was transporting the body." He peered closely at his wristwatch. "Well, gentlemen, if there are no further questions I suggest we call it a day. We'll be issuing a statement as soon as we've picked up the owner of the Granada." He gave a smug smile. "Right. Now if you will just keep to the path again on your way out, please – "

The BBC men made a dash for their van, and the *Advertiser* reporter took the opportunity to pigeonhole the Inspector in an attempt to get some additional titbit of information out of him. I don't think he succeeded. I walked back to the Mini alone, thinking that somewhere there was a husband missing a wife, possibly a child its mother, and that it was odd that no one had so far reported this fact. If I'd lain dead in Cottis Wood since Tuesday night, quite a few people would have started to wonder where I was – even if only because they wanted to know what had become of their ironing.

I was about to cross the road to my car when a man on a bike without lights swerved to a sudden stop in front of me.

"Hello. You from the telly?" he asked.

I was flattered.

"No. *Tipping Herald*."

"Oh." He looked disappointed. "I'm the one that took the car number. Want to interview me?"

Actually, I wanted to go home, but this seemed too good an opportunity to miss. He told me his name was Mr Blunt, and that he was forty-two. In fact, he looked the wrong side of fifty, but I didn't argue.

"The police must be very pleased with you," I said. "Tell me, what made you take the number of the Granada? Did you actually see the man carrying the body, or something?"

"Well, no, not exactly," he admitted, reluctantly. "I live along there, see, just outside Manning Green. I come out about – what? – half-eight last Tuesday with me old dog. He's gettin' on a bit now, like – in the old days he used to take himself off for miles – come back with the odd rabbit or two, an' all!" I shifted from foot to foot, cold and impatient. "So as I come along I seen this car parked in the layby – right there," he added, pointing to where a police car now stood. "Well, I lets me dog off up the track to do his business, like, and I gets out me torch to have a look at the car."

"Why?"

"Well." He looked down at his bike pedal uncomfortably, and kicked it. "Thought it was a courting couple, didn't I? Sometimes you get a right eyeful – better'n Channel 4!"

"I see."

"Well, there wasn't nobody in the car. He must've been off, see, in the woods with the body, doing whatever he does to them," he added, with gruesome speculation. I gave him no encouragement. "So when me old dog comes back, I turns to go. I gets to that tree down there, see – " He paused dramatically. " – and there's this almighty bang. I thought it was one of them electricity substations blowing up, didn't I, so I runs off home to the missus. My missus looks better in the dark," he added, laughing and leaning forward to nudge me. He looked me up and down searchingly. He was exactly my idea of a Peeping Tom, right down to the cycle clips and trousers secured beneath the armpits by a piece of string.

"So you wrote down the number of the Granada," I prompted, sharply.

He moved closer, his breath steaming into my face.

"Not me, missus. I'm a dab hand with numbers. Once seen, always remembered, that's me. I know all me friends' phone numbers. I know the number of the milkman's van and the postman. Go on, try me – ask me one."

I took a step backwards.

"And I take it there weren't any other cars parked nearby?"

"Why should there be? There's nothing here except the wood. Those two cottages over there, there's an old couple living at No. 1. They've got kids but they never come visiting. And her at No. 2 – well, she's a weirdo, know what I mean?" He waved a finger close to his head in a circular motion. "No – that car what I saw – that was the killer's car, all right. I should've known he was up to no good, a night like that. It'd been pouring with rain all day, and the mud was ankle deep. I should've known it was too grim for courting. They save it up for spring, don't they? You should see some of the things – "

Clearly, this was a topic best not pursued.

"Thank you," I said, retreating. "You've been most helpful."

"Don't I get no fee?" he shouted.

"Sorry!" I called, getting into the car.

I did a three-point turn and got away from there, fast. I didn't like the place one bit. I didn't like the image I was going to be left with of a woman's foot sticking out from beneath a tarpaulin, and I didn't like the thought of all the hatred that had put her there. I also didn't much like the man whose allegedly photographic memory looked set to lead the police to the Face Murderer; if I was a detective I would certainly not place much credence on the testimony of someone whose trousers were held up by string.

Still, one way or another, it looked as though Mr Heslop was going to get his big story.

2

The kitchen was barely visible for boxes and carrier bags stacked precariously on every inch of worktop. Sun streamed in through a window hazed with someone else's ten-year build-up of cooking fat, and I sat at the kitchen table with Pete's pyjama top wrapped round me, drinking coffee. Pete was scrambling eggs and cooking toast. I felt like eight out of ten cats who've just spent a night at the Whiskas factory.

"Do you realise," I said, warming my hands on the coffee. "That that was the first night we've ever spent together?"

"No, it wasn't. Don't you remember that night you came round to my flat at three a.m., after Keith came home drunk and tried to drag you into his bed? You put your coat on over your nightie and turned up in the middle of the night."

"Oh." I thought I'd succeeded in erasing that memory. "All right, but we didn't actually *sleep* much that night, did we?"

He smiled and traced the dark circles under my eyes with a gentle finger. "We didn't actually sleep much last night either," he said. "Which is why I want to put lots of protein into you this morning, or you won't keep up the pace."

"Oh!" I exclaimed. "Promises!"

He tipped a mountain of scrambled eggs on to a plate and surrounded it with halved slices of toast. He was wearing a torn tee-shirt and a pair of Marks and Spencers briefs, and he needed a shave, but when he leaned over me with the plate the scent of his skin and yesterday's aftershave went straight to the lower regions of my stomach.

"You spoil me," I said, kissing the small black hairs on his forearm.

"Don't kid yourself, darling. All my girlfriends get this the first morning." He sat down and looked searchingly at me. "No regrets?"

"No. Well – just the odd pang, perhaps. But I'll feel fine once we get this place sorted out," I added quickly. "How about you?"

"Don't be silly! What could I possibly regret?"

I shrugged. "Loss of freedom?"

"Loss of freedom – loss of freedom to do what? Sit at home and wonder what it's all for, or go out to the pub and watch people twenty years younger than me doing all the things I did twenty years ago? Don't be daft." He switched on the radio. It was playing Elvis Presley's "The Wonder of You", and for two blissful minutes I let myself listen to it and believe in it and eat my eggs and feel absolutely wonderful.

"Right," said Pete, whisking the plates away. "So what are we doing today?"

I was galvanised into action. "I've got to get Julie's bedroom sorted out before she comes home on Monday. And we ought to make downstairs look reasonable in case anybody comes. Have you got a Payless catalogue?"

"A what?"

"A Payless catalogue. Or B & Q or Wickes, or any of the big DIY stores. Only before we decide where everything goes I think we ought to give a thought to colour schemes and shelves, and have you noticed – " I went on to categorise various defects I'd noticed in the décor of the house.

He dropped a spoon into the washing up bowl and stared at me in mild astonishment. "Oh yes," he said. "I'd forgotten about all that."

The voice of the radio newsreader echoed among the packing cases.

". . . *You're listening to Three Counties Radio this fine Saturday morning, and here is your local news bulletin.*

"*Hudderston police are confident that it's only a matter of time before a man is arrested and charged with the brutal murder of a woman in Cottis Wood last Tuesday night. The woman, who has still not been identified, is thought to be the fifth victim of the killer known as the Face Murderer, although Hudderston police will not confirm that at this stage. They say thanks must go to sharp eyed local resident, Mr Charles Blunt, who took the registration number of a Ford Granada parked*

19

at the scene. We go over now to our reporter Linda Craven, who spoke to Mr Blunt at his home earlier this morning.

"*Well,*" said the voice of he with the cycle clips and precariously secured trousers. "*I was walking me old dog like I does every night when I sees this . . .*"

I turned the volume down on Mr Blunt.

"Did you hear about our murder?" I asked. Pete had recently left the *Tipping Herald* for a job on a national newspaper. In common with most people who finally get what they want, he was doing his best to like it.

He laughed. "You know, you really are sweet. Only someone who'd spent all their life in Tipping would want to claim a murder as their own."

"Don't be patronising. I was out at Cottis Wood last night. I saw the body."

"The Face Murderer," said Pete. "I think I've got some cuttings somewhere on him. I'll look them out for you. Is he the one who bashes women over the head? The police think he might be a lorry driver, don't they, because he usually strikes near motorways?"

"I don't know. *We're* not near a motorway."

He carried on washing up in silence and I was beginning to feel guilty, when he said, "While we're on the subject of mindless cruelty, you don't mind if we pop over to Maidstone this evening so I can introduce you to Lucrezia Borgia?"

I grimaced. "That's not a very good start, talking about your ex-wife like that. And I don't really want to go. I want us to be alone together without anything spoiling it. And there's so much to do here. Couldn't we put it off for a week or two?"

He took his hands out of the sink and dried them on a tea towel.

"Darling, nothing's going to spoil things between us. The truth is, I haven't seen the kids since the summer. I missed Catherine's birthday. I want you to get to know them so they can come and stay occasionally – in time, that is. I know they'll like you. I want to make a new start with them, and I'd like them to be in on us right from the beginning before they hear about you from someone else. Don't you think that's best?"

I relented guiltily. "Yes, of course. You're absolutely right."

We had driven for two hours along rainswept motorways to Maidstone; my legs were cramped and my eyes dazzled by oncoming lights – and then Pete made his confession.

"I don't believe this," I said. "I just don't believe it. How could you drive all this way without phoning them first to ask if it was OK? You said you'd arranged it."

Our headlights picked out the signboard at the end of his ex-wife's road. With the ease of someone who has made the same manoeuvre many times, he followed the wide arc of the bend and swung quickly into a driveway, stopping inches from the rear of the car already parked there.

"I *was* going to phone. I did try. Twice. But both times I put the phone down before anyone answered. Honestly, telling them about you over the phone just didn't seem the right thing to do." He flashed me his beguiling smile. "They'll be delighted to see us, believe me."

"I won't forgive you for this," I hissed, thinking that I almost meant it.

We got out of the car. We were standing in front of a very nice detached house – double glazing, Elizabethan style front door, the works. Almost exactly the sort of home Keith and I had hoped to own. And once it had been Pete's, but if he was experiencing any twinges of nostalgia, he kept them to himself.

The doorbell was answered by a small blonde woman wearing a scruffy grey tracksuit and eating a doughnut. Her chin glistened with sugar grains. It dawned on me very slowly that this must be Helen, because from Pete's description of her I'd built up an identikit of a woman who was a cross between Medusa and Attila the Hun, complete with blood red fingernails and a dagger in her right boot. "*Pete?*" she queried, her expression changing from surprise to incredulity. "What on *earth* are you doing here?"

He leaned forward and kissed her on the cheek.

"It's been a long time, darling, and you still taste sweet," he said. "How are the kids? Are they in?"

"Yes, of course they're in. They're watching the – Look, you weren't supposed to be coming this weekend, were you? Have I forgotten?" She pushed the remains of the doughnut absently into her pocket, and wiped her hands on her trouser leg. Then she noticed my hovering presence.

"This is Chris," said Pete. "Chris – Helen."

We shook hands stickily.

"You'd better come in," she said, beginning to look cross. Her hair was tucked into a paint stained headscarf, and her eyeshadow had formed thick blue creases in her eyesockets. She opened a door. "*Your father's here*," she hissed threateningly to the occupants of the room. There was no response. "*Catherine*!" hissed Helen.

"Sssh, Mum!" croaked an adolescent male voice angrily. "Give us the remote, Andy, I can't hear a bloody word!"

Pete took my hand and led me into the room. He pushed me in front of the TV screen, a move that provoked instinctive protests from the three children sprawled on the sofa amid a welter of crisp packets and torn pages of the TV Times.

"This is Chris," said Pete, smiling at me and kissing my forehead. "Chris is the new lady in our lives. We're thinking of getting married."

There was silence. "*Asshole*," said the TV set. "*If you and that pile of shit ain't out of my yard by the time I count to three they'll be picking up bits of you in Miami. One – two –*"

Three pairs of eyes raised slowly to our faces.

"Oh – Hi, Dad!" one of the boys said.

"*Three, asshole*!" said the television.

"Oh God!" said Helen, and walked out of the room.

The children eventually managed to tear their eyes away from the TV screen long enough to open the presents Pete had brought them, and to shake hands with me. They didn't look particularly enthusiastic about either me or the presents, but they were achingly polite. If Pete was disappointed, he hid it well.

"I really don't know what you expected, Pete," Helen said

resignedly, as we left the children to their sanctuary. "They haven't heard from you for ages, and you suddenly turn up out of the blue and tell them this! You can't expect them to take an interest in you if you don't show any interest in them."

"I've always been interested in them, you know that," he protested, hurt. "The fact is, I've been very busy. I was winning this fair lady away from her husband."

"I'm sure," she agreed, tartly. She gave him a searching look.

"I'm very pleased for you," she said. "John'll be back in a minute. He took next-door's hot air paint-stripper back. We were going to spend the evening decorating the extension. Would you like to see it?"

We stepped over cans of emulsion paint and baled up dustsheets, and I made the right sort of noises about the extension. The smell of fresh paint filled me with enthusiasm for our new home, and I hoped it was having the same effect on Pete.

Our stilted conversation was suddenly interrupted by the sound of the front door opening and closing.

"You won't believe this, darling," came a deep male bellow from the hall, "but there's a car blocking our drive *exactly* like that old rustbucket your dearly beloved, thank-Christ-long-since-departed ex-husband used to run people over with. What these middle-aged would-be James Deans see in clapped out old MGBs beats the hell – " He stopped in the doorway, staring at us open-mouthed.

"Pete's here," said Helen, unnecessarily. "And this is Chris, his – er – his new fiancée."

"Ah," John said, dropping several rolls of wallpaper and watching them scatter across the dustsheets. "Ah."

"Hallo," I smiled and patted the middle-aged James Dean's arm soothingly. "I'm awfully sorry we didn't let you know we were coming – "

"That's all right. No problem," said John, eyeing Pete warily. "No problem. Sorry about the mess. Well, well. This is a surprise. We often wonder what old Pete gets up to. Well, well."

Pete smiled disarmingly. "I've sold the flat," he said.

"We've bought a house. It's a bit smaller than this one – "
A lot smaller than this one. " – but there are two spare
bedrooms. Chris's eldest son has left home and her daughter
is about Catherine's age, so they could share. Maybe we
could fix something up around Christmas time."

Everybody present looked alarmed, including me.

"Ah," said John again, exchanging glances with Helen.
"Well, of course this all needs sorting out. You're not still
living near Hudderston, are you?"

"Yes, Tipping," I said. "It's about six miles from
Hudderston. Do you know it?"

He shook his head.

"Don't you really?" queried Helen. "I thought you knew
everywhere. John's Business Development Manager for Zircon Water Softeners," she explained. "He's like a walking
road atlas at times. You know where Tipping is though,
don't you?"

"I know where it is, but – "

"Oh, the Face Murderer!" exclaimed Helen, suddenly.
"The latest Face Murder was in Hudderston – I knew
something had made me think of Pete this morning!"

"Thank you very much, darling," Pete said, ironically.

"Do you know, I'm not a feminist," began Helen.

"Yes, you are," interrupted Pete.

" – but I've always thought that if people went round
picking *men* off the streets at random and killing them
there'd be such an outcry something would get done."

"For a start, you'd give them a medal, wouldn't you,
darling?"

"Shut up," said Helen. "You don't change, do you?"

John cleared his throat. "Why don't we open a bottle
of something to celebrate?" he suggested. "How about
all that sparkling stuff we brought back from France last
summer?"

I expect it was the wine that did it, but we all got along so
well after that that Pete and I ended up spending the night
under a duvet on the Redferns' sofa bed. This wouldn't have
been my first choice for enjoying a romantic second night
with my new lover, but there wasn't a lot I could do about

it. I suppose that's the difference between being twenty and being forty: you've learned not to pout openly.

In the morning I was trying to look competent in Helen's kitchen, when she appeared, clad this time in a very smart cerise jogging suit.

"Sorry," she said, "about last night. I hope I didn't seem unwelcoming."

"You didn't, really."

"I hope we can be friends," said Helen, adding, "God, isn't that pathetic! Why shouldn't we be friends? Actually, it's the children I worry about." She sat down on a kitchen stool and lowered her voice the way people do when they're about to utter some sort of truth. "Look, Pete thinks I've turned the kids against him, but I haven't. It's just that John's here and he's not and John's the one who's been a father to them for the last five years. That's a long time for a child. Is he still drinking?"

"Well – "

"Yes, and he's still charming," said Helen acidly, folding her arms. "I don't want them to have to go through all the hurt of being picked up again and then dropped."

"Oh, I'm sure he wouldn't!" I protested, wishing I hadn't been drawn into this conversation.

"Yes, but you don't know him as well as I do, do you?" she said, and I wished even more strongly that I wasn't having this conversation. "He put me through hell, I can tell you, and if it hadn't been for John coming along when he did I don't know what would have happened to us. Sorry to sound so dramatic, but you see my position, don't you? So if – "

Our attention was suddenly caught by a man in police uniform walking across Helen's back garden. He was talking into a radio, and appeared to be signalling to someone just out of sight behind him.

"My God," said Helen.

"I don't want to worry anyone," John said, putting his head round the kitchen door. "But two police cars have just pulled up out front."

Helen touched a hand to her mouth. "I expect it'll be one of Pete's little traffic misdemeanours," she murmured.

There was a heavy pounding on the front door, accompanied by the shrill insistence of the bell.

"I'll go," said John. Helen and I followed him out.

Standing in the porch was a man in a blue suit. I knew I'd seen him before, but it took a few seconds for the memory to punch itself into the right holes.

"Mr John Redfern?" It was DI Carver, and he was one hundred and fifty miles from Hudderston Central.

"Yes."

My imagination raced into overdrive. The Face Murderer – Julie – an accident – Richard –

"Mr Redfern, I'm Detective Inspector Carver of Hudderston Central police station. Is this your Ford Granada, sir, registration E969 CPK?"

Behind DI Carver, in front of Pete's dark green MGB, and flanked by two uniformed officers, I saw for the first time a maroon Ford Granada.

"Well – yes," agreed John, frowning.

The Inspector regarded him suspiciously, as though this reply had not been as positive or as full as it might have been. He nodded.

"I see, sir. In that case, I would ask you to get your coat and accompany me to my vehicle, sir. I shall be taking you back with me to Hudderston, so it would be appropriate for you to advise your wife accordingly.

John's mouth dropped. He paled visibly. "Why? What for?"

Helen said, "The Granada's a company car, Inspector. I can give you the name of the rental people, if you like. We don't have anything to do with getting the tax or – "

"Thank you, madam, that won't be necessary," DI Carver interrupted. "This *is* a matter concerning the car, but I'm not interested in the documentation at this stage."

Oddly, John's colour returned. If a policeman had questioned me about my car, my mind would have rewound itself along every road where I'd breathed in while passing a line of parked cars. But as I stood in the doorway watching a young Detective Constable take possession of John's Granada, I could think of only one thing: a senior CID officer would not give up his Sunday morning with the

26

Telegraph, or his pre-lunch gin and tonic in the lounge bar of the Crown Hotel, for anything as minor as a knocked off wing mirror or a road fund licence. He would not give up his Sunday morning lightly at all – not for anything less than a murder.

3

I found the paracetamol tablets, packed in the same tea chest as the bathroom scales.

"It's absolutely unbelievable," I remarked, for probably the sixth time that morning. "The police picking up someone like John, purely on the strength of one witness's statement. That man obviously remembered the number wrongly. You'd think they'd do some checking before disrupting people's lives like that. How long do you think they'll keep him?"

Pete was sitting on the stairs, reading through his little book of phone numbers. He glanced up, and said patiently, "You're not looking at it from DI Carver's point of view, are you, darling? Look, every force in the country would sell their Chief Constable's grandmother to nail the Face Murderer. There'd be promotions all the way along the line."

"What will happen now?" I persisted.

He thought about it. "Oh, DI Carver will go home and kick the cat, or the wife, or both – yes, both I should think. And then he'll issue a new statement to the effect that the police are following up other lines of enquiry." He produced a pen from his pocket and circled an entry in the book. "That's the guy," he muttered.

"I *meant*, what will happen to John?"

He grinned, and there was a hint of malice in it. "They'll give him a tight lipped apology and his rail fare home. Don't worry, they only use rubber truncheons these days."

The paracetamol wasn't helping my head at all. "You don't seem to be taking this very seriously," I said sharply.

"Of course I'm not! You don't imagine John could be the Face Murderer, do you? Believe me, this time next week he'll be sitting in his favourite spot at the Royal Oak downing free pints on the strength of his 'how I was wrongly arrested by the police' story. He'll dine out on it for ages."

I was feeling cold as well as hung over. I turned up the thermostat on the hall wall, noting the pattern of greasy fingermarks that surrounded it. They were alien fingermarks, and not nice to look at.

"*I* don't think John could be the Face Murderer," I said, thoughtfully. "But it occurs to me that if the police are looking for someone who uses motorways a lot – and because they don't know John like we do – " Pete lifted the telephone on to the step next to him and began dialling a number. "Well, I don't know. One hears these things – "

He shook his head impatiently. "Make me a cup of coffee, will you, darling?" he said.

"Who are you ringing?"

"A DC I know at Hudderston Central. Here." He reached into his jacket pocket and brought out a small silver flask. "Put a drop of that in the coffee, will you? Oh, morning." He smiled pleasantly into the telephone. "It's a busy day down there, is it? Is DC Dave Barrett in, by any chance?"

I went into the kitchen and filled the kettle.

"Oh, hi, Dave," Pete said. "Pete Schiavo. Remember? – Yes, that's right – And last Christmas, as well, at the Bull's Head – " There was a long silence. "Yes. I remember. You're kidding! What, not the one whose husband had just had a vasectomy? Jesus! In the back of a bloody Panda car as well! You boys have all the luck – Listen, I wonder if you could do me a small favour – "

So that's how it's done, I thought. I made the coffee and took it out to him. He covered the mouthpiece with his hand.

"They're questioning John now," he said. "They can't tell me much, but – " He returned to the phone. "Thanks, Dave. Yes, that's great. I've got it. I owe you one." He put the phone down, looking pleased with himself. "Thanks, darling. We're in luck. The victim's husband has just identified her. She was a Mrs Rosemary Tindall and I've got her address – Tucker Hill Road, Hudderston. Do you know it?"

"Yes, but I don't really see how this will help John."

He smiled patiently. "Please don't worry about John. This

is obviously a case of mistaken identity – I doubt if he'll even need a solicitor to sort it out for him. Come on, get your coat. Let's get in first with an exclusive on the victim."

We cruised slowly along Tucker Hill Road, which was deserted, except for a red-faced jogger and a couple of learner drivers attempting hill starts. It was one of those streets that appear to have happened by accident and to have always been part of the landscape: the houses were not identical, and instead of standing to attention in regimented rows occupied tasteful poses amongst well established trees. It was a street I wouldn't have minded living in.

Pete produced his notebook, and we studied Rosemary Tindall's house. It was a large chalet bungalow with a conservatory in the front. A Swiss Cheese plant pressed its leaves against the conservatory window, as though seeking escape, and the front garden was darkened by the spreading branches of a monkey puzzle tree. Pete made notes in his book. He got out of the car.

"You stay here," he said, as I began to follow him up the garden path. "And watch to see if anything moves when I ring the bell."

He climbed the steps to the front door and pressed the bell. Somewhere, distantly, a dog barked and one of the learner drivers revved desperately. Inside the bungalow, as far as I could tell, nothing moved. All the curtains were drawn.

"Anything?" called Pete.

I shook my head.

He shrugged, cupping a hand to the glass and attempting to peer inside. "Maybe they're in, maybe they're not. Let's take a look round the back."

I opened my mouth to protest, but he'd opened the side gate and I went through it. All the curtains at the rear of the bungalow were closed too, and the small back garden looked stark and empty apart from a rotary clothes line bedecked with blackened pegs. A half filled rubbish sack lay next to the back door, and there was a tangle of hose pipe attached to an outside tap. I touched it with my foot, and the coils shifted to reveal their outlines etched in dust and leaf debris. Someone had neglected to sweep the patio and tidy up after the summer.

The garage was separate from the house and Pete opened a side door and looked inside. In the gloom, we could make out the shape of a bright yellow 2CV, a lawnmower, and a cardboard box almost full of newspapers.

"When was this woman killed?" asked Pete.

"Last Tuesday."

"Hmm. That means she was missing for almost six full days before the husband bothered to report it. Why do you think that was? I think they must have been separated, don't you? Let's go and have a chat with the neighbours."

Two doors up the hill from the Tindalls' bungalow a man in smart overalls was shampooing a blue Sierra estate car. A sharp north wind rattled the dry clusters of seed pods on the laburnum tree, bringing down scatterings of leaves. Her brow furrowed with stoic determination, a woman in matching overalls pulled a garden rake vigorously across the front lawn in pursuit of the leaves.

"Hallo," said Pete, smiling. "We're with the Press, and – "

"Oh! We're with the Woolwich!" exclaimed the man, and turned round to see if his wife had appreciated his humour. She hadn't. He laughed anyway. So did Pete.

"Do you know the Tindalls at No. 53?"

He shrugged. "Yes, I suppose so. Why?"

Pete pretended to be searching his pockets for something. "Have they lived in the bungalow long?"

The man looked puzzled and suspicious. "About three years, I think. Why? Have they won the pools or something?"

Pete smiled again, and almost nodded. "I just want some general information – their ages, number of children, that sort of thing."

The man looked to his wife for assistance. He tossed the foam laden sponge on to the roof of the Sierra and placed his hands on his hips.

"Look here," he began. "I know my rights. You can't – "

"Did you know you've got a couple of scratches here?" interrupted Pete, delicately stroking the side of the car. "It looks like it's been reversed into a bush."

"*Does it?*" He turned to his wife again, this time with menace.

"I should try some T-Cut," suggested Pete. "It's magic, that stuff. How old did you say the Tindalls were?"

"Oh, I don't know. Mid to late twenties." He walked round the car to examine the scratches. "Bloody hell, Margaret, how did you do that?"

"And how many children have they got?"

"They haven't got any bloody kids! *Margaret!*"

"*I* didn't do that!" countered Margaret, defiantly, handing me her rake. "It must have been that hydrangea by Mother's front gate."

"Are you telling me the hydrangea was driving the bloody car? Is that what you're saying?"

"No – I – "

"Do they get on well together?" interrupted Pete.

"What do you mean?" asked Margaret.

"Well, would you say they were happily married?"

"Oh, yes, definitely. I'm always remarking on that to Frank – aren't I, darling? – on how close they are. They do everything together. Do you know, I've even seen him helping her hang out the washing. And the shopping. He always goes with – "

"There's a dent here!" shouted Frank, suddenly. "A bloody great dent! How did you do that?"

"So you'd say they were a devoted couple, would you?" persisted Pete.

"Oh, absolutely! It's so rare to see it," Margaret added, scowling at her husband.

"Will you kindly tell me how you managed to put a dent like this in my car without noticing?" demanded Frank. "Look at that!"

"Oh, don't be silly, it's just a tiny little knock – nothing to get excited about. I expect Mother's gate blew on to it, or something. If you don't mind I'm talking to this gentleman."

Pete winked at her sympathetically. "And what do they do for a living?"

"He's a computer programmer," she said. "And she's a secretary. They're very quiet and keep very much to

32

themselves. She sometimes comes round collecting for the Church or delivering the parish magazine. I wouldn't have thought they were the kind of people to do the pools. I say, shouldn't you be asking *them* these questions?"

"I'd love to, darling, but they seem to be out and I've got a deadline. Who did you say she worked for?"

"She works for Taylors, the heating people. They used to service our boiler for us, but I understand they've stopped doing maintenance work these days. Just as well, really, because *Frank* was always arguing with them about their bills and it could have been embarrassing, couldn't it, with Rosemary working for them."

"Oh, I know Taylors," I remarked. "*My* husband used to argue with them about their bills as well." And then I blushed, because this was a stupid thing to say.

Pete frowned at me. "You've been very helpful," he said to Margaret, gratefully. "One last thing – did it come as a great shock to you, in view of what you said, when you realised the Tindalls were no longer living together?"

Margaret's mouth gaped in surprise. "Not living together?" she repeated. "Aren't they really? But – " A light dawned in her eyes. "Now you come to mention it I suppose I haven't seen him this week. Or her, either." She took a step backwards, craning her neck in the direction of the Tindalls' bungalow. "Well, I never. That *is* a shock. And you say they've come up on the pools as well? Gosh – "

"Margaret, shut up!" snapped Frank. "Don't start speculating about other people's affairs. What *is* all this, anyway?"

"Thank you," said Pete, snapping his notebook shut. "You've been very helpful. Come on, Chris. And by the way, I wouldn't worry about that dent, mate – you should see some of mine."

We made a hasty departure in the MGB just as a small convoy of police cars arrived from the direction of Hudderston town centre.

We headed towards the by-pass, and Pete said, "I wish you wouldn't do that."

"What?"

"Bring up your husband at every opportunity." He flashed the driver in front, forcing him into the slow lane.

"I don't," I protested, weakly. Pete remained stony faced.

"Anyway," I said. "Why didn't you tell them what had happened to Mrs Tindall? Why did you let them think the Tindalls had won some money?"

"It's not up to me what they think, but if I'd told them the truth they'd've got very uptight with righteous indignation and refused to tell us anything at all. Then tomorrow they'd've rushed out to buy the *Sun* to see what dirt they could dig up on their neighbours."

"They didn't really tell you anything, anyway."

"Yes, they did, they told me quite a lot. And what's more I know they were telling the truth. If they'd known Rosemary was dead the one thing you can be sure of is that they wouldn't have said anything unpleasant about her. As it is, they told me she was a clean living, happily married young lady who did charity work for the Church. Not exactly earth shattering, but certainly the truth as they saw it. One can't ask for more than that."

"I see. And you don't think it's odd that Mr Tindall didn't report his wife missing for nearly a week? You didn't notice the air of neglect the bungalow had – the garden hose not put away or anything?"

He took his eyes off the road long enough to give me an astonished stare, then said, "Shit! Oh, shit, I forgot to get the husband's Christian name."

We were sitting at the dining table eating a very late Sunday lunch of ham sandwiches and packet tomato soup, and studying newspaper cuttings on the Face Murderer, when the doorbell emitted three urgent sounding rings. I got up eagerly, expecting to find Julie, or Richard. Instead, I was confronted by a distinguished looking man in a sheepskin coat. Helen was with him, and she was clinging to our porch support and looking tearful.

"Are you all right?" I asked, anxiously.

She nodded. She'd changed out of the cerise tracksuit into a sombre grey pinstripe suit, and I noticed with a twinge of disappointment that she had very nice legs. I'd always believed that God punished those women whose bottoms looked good in trousers by giving them rotten legs.

"Our solicitor," she said, indicating her companion. "Mr Hurnell."

Mr Hurnell shook my hand unenthusiastically. "We're hotfoot from Maidstone," he explained. "En route to Hudderston Central police station. Mrs Redfern felt in need of freshening up and a glass of water. Nasty business. Er – will my car be all right there?" He glanced unhappily towards a silver Volvo which had been parked with a shoe horn between a skip and an old Citroën. I think his main concern was probably whether a client whose friends lived in streets full of skips and old Citroëns was quite the sort of person he wished to represent.

"It'll be fine," I said. "Do come in."

I led them past the tea chests to the dining-room, which was marginally tidier than the rest of the house. I felt awful about the threadbare carpet and the seat covers not matching.

"We're going to completely redecorate," I said apologetically, but, of course, no one was interested.

Helen made straight for Pete and grasped him by the hands. "This is so terrible!" she said, distraught. "I can't believe it's happening. After you'd gone the police came back and went through the house. They opened all my cupboards and they took away some of John's clothes. They've taken the car away! They think he's a murderer!"

Pete looked surprised. "Did they have a search warrant?" he asked.

"No," said Mr Hurnell. "But in the circumstances I advised Mrs Redfern to cooperate fully. It really is the best thing."

"They want John's office diary," Helen said. "They want me to verify where he was on certain dates!"

Pete hastily collected up the Face Murderer cuttings and hid them under *The Sunday Times* colour supplement.

"I don't know why you're worried, darling," he said soothingly. "Once John's told them he was nowhere near Hudderston on Tuesday night and they've had a chance to check out his story, they'll admit they've made a mistake and you'll be sitting together over a double whisky and laughing about all this."

Mr Hurnell cleared his throat.

"Unfortunately," he said. "It isn't quite as simple as that. Mr Redfern has already made a preliminary statement, and it seems he's admitted he spent the night of Tuesday, 10th November at the Eldon Lodge Hotel. Do you know it?"

We shook our heads.

"Well," he said, reluctantly. "Apparently it's a small hotel on the northern outskirts of Hudderston – not ten minutes' walk from the home of the victim."

4

After Helen and Mr Hurnell had left, we sat at the dining table gazing at the crusted rings of tomato soup in the bottom of our mugs. It had been a long day.

"Well," said Pete. "She's got great taste, hasn't she, my ex-wife? First she marries me, then a serial killer."

"Oh, for heaven's sake, don't talk like that!"

"OK. *You* explain it then. We were drinking together last night, discussing Hudderston and the murder, and John didn't once mention the fact that he'd *been* in Hudderston last week. Tell me why that is," he demanded, grimly.

"Well – you heard what Helen said. He travels a lot. Probably he doesn't remember exactly when and where he's been." I was floundering. "Salesmen stay in lots of hotels. They don't – "

"Not Hudderston," said Pete flatly. "I distinctly remember him saying he didn't visit Hudderston or Tipping." He closed his eyes and leaned back, thinking.

I groaned inwardly. I couldn't believe that such a normal seeming Sunday could have turned into such a nightmare. There wasn't the remotest possibility that John could be the Face Murderer. Why were we wasting what was left of our afternoon in trying to explain away that possibility?

Pete said, "What was the name of that hotel?"

"The Eldon Lodge."

"Right. Let's go and find it."

This time I groaned aloud. "But why?"

"Because I've had an idea. Because it's better than sitting around here doing nothing. Come on."

It was getting dark as we drove over to Hudderston for the second time that day. I knew the route well. Sometimes, before Keith got his company car, I used to drive him to work in Hudderston so I'd have the car to myself all day.

37

Then I'd have to collect him in the evening. I remembered the junctions where he always yelled at me, saying I was too slow to pull out and how embarrassing it was to have an irate convoy of cars collecting behind us.

We approached Eldon Road from Tucker Hill Road, and I glanced up towards the Tindalls' bungalow. I couldn't tell whether there were any lights on or not, because the monkey puzzle tree hid the house from view. The Eldon Lodge Hotel was indeed less than ten minutes' walk away; as we turned into Eldon Road we could see its neon sign proclaiming "Eldon Lodge Hot". In the dim glow of what remained of this sign, it didn't look inviting. A painted signboard nailed to the gate announced with an air of desperation "Recently modernised, large car park at rear", and a ladder had been left propped against a broken drain pipe. I guessed that the modernisation referred to on the signboard probably had something to do with the lengths of plastic guttering and paint pots lying in a flower bed, but maybe I was being unfair.

The hotel foyer smelled of starched linen and bacon fat. A short, bald man sat at the Reception desk, smoking a large cigar and nodding impatiently into a telephone.

"Yes, yes. I heard you the first time," he snapped irritably. "And what *I* said stands. The cheque's in the post. I want your men back here *tomorrow, first thing*, or you'll never get another order from me, and I want my frontage completed before anyone so much as looks at a cup of tea." He nodded again, releasing clouds of blue smoke in our direction. "No problem. No problem. Your signboard goes up beneath the hotel sign – yes, that's not a problem. Let's all get what we can out of this. Right!"

He directed an insincere smile at us in pursuit of the smoke, then added several more "no problems" into the telephone. He replaced the receiver.

"Right, lady and gentleman, what can I do for you? A double, is it? I can do you a nice one at the front – Would you be interested in our massage bed, at all?"

"No, no," said Pete. "We're Press. We'd like to ask you a few questions about one of your guests."

The smile took on a new sincerity.

"No problem! Here, I'll give you one of our cards. Our new tariff is on the reverse, you see? And you'll be sure to give us our full name, won't you? We don't want to be confused with the – "

"Er, Mr – Fredericks," interrupted Pete, reading the name off the card. "We're interested in a guest you had staying here last week, a Mr Redfern. Tall guy, lots of thick grey hair. He may have used a different name – " I shook my head in puzzlement. "It would be last Tuesday, the tenth."

Mr Fredericks nodded again, and opened the hotel register at a page marked by one of the hotel's cards. He turned it round for us to see and placed his finger on an entry.

"There you are, that's the one," he exclaimed. "You see, I'm ready for you gentlemen of the Press. We had the police here this morning, questioning us about Mr Redfern. They wouldn't tell us what it was in aid of at first, but my chambermaid got it out of one of their young DCs." He winked. "Exciting, isn't it?"

I read John's name and address. Pete perused the entries for the day, then flipped casually through the pages.

"You're not exactly full most nights, are you?" he remarked.

Mr Fredericks' smile vanished. "Bit of a slack time for us, yes," he admitted. "A lot of our regulars not travelling at the moment. Once people have found us they keep on coming back, but of course we're located on the wrong side of Hudderston for most of the through routes. A bit of extra publicity, that's all it takes." He rubbed his hands. "Ah, here she is, the lady of the moment. Come round here, Joyce."

Joyce was a small, dark girl with a nervous smile and spots. She flinched away from Mr Fredericks' arm.

"Joyce was the receptionist on duty last Tuesday night," explained Mr Fredericks. A telephone trilled plaintively from behind the door marked "Private". "Joyce will tell you anything you want to know about Mr Redfern – won't you, Joyce? She's been down to the police station this morning. Sorry about the phone. My private line," he added, reluctantly departing to answer it.

Joyce took off her raincoat. Beneath it she was wearing

a blue checked overall, with a button strained to breaking point over her sweater clad bust. She was shivering slightly, and blew her nose on a crumpled tissue.

"Hallo, Joyce," said Pete. "Don't look so worried. We don't bite. Can I ask you a few questions about Mr Redfern?" Joyce nodded. "Do you actually remember Mr Redfern, or are all hotel guests much of a muchness to you?"

"Oh, I know Mr Redfern!" said Joyce, positively.

"Do you?" I asked, surprised.

"Yes. He's – well he's stayed here lots of times before." She looked down at the tissue in her hands. Pete and I exchanged glances.

"Mr Redfern has stayed in this hotel on several previous occasions," Pete said. "You're sure about that?"

"Yes." She smiled at him, then blushed becomingly.

"All right," said Pete. "Tell me about last Tuesday. What time did he check in?"

"Well – " She glanced from one to the other of us warily. "I already told the police. Am I supposed to go over it again? Can't you ask them?"

"We'd like to hear it from you, darling. You're an eye witness. You may end up on Page One."

She looked less than thrilled at the prospect of ending up on Page One. I began to get the feeling that Joyce was frightened of something.

"He checked in at six thirty," said Joyce, absently shredding her tissue. "Same time as my shift starts. That's how I remember for sure – that's what I told the police."

"Had he booked a room? Was it a single or a double?"

"People don't book here. They just turn up – usually when they can't get in anywhere else," said Joyce, and then glanced, aghast, at the door marked "Private".

Pete laughed. "Never mind. Was it a single or a double? Did he arrive by himself, did someone join him later, or what?"

"Oh, he was by himself, in a single room," said Joyce. "He said he had a lot of paperwork to do, and he asked me to have some sandwiches sent up to his room. He said he didn't want to be disturbed." She reddened suddenly, and concentrated her efforts on destroying the tissue.

"All right, and what time did he go out?"

"Oh, he didn't go out!" Her blush deepened. "I told you, he had a lot of paperwork to do and he stayed up there doing it. He never went out. He always liked to be quiet in his room and get on with his paperwork."

"I see." Pete looked mystified. He also looked as if he didn't quite believe Joyce. He seemed disappointed.

"He came downstairs just after ten," blurted Joyce suddenly. "And had a whisky in the bar."

"Who did he meet in the bar?"

She hesitated. "Well, it was the end of my shift. I was just knocking off. He bought me a sweet Martini."

"He bought you a sweet Martini. Is that what he usually bought you, Joyce? Or do you occasionally like something different? I bet you like Tia Maria, too, don't you? Did he sometimes buy you that?"

"I don't know. I don't remember. How d'you know I like Tia Maria?"

"I've got psychic powers, darling. Mr Redfern usually got you what you like, did he?"

"Yes."

"And you liked him, didn't you? What time did you go up to his room with him?"

She looked shocked. "I didn't," she said. "Honest. We just had drinks."

He smiled. "Oh, come on, you're a pretty girl, this is a crummy hotel. Why shouldn't you have a little fun from time to time? I bet Mr Redfern treated you like a lady, didn't he?"

"Yes, he did," agreed Joyce, by now completely scarlet. "But I never went to his room. I've got a little boy at home. I have to earn for both of us – I do two jobs!"

Pete studied her thoughtfully for a moment. "I'll bet Mr Redfern sometimes gave you money for your son," he said.

Joyce's eyes did a half circuit of their sockets and she dropped her gaze to the hotel register.

Pete said, "Have you told either the police or Mr Fredericks about your relationship with Mr Redfern?"

She gulped. For a moment she looked torn between fear

and artfulness. She'd begun to suspect that just for once she was in a position to affect someone else's life. Finally, she settled on tears. "No," she whispered.

"Well, this may surprise you, darling," said Pete, reaching into his pocket. "But I hope as much as you do that we can keep it that way." He opened her fingers and closed them again over a ten pound note. "For your little boy," he said.

Mr Fredericks emerged from his office just as the money changed hands.

"Have you finished?" He sounded dismayed. "Don't you want to see his room?"

"Whose?"

"The Face Murderer's!"

Pete laughed. "I don't think you're in a position to show me that," he said.

"Why not? No one else has stayed there, it's all exactly as it was. Except for the linen, of course."

"Well, maybe you should put up a plaque – 'the Face Murderer stayed here', how about that?"

Mr Fredericks was uncertain how to take this remark.

"When do you think we can expect the TV people?" he asked. "I'm a bit worried about my frontage. I had a slight artistic disagreement with my painters."

"Don't worry, Mr Fredericks," said Pete. "You really don't need to worry about that."

We walked in silence to the car. It had started to rain. Pete put the key in the ignition but did not switch on, staring instead at Mr Fredericks' decaying frontage.

"Bastard," he muttered. "You'd think he'd have a bit more style. Christ, Helen deserves better than that."

"What did you expect? Is that what you were expecting?"

"I don't know really. I don't know what I expected." He turned the engine on. "Yes, I do. I thought John had probably booked in here under the name of Smith. I thought he'd probably had someone else's wife booked in here with him. It was the only thing I could think of to explain why he'd stay in Hudderston and not want anyone to know about it. I didn't anticipate someone like Joyce." He manoeuvred slowly across the car park.

"What *I* don't understand," I said, "is how his car can have been seen in Cottis Wood if *he* spent all evening in his room."

"Well – " He turned on the windscreen wipers, and the lights of the houses in Tucker Hill Road trickled down the edge of the windscreen and swished across it with the wipers. "I don't understand it either, but it doesn't matter, does it? John can't have been in two places at once."

"No. No, I suppose not. And what are you going to do about John and Joyce? Are you going to tell Helen?"

"No, of course I'm not. It's not my business, is it? Would you tell Keith if you found out his ladyfriend was playing around?"

I thought about it. "I don't know," I said, truthfully. "I'm not sure."

He turned towards me. "And that's because you still haven't decided whether it's your business or not," he said, sharply.

As we pulled into our drive again with a mutter of displaced gravel, I saw next door's curtains twitch. Our new neighbour was pretending to dust the leaves of her African violet. With a sinking feeling, I realised we had already gained her seal of disapproval.

Pete rang Hudderston Central again while I made tea.

"They've let him go. He's on his way back to Maidstone with Helen and Mr Hurnell," he said, and laughed. "Do you know, I'm almost beginning to believe in divine retribution?"

"Why? What's happened?"

"Well, it seems that while John was sitting in his room last Tuesday waiting for the lovely Joyce to finish her shift, someone was busy nicking his car from the hotel car park. He told the police he left it by the kitchen entrance when he checked in, but when he came down in the morning it had been moved. He reckoned there was an extra six or seven miles on the clock, but as nothing seemed to have been taken or damaged he didn't bother to report it."

"Oh. You mean the *Face Murderer* borrowed John's car to dispose of Rosemary Tindall's body? How horrible!"

43

"Yes. The police are keeping the car for forensic testing."

I thought about it. "I see," I said. "The murderer didn't want to risk being seen putting the body into his own car, so he took one from the car park. That means Mrs Tindall was probably killed close by." I shuddered. "But you'd think John would have noticed something – bloodstains or something." I prodded the teabags thoughtfully. "I don't think the Face Murderer's ever gone in for stealing cars before."

He shrugged. "One thing's for sure – it'll be a while before John visits Joyce again. See what I mean about divine retribution?"

I thought about John, sitting in the silver Volvo on his way back to Maidstone and trying to explain things to Helen. I almost felt sorry for him myself. The scenario he'd been faced with must have gone beyond even the most nervous adulterer's nightmare. *I'd* been pretty good at dreaming up this sort of thing: when I kept secret assignations with Pete I was terrified in case his flat burned down and I'd have to explain from the Burns Unit what I'd been doing there. I used to run a hasty check for loose wires and leaky gas taps before taking my clothes off. Somehow, I'd got a feeling John would get away with it.

Mr Heslop rifled through the piles of paper on his desk, looking for his new glasses. He found them, put them on, and gazed into his wife's picture, tilting it this way and that to get a better reflection.

"Right," he said, his face totally hidden from view by the photograph. "Update me on the Cottis Wood murder."

I hesitated. "They took a man in for questioning and they've released him without charges."

He looked at me over the top of the picture. "Well, I know that. Anybody who listens to Three Counties radio knows that. I hope you haven't been so deeply immersed in your love nest that you've failed to keep tabs on things."

"Actually, it's a bit awkward," I said. "The man they took in for questioning was – well, it was Pete's ex-wife's second husband."

44

He looked away from me for a moment, working this out. Then he put the glasses back on and leaned forward, elbows on the desk, looking thoughtful.

"I've often wondered what it feels like to suddenly find that someone you're related to, however distantly, has committed a violent and inexcusable act. It must totally alter your view of the world. Scary stuff. As a matter of fact I sketched out the rough plan for a novel on this theme, but – " He waved his hand, sighing. "One doesn't have the time in this job."

I took a deep breath and prevented myself from saying something I'd regret.

"Look, this is likely to be our only chance of a big story between now and Christmas," he said earnestly. "I want you to get on to Hudderston Central and establish a contact there – buy someone a few drinks if you have to." He thought about this, then added hastily. "Of course there's no need to go to extremes. I don't ever want to see any more expense slips like those of your paramour." He gave an involuntary shudder. "And take a camera and get me a couple of shots of the murder scene. You only need to point the bloody thing at a few trees," he said, to silence my protest. "And while you're over there do an interview with the person who found the body, that should go down well. Let's see, something like 'There amongst the blue of the bluebells, a splash of scarlet lifeblood – '"

"It's November," I interrupted, patronisingly. "You don't get bluebells in November."

"Whatever." He was unabashed. He rubbed his hands gleefully. "The victim lived on the bloody Dragon Lady's patch, didn't she? So she'll be blazoning her front page with another diatribe on the streets of Hudderston not being safe for women to walk." "The Dragon Lady" was one of his more polite epithets for Fiona Lomax, the editor of the *Hudderston Advertiser*. "And think of all those ads for martial arts courses she'll pick up – Oh well, we'll give 'em a good human interest story. You're good at that, Chris."

"Am I? Thank you," I said, flattered.

I went back to my desk. I sat and looked at my notes on Rosemary Tindall. I'd got a funny sort of feeling about her. Of course, it was quite irrelevant to her murder, but I just couldn't reconcile the picture of the happily married woman her neighbours had given me, with the one of the husband who'd failed to report her disappearance for nearly a week. And then there was that neglected garden. Happily married young couples in a street like Tucker Hill Road took pride in having well-stocked gardens. They might occasionally neglect them in order to sit in deckchairs consuming chilled wine and badly charred chicken legs, but they didn't completely abandon them. The Tindalls' garden looked as if it hadn't been touched for months.

I dialled the number of Hudderston Central police station, and asked for DI Carver. After a lot of clicks and bad-tempered male voices telling me to hang on, I was put through to a Detective Sergeant Horton.

"Hallo," I said, doing my best to sound like the sort of person a busy detective sergeant would enjoy talking to. "I'm Chris Martin and I'm with the *Tipping Herald*. I've been assigned to cover the Cottis Wood murder, and I wondered if you could update me on the latest developments."

"The *Tipping Herald*!" exclaimed DS Horton, with a gasp of mock awe. "My, my! Fame at last."

I laughed obligingly, then said. "I understand you've released your only suspect so far without charges."

He whistled. "You're a cruel woman! Tell me, do you go in for black leather and whips and all that? If so, we've got an endless supply of good quality handcuffs up here. One size fits all, but if you'd give me your vital statistics I'd be happy to – "

I decided there was no point in pretending to be the sort of person a busy detective sergeant would enjoy talking to.

"Look," I interrupted, unhappily. "All I wanted was to – you know – find out which way the investigation was going, and I thought perhaps you and I could sort of – "

"I hope you and I can 'sort of' as well," agreed DS Horton, suggestively, "because you've got a really nice voice, but the problem is, I'm not supposed to talk to reporters. Hang on." The line appeared to go dead for a moment, and when he spoke again his voice was muffled. "Chrissy? Listen. We're conducting a house-to-house this morning in the Tucker

Hill Road area, and forensics are going over the vehicle we believe was used by the murderer – You give me your number, love, and if you're very lucky I might be in touch soon, with something hot and promising."

I forced a smile into my voice, and gave him my number.

I had just finished making up a file on the Cottis Wood murder when Gillian pushed a piece of paper in front of me.

"Mr Heslop wants you to interview this person," she said. Then she stood back and stared at me with an expression of awed admiration. "Gosh," she said. "I think it's wonderful how you always know what to say to people."

I looked at the piece of paper. It said, "Graham Tindall, 53 Tucker Hill Road. Before 11.30, please." An interview with a bereaved relative. My stomach turned over, but I smiled at Gillian and said nothing.

I drove through Hudderston town centre, which was partly blocked by a lorry and a hoist and men wiring up Christmas lights. In shop windows, the first glittering baubles and exhortations to "beat the rush" had begun to appear. Ever since joining the *Herald* I had lived in dread of having to interview a bereaved relative. I once hid in the Ladies' room for half an hour when reports came in of a house fire, in case there might have been fatalities (there weren't). But there was to be no escape this time.

A large police van had parked at the bottom of Tucker Hill Road, and policemen in waterproof jackets were searching an open space signposted "Tucker Gardens. Private. Residents only." Several women and small children had gathered to watch them. I drove slowly up the hill and parked behind the panther-like presence of a sleek black Renault GTA. There was a time when all cars looked alike to me, apart from colour and number of doors, headlamps, etc, but Pete was fond of lecturing me about engine capacity and power to weight ratios (usually as we overtook something at high speed). What particularly surprised me about this car was that it had "Nuclear Power No Thanks" and "Stop the Bloody Whaling" stickers on its back window; I don't think I'd ever seen this type of sticker on a car costing more than ten thousand pounds.

I parked at a respectful distance from the Renault and walked straight up the front path of the Tindalls' bungalow. If I'd hesitated I would have been lost. As I raised my finger to the doorbell the door opened, and a man in a grey suit emerged. He was in his late forties, with a hairline receding gradually into memory.

"Ah," I said, trying to prevent my face twitching into an automatic smile. "I hope I'm not late. You were expecting me. I'm so awfully sorry about – "

He frowned. He looked me up and down as though I reminded him of someone else, someone he disliked.

"It's good of you to see me," I stammered. "Chris Martin, *Tipping Herald* – "

"Excuse me," he muttered, pushing past me. "I'm extremely late already." On the damp morning air in his wake, I detected the lingering scent of wintergreen.

He strode down the path and climbed into the expensive Renault.

"Are you from the *Tipping Herald*?" asked a voice behind me. I jumped.

"I'm Graham Tindall." He stood just inside the conservatory, next to the Swiss Cheese plant which clung to the glass amid tears of condensation. He had uncombed sandy hair and a pink overheated complexion.

"Oh, I'm so sorry," I exclaimed, unable to prevent the automatic smile from attaching itself to my lips. "When the other gentleman opened the door I thought he must be you. How silly of me."

"No. He works for the same firm as my wife. He called round to offer their condolences. They've been very good. Everybody's been very good. They thought Rosemary had brought a file home, or something, but she hadn't. I don't know how they'll manage without her," he added, gazing at the departing Renault.

I knew this wasn't going to be easy. "Shall I come in?" I prompted.

"Oh, yes, of course, I'm sorry." He stood aside, ushering me through the conservatory into a large hall sparsely strewn with Persian style rugs. "The doctor gave me valium, you know. I didn't want to take it, but I need to be able to cope. The lady next door brought me round a shepherds pie and offered to do my washing. People are so kind."

I felt guilty, because of course I was offering him nothing.

"Do sit down," he said, indicating a small cane sofa. He plunged his hands into his pockets and took a deep breath.

"I told your editor I'd agree to see someone," he said, "because he told me you were thinking of doing a piece about Rosemary's life – not her death." He bit his lip. "Yesterday, somebody came round from the national press. He was trying to get my neighbours to say that Rosemary and I had marital problems – I'm sure you can understand how upsetting that is." I bent my head over my notebook, horrified. "I first met Rosemary when she was fifteen," he went on, "and I knew straight away she was the woman for me. I never had any doubts. Of course, it took me a long time to convince her – " I risked glancing up at him. He was staring off into space, recalling the past. "But we never regretted our marriage."

The ridges of the cane sofa pressed uncomfortably against my thighs. I shifted position.

"Can I ask you if you've got any message for anyone who might know anything about the person who did this to your wife?"

"You can ask me," he said, "and then you can write whatever you like for an answer."

In the silence that followed, I wrote down in careful shorthand "he would like anyone with information to come forward", because I supposed that was what he meant.

"Um, I wonder if you could tell me – " I began. "Why was it so long before you reported your wife missing?"

He shook his head, his eyes closed. "I didn't know she was missing. I had to attend a course last week in Shepton Mallet. On computers. I'm a computer programmer – we need to update ourselves constantly – I didn't get home until Friday evening."

I waited. He didn't go on. "But you didn't report your wife missing on Friday, either."

His eyes were still closed. "No," he said. "I didn't, because as it happened my wife was due to be away last weekend anyway. She was supposed to be looking after her friend's shop – Tropaquaria, in Hudderston – Do you know it? Rosemary and Tania used to share a flat together, and occasionally when Tania has to go away for the weekend Rosemary minds her shop for her. I believe Tania once had a very unpleasant experience with vandals."

He was having an understandable problem with his tenses.

I said, "What sort of shop is Tropaquaria?"

"It's a tropical fish shop."

"And – wasn't Tania worried when Rosemary didn't turn up? Didn't she phone to find out what had happened?"

"No. You see, I didn't know this, but apparently Tania had changed her mind about going away, and she'd told Rosemary not to come. So for the entire weekend Tania assumed Rosemary was at home with *me*, and *I* thought she was in Tania's flat."

I had expected there to be some logical explanation, but somehow this one seemed to raise more questions than it answered. I was moving some of them around in my head, when Graham continued.

"I thought Rosemary would be home Sunday morning after Church. I waited – we always used to do a roast together on Sundays. It was something we liked to do together – we looked forward to it. Anyway, when she didn't come home I rang Tania, and there was this report on the radio about a woman's body being found – "

"Yes, I see," I said, quickly. "I do realise how awfully painful this must be for you. Can you tell me where Mrs Tindall was going when she left home on Tuesday evening?"

He shook his head. "I've already told the police, I haven't the faintest idea. I suggested they ask the Reverend Hollingsworth. He's Rosemary's vicar. She'd become very religious, you see, and she sometimes used to go out in the evenings to chat with people who were on their own – that sort of thing. She was a very caring person. Look," He handed me a large buff envelope. "There are some photographs of me and Rosemary in here, and a copy of the parish magazine she used to distribute. You can ask me what you like about her, and I'll try and help you, but I think these pictures will give you a good idea of what Rosemary was really like."

"Thank you," I said. I pulled the photographs from the envelope and looked at them. Most of them were of Rosemary and Graham posing stiffly for the camera. Her face had been pretty, I realised with a flinch – the sort you might rest your eyes on in a railway carriage and know would smile back self-consciously if she caught you looking. She was what I'd describe as a pale English blonde: bland by choice, when she might have made herself glossily attractive. In fact, at first sight, she and Graham looked well matched. Certainly in each of the photos he seemed to be gazing at her in adoration. Dog-like adoration. I wasn't sure I'd want anyone looking at me that way. I picked out a photo which appeared to have been taken in a tulip field.

"Were you keen gardeners?" I asked. "This looks like Holland."

"Oh, yes," said Graham. "That was the spring before last. We loved our garden."

I nodded.

Graham told me they'd been married for three years, and that they treated themselves to a trip to the Dutch bulb fields whenever it could be fitted in. Rosemary's life, he said, had revolved around him, the Church, and her job at Taylors, where she'd worked since their marriage. Prior to that she'd worked for a local solicitor. It all sounded very routine and unsurprising: just the sort of trauma-free life most mothers would wish for their daughters – until, that is, last Tuesday.

I got up to go. I wasn't going to ask him the question, "What do you feel about the person who killed your wife?", and I also wasn't going to ask, "Why did you neglect your garden of late if you loved it so much?", but there was one question I just had to ask.

"Mr Tindall," I began, thinking that his complexion was just like that of the pink plastic pigs my children used to have in their farmyard sets. "Can I ask you one thing more? You said goodbye to your wife on Monday morning and spent five days in a hotel on some kind of seminar, you returned home on Friday to an empty house – your wife was not three miles away at Tropaquaria – or so you thought. Why didn't you contact her during all that time?" And then I steeled myself, because he'd answered all my questions reasonably and this one was merely impertinent.

Graham Tindall had his back to me and I thought his shoulders tensed just a little. "That's a very reasonable question," he said, confounding me. "It's like I told the police. I was on a very intensive course, and I had a lot of notes to catch up on. My wife and I loved and trusted each other. We didn't need to live in each other's pockets." He opened the front door and extended a hand to me. "Thank you for being so sympathetic," he said.

"Thank you," I said, and made another stumbling attempt at offering him my condolences.

I sat in the Mini, out of sight of the Tindalls' bungalow. I'd always dreaded doing an interview with a bereaved relative, but I'd come away from this one with an odd sort of feeling. Graham Tindall was definitely bereft, there was no doubting that, but there was something about his story that simply didn't add up. You couldn't claim on the one hand to look forward to spending your Sunday mornings helping your wife to peel potatoes, while on the other claiming that you could manage to spend six days quite nicely, thank you, without hearing that same wife's voice on the telephone. It wasn't logical, and men – so I'd been led to believe – were always logical. I sat in the car with my pen poised over my notebook, searching for a few apt words to describe my impression of Graham Tindall. None came. I tossed the book in the glove compartment and drove away from Tucker Hill Road.

5

I collected Julie after work that evening from her friend's house. She came out into the porch, breathless, wearing an oversized anorak and carrying her school bag and two plastic carriers, from one of which a pair of unwashed tights billowed forlornly. She looked like a refugee and my heart turned over.

"Thank you so much," I said to the friend's mother. "I can't tell you how much this has helped."

The friend's mother, accompanied by the friend's father hovering in the background, gave me a saintly smile.

"Anything exciting happen while I've been away?" asked Julie, tossing things on to the back seat.

"Not really," I replied, carefully. "Did you have a nice weekend?"

"Brilliant," said Julie. "Stephanie's Mum and Dad got next year's holiday brochures and we spent hours going through them – I brought one home for us. What do you think about Tenerife for next year?"

I was tempted to give my usual speech about money not growing on trees, and especially not when people were getting divorced, but I didn't.

"Richard phoned," announced Julie, suddenly.

"What – he phoned *you*, at Stephanie's?" I asked, surprised. "From his flat? Why didn't he phone me? He knows the number."

"Don't know. He was in the middle of a party or something. He wants you to phone him some time but he says it's not urgent."

I manoeuvred the car up against the kerb outside our house, noting that the garage doors were open and that Pete's car was absent. We walked up the path in a rather gloomy silence.

"Well, here we are, home sweet home," I said, as I unlocked the front door, and hoped I didn't sound ironic. I turned on the light. Julie stared at the tea chests and the brown, geometric patterned wallpaper, and stuck her finger in a screwhole in the wall.

"What time does Pete get home?" she asked. She liked Pete. She'd allowed him to collect her from school a couple of times and announced proudly to her friends that he was "Mum's new boyfriend". I don't know how the "new" crept in.

"I'm not sure," I said. "It'll take a while for us all to get used to each other's routines. Let's go up to your room."

I led her upstairs to her room and turned on the light dramatically. I'd unpacked most of her things and stored them neatly in the fitted cupboards, but there was no place for her twin stereo cassette deck or her record collection, so I'd balanced these on top of two upended suitcases with a table cloth draped decorously over the front.

She stared at the result of my efforts in silence.

Her nose started to wrinkle into its accomplished pattern of disdain, but another thought prevailed. "Oh," she exclaimed, delightedly. "It's just like living in a grotty bedsit, isn't it? You wait till Steph sees this!"

I made a start on my story about Rosemary Tindall first thing on Tuesday morning. Somehow, I was going to have to make a virtue out of the fact that she'd led a singularly uneventful life. I wrote down "happy marriage" and "willing worker for the Church", as the main points of my story. The parish magazine Graham Tindall had given me contained a lot of family photographs of people I didn't recognise, and the intriguing headline "Scoring for God", which turned out to be an item about the Church football team. I decided to give the Reverend Hollingsworth a ring. He answered the phone with his mouth full of toast.

"Rosemary Tindall," he repeated, chewing noisily. "I'd be delighted to tell you about her. She had so much to give, and she'd only just started to give it. I shall of course be saying prayers for the soul of her murderer, as well as for her, but I must confess it's hard sometimes." He tut-tutted to himself. "She's certainly a great loss to our Church, I can tell you. Did you know she was considering becoming a full-time Pastoral worker for us?"

"No, I didn't."

"Yes. I'd broached the idea only recently, and she seemed very keen. I don't know what her final decision would have been, of course, because it was a big step. The job certainly wouldn't have been as lucrative for her as her present position. It's so rare these days to come across people for whom money isn't a major consideration," he added.

"Had she discussed taking the new job with her husband?" I asked.

"I've no idea. Unfortunately he wasn't a member of our flock so I didn't have the opportunity to discuss it with him. I hardly knew him."

"When did you last see Rosemary?"

"Actually, it was the Sunday before her death. We had a word or two about the Christmas Fair she was helping to arrange in our Church Hall. We'll be having all the usual stalls, plus Father Christmas. The ladies work extremely hard for it." He paused, as though expecting some comment from me. Finally he said, "Well, it would help if you could just slip a mention of the Fair into your article. I know Rosemary would have been pleased. The proceeds will go towards our tower restoration fund. We have to work *so* hard these days to compete with major disasters – they get all the publicity, you see."

"Yes, of course, I'll do my best. Were you able to tell the police where Rosemary was going the night she died?"

"Unfortunately, no. As a matter of fact Rosemary seemed a bit preoccupied the last time I saw her, and we didn't talk much. Of course, I deeply regret that now, but – " He sighed. "Anyway, I'm fairly certain she can't have been on her way to visit anyone connected with the Church. They'd've come forward by now. We're a very tight knit little community, you know."

My pen hesitated over the page. "You say Rosemary seemed to have something on her mind that last Sunday but you don't know what it was? Could you give me the name of someone else in the congregation I could talk to about Rosemary?"

The Reverend Hollingsworth wiped his mouth noisily. "I'd be delighted to. Rosemary used to be very friendly with Sally Wallace. Harry Wallace, like Graham Tindall, couldn't be prevailed upon to attend Church, so the two ladies naturally palled up. Ready? I've got the address here." He slowly dictated an unfamiliar address that ended with the depressingly unhelpful word "Auckland".

"Auckland?" I queried, dropping my pen.

"Yes. The Wallaces moved to New Zealand about four months ago. I was sorry to lose Sally, and I'm sure Rosemary was. I do hope they'll be able to settle. I wonder sometimes if people – "

"Look, isn't there anyone else Rosemary was friendly with? Anyone she might have confided in?"

He took a few moments to consider. "You know, I really can't think of anyone. Not that we don't all offer our hearts and minds to one another, of course, but I really don't think Rosemary formed an attachment to anyone else after Sally left. We're a very reserved lot, the English, aren't we? Still, personally I'm heartened by the fact that Rosemary returned to the fold before she died."

The screwed up Auckland address hit the rim of the wastepaper basket and bounced inside. "Returned to the fold?" I queried. "What do you mean by that exactly?"

"Well," he hesitated. "I suppose we all suffer doubts. Her attendance dropped off for a while last summer, but she was back amongst us and that was why I jumped in with the job offer when I did. Strike while the iron is hot, that's my motto."

"Yes, I see," I said. "Well, thank you for your time."

"November 28th," said the Reverend Hollingsworth. "November 28th for the Christmas Fair."

"Thank you," I said. "I've made a note."

I sat still for a moment, tapping my pen rhythmically against my teeth. Investigating Rosemary Tindall was like doing one of those magic pictures where you rub a pencil over an apparently blank piece of paper until an image appears. And the image I was getting of Rosemary Tindall, blurred though it was, was of a woman at some kind of turning point in her life.

I was still gazing at these imaginary pencil marks when my phone rang.

"Hi, there," breathed a disturbingly sexy male voice. "I'm young, handsome and available, and I've got something in my hand you would just *love* to get hold of."

There followed the muffled thud of a telephone receiver being dropped and a chorus of raucous male laughter and shouted encouragement. I blushed. I wasn't in the mood for this.

"I should warn you," I said, stiffly, "that all our incoming calls are taped and this one will certainly be played to the police."

The laughter choked off. "Oh Jesus!" begged the voice. "Don't do that! This *is* the police. Don't hang up. This is DS Horton of Hudderston Central, your friendly neighbourhood police station. You wouldn't want to ruin a promising career, would you?"

I counted to five, slowly. "What do you want?" I asked, primly.

"To do something for you, love. No – seriously. Shut up, you – " The receiver went dead for a moment. "I've got the post mortem report on Rosemary Tindall, and it contains a bit of a bombshell. What say we make it lunch at twelve in Perry's Wine Bar?"

"Well – "

"Bring your American Express card," said DS Horton. "You'll recognise me – I'll be the incredibly handsome guy wearing the Mr Happy badge."

Perry's Wine Bar was situated in a Hudderston side street, and I remembered it better in its previous incarnation as "Betty's", a small café modestly shaded by net curtains, where ladies with shopping trolleys would gather to discuss their friends' affairs, financial and otherwise. Now, the nets had been swapped for crimson velvet and a smudged blackboard menu, and it was a place where people with document cases would gather to discuss their friends' affairs, financial and otherwise. DS Horton was leaning against the bar, and he wasn't kidding about the Mr Happy badge. Devastatingly handsome was a bit of an overstatement, but he was tall and athletic and thirtyish and he inspired in me a nostalgic twinge of something or other. I hesitated in the doorway. I'd got this awful feeling he expected me to be something I wasn't – namely a slim-hipped blonde with a short past.

DS Horton glanced in my direction and noted my interest in him.

"Are you Chrissy from the *Herald*?" he asked, surprised.

I nodded, feeling the creases beneath my eyes lengthen like evening shadows.

"Well, well, and I'd've sworn you had a brunette voice."

Now it was my turn to be surprised; I hadn't expected tact to be one of his qualities.

We ordered lunch and sat at a corner table.

"Here's to the *Tipping Herald*, Chrissy. Do you mind if I call you that?" He had longish brown hair which had been highlighted, and very perceptive eyes.

"I'd prefer Chris, actually."

"OK. I'm called *Wayne*. I think my mother must have been frightened by a poster for a Western movie."

"Well, just be thankful it wasn't a Roy Rogers film," I said, but I don't think he'd ever heard of Trigger.

A couple sat down at the table next to ours and held hands over the ash tray. Wayne glanced at them and smiled wistfully.

"So – what's your bombshell?" I asked.

He sniffed the wine bottle and began pouring.

"The bombshell," he announced, "is that we were all wrong in thinking Mrs Tindall was killed by the Face Murderer."

I raised my eyebrows. "Really? How do you know?"

"Well, I'll tell you. The Face Murderer despatches his victims by hitting them over the back of the head with a blunt instrument, and then blasting off their faces with a sawn-off shotgun."

I nodded, sipping my wine.

"OK. Well, for a start Mrs Tindall wasn't shot with a sawn off shotgun, she was shot with an ordinary shotgun and from a different angle. I've got some nasty comparison photos but I don't suppose you really want to see them. Ah, here come my snails."

I didn't want to see the photographs. I waited while Wayne inspected the snails.

"Also, the positioning of the head wounds on previous victims suggests the original Face Murderer is almost certainly left-handed. This guy looks to have been right-handed. So we think we're looking for a copycat killer – someone who was turned on by the Press reports of the Face Murders."

I thought for a moment. "Don't you think it's a bit odd the killer set out to copy the Face Murderer – and then didn't? Everyone knows the Face Murderer uses a sawn-off shotgun. It's not difficult to saw off the barrel of a shotgun, is it?"

He grinned. "I take your point, but I don't see its significance."

"Well – " I wasn't sure *I* did. I shrugged.

Wayne said, "I hope I won't put you off your food if I tell you the rest of it. The woman was killed instantly by a massive blow to the back of the head with a piece of piping, just like the Face Murderer's last three victims. As for time of death – " He shrugged. "Bloody pathologist won't commit himself. There's a lot here about loss of body fluids and fluctuations in ground temperature – what it comes down to is that the body could have been in those woods for anything up to six days."

I dipped into my winter vegetable soup and tried not to speculate on the body fluids.

"Well, it's been dead cold for November, hasn't it? Cold and wet," went on Wayne. "So we're going to have to rely on witness reports to fix the time of death as near as we can. I'll be asking you later to help us with an appeal for sightings."

I had a sudden inspiration. "About the shotgun," I said. "Supposing that was a mistake? I mean, supposing whoever killed Rosemary did it in a fit of anger and decided *afterwards* to make it look like a Face Murder. They might have been in too much of a hurry to saw off the barrel of the gun."

Wayne almost choked over a snail. "Jesus!" he said.

"What illegal substances have you been sniffing? You'd better keep your handbag out of my sight, love. Who on earth would have wanted to kill a nice girl like Rosemary Tindall?"

I dabbed wine from my lips with a napkin. "Her husband, perhaps."

"Oh dear, not another refugee from an unhappy marriage, are we, Chris?" he asked, running his eyes over me. He didn't wait for an answer. "Matter of fact, we checked out the husband's movements for last week. Routine, really – husbands are never totally above suspicion. Heartening, isn't it?" He pushed away the tray of empty snail shells and pulled a sheaf of papers from his pocket. "Graham Tindall went off to work as usual on Monday morning. He left his office at five and drove straight down to Shepton Mallet, checking in to his hotel at ten thirty that night."

I frowned. "Does it really take five and a half hours to drive from here to Shepton Mallet?"

"No, it doesn't. It normally takes three – two if you don't bother about speed limits. He had trouble with his car – had to push it up a hill or something. Some of the staff remember him arriving all wet and muddy. I sympathise. My wife used to have one of those bloody kiddy cars. Anyway, on the Tuesday evening, at the time which concerns us, he was still in the Conference Room discussing computer viruses."

"Have you worked out exactly when she was killed then?"

"More or less, yes. There's a very helpful old lady in Tucker Hill Road who runs a neighbourhood watch scheme, and she saw Mrs Tindall leave home at six thirty and walk down the hill in the direction of the bus stop. We don't know where she was going, but we do know she didn't get on the bus. In fact we think the murderer was lying in wait on the wasteground by the bus stop. We think she was dead within minutes of that last sighting."

The couple at the next table began to kiss noisily over their mackerel pâté.

Wayne continued. "The Ford Granada used in the commission of the crime was parked by its owner in the Eldon Lodge car park at six twenty-five, and the owner didn't see it again until the following morning. He noticed it had been moved but the silly bugger didn't report it."

"Well, I can't say I blame him," I retorted. "*My* car was stolen by joy-riders once. I reported it and the police weren't in the least bit interested. I found it myself, eventually – abandoned in Tesco's car park."

"Yes, well – " muttered Wayne, frowning. "It's a pity, because if he had reported it and we'd taken a look at it we might've found something. As it is he apparently took it to be *valeted* the following day. Still, we'll give it a good going over. Rosemary Tindall's head was split open like a coconut. Even if the guy wrapped her in the most leakproof dustbin liner known to man we're bound to come across the odd bloodstain."

The couple at the next table were staring fixedly at one another. I don't think I was ever so involved with someone that talk of heads split open like coconuts wouldn't have caught my attention.

Wayne glanced at his watch. "So, to wrap things up – we think the murderer killed Rosemary between six thirty and six forty-five. He must've hidden her body temporarily in the bushes, then nicked the car from the Eldon Lodge car park and come back for the body. So what we'd like from you is an appeal to the public for any sightings of Rosemary Tindall on the Tuesday evening – we particularly want to hear from anybody who was expecting a visit from her that night. In fact we'd like people to come forward if they saw anything unusual in Tucker Hill Road last Tuesday, no matter how insignificant it might seem, and if anyone saw a man acting suspiciously in the Eldon Lodge car park they'll get a marriage proposal from DI Carver."

I wrestled my notebook out of a clinch with my cheque book, and made notes.

"It'll go in this week's edition," I promised.

The couple with the mackerel pâté suddenly sprang apart.

"Oh, Christ, Ann!" shouted the man. "What did you have to bring that up for? I thought I explained all that to you in Sheffield."

Wayne glanced at them and grinned at me.

"I've enjoyed your paying for my lunch," he said. "We must do it again some time. As a matter of fact, I've never been able to get on with Fiona Lomax and her team of harpies. Do you know – " He leaned forward, and was just about to impart some juicy piece of gossip concerning the staff of the _Hudderston Advertiser_, when our table was almost knocked off its feet.

"You bastard!" shrieked Ann, knocking over our wine bottle. "I hope your wife sues you for every penny you've got! You're the biggest creep that ever walked this earth!" She picked up a piece of French stick, aimed it accurately at the nose of her ex-lover and stormed off. If her mood and the strength of her arm were anything to go by, he probably had a lucky escape.

"Love," remarked Wayne, surveying the mess. "Not worth it, is it? Sometimes I think life would be a lot easier if we were all self-pollinating. Like apples."

"I think it's certain varieties of cherry, actually," I said, but I knew what he meant.

I left Wayne outside Perry's, and walked slowly back to my car. I felt good. I'd met a police informant in a wine bar, paid for his lunch, and got quite a few notes for my story. Not so long ago I wouldn't even have dared set foot in a wine bar without a companion. I breathed in fresh November air and exhaled red wine fumes. Just to finish off the exercise I'd drive over to Cottis Wood and take a couple of shots of the murder scene.

I parked in the lay-by opposite the cottages, exactly where the murderer was supposed to have parked John's car. I got out my camera and tried to pick my way through mud thoroughly churned up by dozens of pairs of size ten police boots. Over in the cottages, someone was watching me. I gave her a cheery wave, in the hope that it would put her off. It did. I held up the camera and played around with the focus on it, wondering how you take a picture of a murder scene and make it look like a murder scene. I could, of course, have walked up the track and entered the actual clearing where the body was found, but that would have meant ruining another pair of shoes, and anyway all these trees looked pretty much alike. Would anyone notice if I just snapped the ones near the gate?

"Local paper?" A brisk female voice cut suddenly across my thoughts.

I jumped, and wished that just for once someone would use the magic words "Fleet Street". Or even "Wapping".

"Yes," I said, glancing at her muddied wellies and labrador dog. "Where did you spring from?"

"Oh, you drove past me in your little car," she said. "Going rather fast you were, as well, if you don't mind my saying so." I didn't. I was quite flattered. She patted her dog, whose rhythmic panting dripped mud and saliva down the back of her leg.

"Nasty business," she said, inclining her head towards the wood.

"Yes," I agreed, trying to look as though I knew what I was doing with the camera.

"I was the one who found the body," she said.

I let the camera rest on its strap. "Oh, *were* you? You must be Miss Corby then. My editor wants me to do an interview with you."

"Fire away," said Miss Corby, obligingly. She was a large woman, elderly but by no means frail, perspiring in a plastic mac. "What paper are you with?"

"The *Tipping Herald*. Chris Martin." I opened my notebook.

"You're jolly lucky to catch me," said Miss Corby. "This just happens not to be one of my WRVS days."

I found a pen in the bottom of my bag.

"Miss Corby," I began, assuming what I hoped was a sympathetic expression. "It must have been an awful shock to you, stumbling over the body like that. Would you mind if I asked you exactly what went through your head when you saw it?"

She frowned. "Well, I thought – Gosh, there's a body."

I decided this wasn't quite what I wanted. "Do you think the murderer had made any attempt at concealment? Was she lying face up or face down?"

"She was on her back. There were a few branches lying around. If he'd tried to cover her with them then he'd made

63

a jolly poor job of it. I saw an arm first, sticking up through some grass, and then the blonde hair. Actually, I didn't look too closely. It was pretty ghastly. Timmy wanted to have a sniff at her, but I called him off because I know how important it is for things not to be touched. Nasty business. You were a good lad, weren't you, Timmy?"

I wrote down "pretty ghastly", and "dog called off".

"Do you often take Timmy into Cottis Wood?" I asked.

"Once or twice a week, weather and time permitting. I'm pretty busy, you know," she said, and she seemed to be scenting the air. I took a step backwards, mindful of the garlic and wine.

"Well – " I knew Mr Heslop was expecting a statement from Miss Corby to the effect that for the rest of her life she would be haunted by visions of the corpse in Cottis Wood. Miss Corby, on the other hand, had the look of a woman who had spent her girlhood ripping up petticoats to bandage soldiers' amputated limbs. Still, I decided to give it one last try. "I suppose the shock of finding her was slightly lessened because you'd already seen her shoe lying beside the track."

She frowned again. "What shoe?"

"The victim's shoe. It was lying in some long grass. I shouldn't have thought you could miss it."

"A black patent shoe, with a little bow? *That* didn't belong to the victim!"

"What makes you say that?"

"Because it can't have done. That girl was killed on Tuesday night, but the *shoe* was there on Tuesday morning. I took Timmy into Cottis Wood for a little run very early Tuesday – I was due in at Oxfam at nine thirty – and I remember seeing the shoe by the track. I thought it quite disgraceful – young people these days have no idea of the value of things. Just dumping unwanted clothing when it could be put to good use!"

I stared at her. "But it *was* Rosemary Tindall's shoe! It fell off her foot while the murderer was carrying her. Are you *sure* it was there on Tuesday morning?"

"Yes. Positive. I know which days I worked at Oxfam."

I took a deep breath and let it out again. Miss Corby's nose wrinkled with distaste.

"Miss Corby, this could be very important. On the Tuesday morning, did you walk past the spot where you later found Mrs Tindall's body?"

"No, I didn't, but that's neither here nor there, my girl!" exclaimed Miss Corby, reddening with annoyance. "The police have established that the woman was killed on Tuesday *night*, so one merely has to be *sober* to deduce that it would be totally out of the question for her shoe to have been there in the morning. You ought to think things through."

"I *am* thinking things through! I questioned DI Carver myself about that shoe, before they took the body away, and he definitely said it belonged to the victim. He said the other one was still on her foot."

She frowned and jabbed a finger towards my notebook. "Look it up," she demanded. "Look it up in your notes and let me see."

"I will," I said, thumbing hopelessly through dog-eared pages. "But some of my notes are in shorthand – "

"Pitmans?" snapped Miss Corby. "I know Pitmans! Let me see it in black and white!"

I found last Friday's notes, crossed through with smudged red felt tip. I could still read them, but there was no mention of Rosemary Tindall's shoe.

"Actually I didn't write it down," I said. "But I distinctly remember seeing the shoe and saying to the Inspector – "

"You distinctly remember," repeated Miss Corby, a glint in her eye. "You should make notes! If you haven't, then your memory isn't worth tuppence. I've been on court duty a number of times. I've seen people try to make nonsense of police testimony. The police don't make mistakes, my dear. They write everything down. If they say the girl was killed on Tuesday night, then that's when she was killed – and the shoe can't have been hers!"

"But – " It was hopeless. I shook my head with resignation and put my notebook away. "I do think perhaps you ought to tell the police about seeing the shoe on Tuesday morning," I suggested.

"Nonsense! The police don't need me to tell them how to do their job. There are far too many people trying to do that already," she added, fixing me with an accusing stare.

Timmy, having sensed his mistress's anger, suddenly lunged forward and barked petulantly at me. A shower of black water droplets descended on my coat.

"Sorry about that," said Miss Corby. "Pull yourself together, Timmy."

After that she agreed to pose by the entrance gate to Cottis Wood while I took a photograph. I took three in the end, just to be sure, and for each one Miss Corby touched the curls protruding from her head scarf and assumed a coy smile. Then she wagged a finger at me.

"I hope we're not going to see your paper starting a round of police bashing," she said, and treated me to a look probably normally reserved for football hooligans, CND supporters, and people who stop at traffic lights with more than an inch of tread over the line.

I got into the Mini, feeling deeply flattered.

It had nothing to do with Miss Corby's lecture, but I drove away from Cottis Wood at a walking pace. How could Rosemary's shoe have been in the wood on Tuesday morning? Because if it had, it could mean only one thing. If Rosemary's shoe had been in the wood on Tuesday morning then Rosemary's body must have been there too. And if it had been, and if her murderer had returned on Tuesday with a shotgun for the express purpose of . . . But it was no good "iffing". The police already had a witness who claimed to have seen Rosemary leaving home at six-thirty on the Tuesday evening. So who was wrong – Miss Corby, the police witness – or me?

When I reached the dual carriageway I turned right, and headed back towards Hudderston, and the witness who lived in Tucker Hill Road.

6

Tucker Hill Road was deserted that afternoon apart from black plastic rubbish sacks standing in conspiratorial groups at intervals along the pavement, and a Gas Board van whose occupants were silently reading newspapers. I parked near the Tindalls' bungalow, noting the drawn curtains, and looked up and down the road. Orange signs proclaiming "Burglars Beware! This neighbourhood is protected by the vigilance of its community" had been attached to several lamp posts. About two years ago, when I still lived in Barrington Avenue as a full-time housewife, some of our neighbours had half-heartedly talked of setting up a similar scheme. They wanted me to act as co-ordinator because, as someone patronisingly remarked, I was at home all day and au fait with the routine comings and goings of local people. What she actually meant was that she'd seen me gazing longingly out of my window whenever something in the street moved (which wasn't often) in the hope that I might witness a little piece of action in the big outside world (I never did). Keith said we shouldn't have anything to do with it. He said that neighbourhood watch schemes were just an excuse for neighbours to spy on each other, and he didn't want any silly old biddies keeping tabs on him. Considering what it turned out he was up to in his spare time, his attitude was fairly predictable.

I got out of the car and tried to decide which house looked most like the residence of a neighbourhood watch co-ordinator. They all looked as though they might have quite a lot to lose. Tucker Hill Road was a "good neighbourhood", the sort of place where you could drop a five pound note in the gutter and someone would donate it to the World Wildlife Fund. I walked slowly downhill, peering into windows and half expecting to see someone peering back at me. Maybe mid-afternoon, the hour of the school collection run, wasn't the best time to call. Then I spotted a small orange "Burglar Beware" sticker on a glazed-in porch. As I started up the front path I heard the depressingly familiar music of an Australian soap opera billowing from an open window. It took me back to where I didn't want to go.

"Yes?" demanded the woman who answered the door. Her eyes had a far away look. She was in Melbourne, Australia, deciding whether or not to marry the Flying Doctor.

"I'm sorry to disturb you," I said. "I'm from the *Tipping Herald* and I'm looking for the person who runs the local neighbourhood watch scheme."

The dustclouds of the outback receded.

"Oh, that's me. Do come in. I'll switch this rubbish off. I only had it on for the local news."

She snapped off the television. "Let me take your coat, and do sit down. My name's Valerie Stubbs," she added, and she spelled it out for me.

I handed her my coat and she brushed an imaginary crumb from the seat of an armchair and fluffed up its cushions. She was in her fifties, and wore the sort of twinset I didn't think they made any more.

I sat down. "Thank you. I won't keep you long. I just wanted to ask you one or two questions about the Rosemary Tindall murder."

"Yes, of course," she exclaimed, assuming an expression of rapt attention. "I'm so glad to be able to help. I watch all the programmes, you know – *Crimewatch, The Bill, Shaw Taylor* – *I* was the last person to see Rosemary Tindall alive."

"Well, yes, so I understand. I believe you told the police you saw her leave home last Tuesday evening and walk down Tucker Hill Road in the direction of the bus stop?"

"Yes, I did. It was just after half past six and the six o'clock news had finished, so I got up and went to the window like I always do." She got up and went to the window, resting her hand on a notebook on the sill. "Vigilance is my by-word. I keep a regular check on what happens out there. Nothing much gets past me."

"You mean you look out of your window regularly, during commercial breaks and in the gaps between programmes?" I suggested.

She pursed her lips. "I don't watch television all the time. I'm much too busy."

On her mantelpiece were photographs of a wedding, a tiny newborn baby with its eyes closed, and a poodle wearing a Christmas hat. She saw me looking at the poodle and walked across to give the frame a polish. "I don't know if you noticed," she said. "But there's a Gas Board van out there, and I'm keeping a careful watch on it. It's been there half an hour. You never know. A friend of mine had all her furniture stolen by some men driving a lorry that said 'Harrods' on the side. Well, you don't question *Harrods*, do you?" She returned to the window. "Those dustmen are very late this week. I shall have to complain to the Council again."

"Last Tuesday, Mrs Stubbs," I prompted. "You say you saw Mrs Tindall leave home – "

"Oh, yes!" She pointed gleefully to the Tindalls' gate. "I saw her come out of her house and walk down the street. She was wearing a nice little red jacket, a grey skirt and high heel shoes – "

"Those were the clothes she was wearing when they found the body."

"Yes. I remember thinking she must be catching the bus, or she'd've needed an umbrella. She looked over her shoulder a couple of times as though she was watching for the bus. I thought to myself, I wonder where *she's* off to, going into town when it's not a Wednesday? Anyway, once she got past those conifers down there she was out of my sight. Do you see them? They hang out over the wall and completely block my view. I've asked the Brownlows to chop them down, but they won't. They're conservationists," she added, meaningfully. "Personally, I think all this nonsense about the ozone layer is a con trick, don't you? I think if people want to buy green washing powder and things then it's up to them, but their crackpot ideas shouldn't be allowed to obstruct other people's health and safety. I had a right old ding-dong with the Brownlows about the footpath on the common. They wanted to leave the nettles for the butterflies, but I said to them – what about the *flashers*? Don't you care about the flashers?"

I blinked. "You wanted to protect the flashers from getting stung?"

"What?" She looked baffled. "It's where they hide, isn't it, in undergrowth – " She became suddenly and deeply worried. Obviously she had never considered the deterrent properties of nettles.

"Anyway," she continued. "I think Mrs Tindall sheltered under the trees on the wasteground while she waited for the bus. I think that's where he got her. I told the police that and they agree with me. I'm going to start up a campaign to get those trees cut down, so – "

"Mrs Stubbs," I interrupted, urgently. "I want to ask you something. Are you absolutely sure when you saw Mrs Tindall walking towards the bus stop that it was *Tuesday* evening? Are you absolutely positive that it wasn't Monday?"

She looked puzzled. "Of course it was Tuesday. That was the day she was killed, I heard it on the radio. The clothes she was wearing – The police were asking about *Tuesday*, not Monday."

"I know, but listen, the six o'clock news is on every night, and buses run at the same times throughout the week, don't they? All you really know is that the last time you saw her she was walking down this street towards the bus stop, and that the six o'clock news had just finished."

Valerie Stubbs assumed a hurt and indignant expression.

"The police were asking about *Tuesday*," she said. "I helped them. I made a statement. Heavens, it was over a week ago – Well, it must have been *Tuesday*, mustn't it?" she ended, desperately.

I decided to take a leaf out of Miss Corby's book.

"Did you write it down?" I demanded, pointing to the notebook on the sill.

She looked shocked. "Certainly not! I don't write down what the *neighbours* do!"

I sighed. She had made up her mind and would not be budged.

"All right," I said, defeated. "One other point – the night you saw Mrs Tindall going out – or in fact any night that week – did you notice Mr Tindall's yellow 2CV anywhere in the street?"

She shook her head. "Didn't you know? Poor Mr Tindall was off in the West Country somewhere while all this was happening. That's why he didn't report his wife missing straightaway. Such a shame, they were a really happy couple. And she was such a charming woman."

"Did you know them well?"

"Well, no, not really," she admitted.

I didn't seem to be getting anywhere, and the dustcart was advancing alarmingly upon my car, so I rose to leave. Valerie Stubbs nodded towards the sacks and a cardboard box piled up by the Tindalls' gate.

"Poor Mr Tindall," she said. "The lady at No. 55 had to put out his rubbish for him. I saw her do it, and she made him a dish of something or other. *Most* of the people in this street are so kind." She scowled pointedly at the Brownlows' conifers, which were obviously the bane of her life.

The wine was beginning to take its revenge on my head, compounding my disappointment. I extended a hand to Mrs Stubbs.

"Thank you for talking to me," I said. "Oh – I just wondered. Why did you say you were surprised to see Mrs Tindall going into town on a Tuesday instead of a Wednesday?"

"Oh, because on Wednesdays she usually went to an Adult Education class at Burymead County Secondary school. I think *somebody* told me it was Creative Writing. She – "

"Burymead?" I interrupted, the name striking a chord.

"Yes. They do all sorts of classes there for adults. I've sometimes wondered if they do . . ."

I stared out of the window. Where had I come across a reference to Burymead School recently? It was somewhere at the back of my mind, hemmed in by reminders to do various things to the new house –

". . . dressmaking for my grandchildren . . ."

Suddenly it cross-referenced itself. Burymead County Secondary School – the anonymous note Gillian had mislaid in

71

her filing tray: "I have information of wrongdoings, all I ask is peace of mind".

". . . some sort of home maintenance course so you wouldn't have to wait for your husband to get round to knocking in nails . . ." went on Mrs Stubbs.

"Did you say Mrs Tindall used to attend a course at Burymead School every Wednesday evening?"

"Yes. Oh, don't forget your coat." She handed it to me, looking with distaste at the mudstains left behind by Miss Corby's labrador.

"Thank you." I started out through the porch. The anonymous letter had asked for someone to ring a telephone box located at the school. I had rung that number mid-afternoon, and spoken to a child; if I'd rung it during the evening it might have been answered by an adult attending an evening course. What better way of making contact anonymously than by using a phone available to hundreds of people? Maybe the letter *hadn't* been a hoax, maybe –

The advancing dustmen were yards from the box of newspapers that stood waiting outside the Tindalls' bungalow.

"Thank you again, Mrs Stubbs," I said, bundling the coat over my arm. "You've been a great help."

She followed me along the path. "By the way," she said. "I don't suppose you'd know, but when they do the *Crimewatch* reconstructions, do they – "

The dustcart was grinding its jaws noisily outside No. 31. Two dustmen were picking over an assortment of iron-mongery, and tut-tutting at a bag of rose prunings. They didn't look at me as I approached the Tindalls' bungalow. The cardboard box was full to its brim with newspaper, topped by several copies of PC Week, still in their poly-thene wrappers. I tossed them aside. The letter had been written two weeks ago – I'd have to go right through the box. Frantically I pulled at it, spilling copies of *Woman's Realm* and Dixon's Amazing pre-Christmas offers on to the pavement. I was probably wasting my time, but I just had to be sure. The last paper in the box was the *Hudderston Advertiser*, and as I tugged at it pieces of pages from the *Tipping Herald* cascaded from its centre. I picked up three loose pages and tucked them under my arm.

"Oi! What's your game?" An irate dustman interposed himself threateningly between me and the newspapers.

"What d'you think you're going to find in there?" he demanded. "Look at that bloody mess! People like you make me sick, trying to jump the gun like that."

"I was only – "

"Oh, don't you give me no hard luck stories. What happened – husband left you for a younger woman and they turned you down for Tesco's checkout? Well, you can try that one on your social worker! You want to make a few bob you can take your turn down the tip like anyone else." He snatched the sack from under my nose, and kicked the newspapers into the street. As an afterthought, he turned and jabbed a finger in the direction of my best Marks and Spencers coat. "By rights," he said, "I ought to take that off you, an' all!"

I had to leave the rest of the newspapers to blow about Tucker Hill Road. I retreated hastily to my car and pulled away from the Tindalls' bungalow. Mrs Stubbs was watching me: she had the look of a woman deciding on her best profile for the *Crimewatch* cameras. On the seat beside me lay three loose pages of newsprint – and they were pockmarked with small oblong holes where someone had cut a number of words from them.

7

I opened my front door, switched on the light, and immediately remembered Richard. It was the sight of the overflowing teachests that did it; they looked just like the drawers in his old bedroom. I got out my diary and dialled his new and unfamiliar number.

The phone rang for a long time, then the ringing stopped, and someone breathed slowly into my ear. It was like a nuisance call in reverse.

"Hello?" I began questioningly. "Is anyone there? This is Richard's Mum."

"Oh." I could visualise Richard's flatmate's acne. "Well, he's not here."

"Isn't he? He asked me to ring him. Do you know when he'll be back? I keep missing him."

"No." I didn't much like Richard's flatmate. He sounded as though he had some kind of breathing problem, and I was beginning to wish it might become terminal.

"Tell him you called, if you like," he said suddenly, and replaced the receiver.

I'd dropped my shopping bag on top of a heap of the day's post. Most of the letters looked like bills, and fortunately most of these were addressed to the previous owner of our house, but there was a long white envelope marked "Confidential" which I recognised immediately. I took it to the kitchen with my shopping and dropped it casually on the table. Then I made a few token attempts at putting the shopping away, but it was no use. Finally I ripped open the envelope and pulled out my solicitor's letter. Mr Keith Martin, it said, had failed to respond to any of their enquiries so far, but they would let me know as soon as he did. Well, at least the letter was short and to the point: communications from my solicitor cost me more per word than Jackie Collins gets for one of her bestsellers. I swallowed my disappointment and began attacking the dishes in the sink.

It was nearly nine when Pete came home, looking tired and dispirited and as though someone had screwed up his shirt and used it to clean out a drain. He glanced at the copy of the Pigeon Fanciers' Gazette I'd placed on the kitchen table for onward transmission to the addressee, picked it up, and tossed it into the kitchen waste bin.

"Christ, what a day," he said, making for the bottles on top of the fridge. "I don't know if I can take much more of this. I spent all afternoon going through a dustbin in an alley full of dogshit. Don't ask me why. Believe me, you wouldn't want to know. Where's your daughter?"

"Upstairs. Do you know – *I* had to go through a dustbin today as well!"

He put his arms round my waist and kissed me and pressed our pelvic regions together. His mouth tasted of stale alcohol.

"I love you," he said. "You don't know how great it is to drive up this road and see a light on in the house and know it's you. Would she notice if you and I went into the shower together?"

I blushed. "Yes. Don't you want some tonic with that?" He'd filled a wine glass with vodka and was preparing to drink it.

"No."

He drank it. I watched uneasily, but said nothing.

"You'll never guess," I began. "You know the Rosemary Tindall murder? Well, apparently she wasn't killed by the Face Murderer at all. The police think it's a copycat killing, but I was talking to this woman who found the body, and I'm pretty certain there's more to it than that. I don't think Rosemary was killed on the Tuesday, I think she was killed on the Monday, and the murderer went back the next day and tried to make it look like one of the Face Murders. He didn't even use the right type of shotgun! I actually suggested this to Wayne, even before I'd found out that – "

"Hold on. Who's Wayne?"

"He's a detective sergeant at Hudderston Central. He's

working on the Tindall case. I took him out to lunch today and he gave me details of the post mortem report."

Pete laughed. "You ought to be careful, you know. Detectives are like journalists – they spend a lot of time sitting around in cars and bars waiting for things to happen, and fantasising about how to lure beautiful female reporters into their beds."

"Do they? Don't be silly. Listen. Two weeks before she was murdered Rosemary Tindall wrote a letter to the *Tipping Herald* anonymously. In it she said she knew something about a Hudderston businessman which she wanted to reveal to the Press."

"Really? You didn't tell me this before. How much did she want for the information?"

I shook my head impatiently. "She didn't want any money, just peace of mind. And I didn't tell you about it before because I've only just discovered it was Rosemary who wrote the letter. The letter got lost in the office."

He laughed. "Oh, well, that's the end of that then. The story has died with her, as they say. I shouldn't worry about it, darling. Most of these things are written by cranks. Probably her husband had been parking that converted pram of his on double yellow lines and she wanted to get him nicked to pay him back for not doing his share of the washing up."

I bit my lip. "You're very cynical about everything."

"Yes. I'm very pissed off with everything. Come upstairs, darling. I've been dreaming about taking a hot shower and rubbing you all over with shower gel."

I thought about it, and blushed again. "I can't. Not with Julie in the house. I'll get you something to eat. I wish you'd listen to me properly when I talk to you." And then I stopped, because I seemed to have said that before, a lot of times, and to someone else.

I turned my back on him and switched on the cooker.

"What's that?" asked Pete, suddenly. He was holding up the letter from my solicitor.

"It's about Keith. He's not answering letters asking for a divorce."

He shrugged. He went to the sink and washed his face and

hands. Having finished that, he picked up a cloth and began meticulously drying forks. I stared at him open-mouthed. It wasn't just the voluntary drying up: how could he show so little interest in my divorce?

"Well, what are we going to do?" I demanded. "This could take years if he doesn't cooperate!"

"So what? You've got away from the bastard, haven't you? You're living with me – what does it matter if there are a few pieces of paper floating around that say you're still married to him?"

"There are lots of bits of paper floating around that say I'm married to him! I don't want to be married to him – I want to be married to *you*!"

"Well, you are – as good as."

I spilled about thirty frozen peas through the electric ring on the cooker. "Oh *God*!" I moaned. "But I'm not, I'm not! You *asked* me to marry you – I thought you wanted us to get married."

"Yes, yes, yes," he agreed soothingly. "And as far as I'm concerned, we are. We're not kids. We don't need proper bits of paper."

"Pete," I said, touching my fingers to cheeks which had gone suddenly cold. "There's no such thing as being 'as good as' married. You're either married or you're not. You – "

"Oh, I almost forgot," he interrupted. "I rang Helen today. John is having to pay for car hire out of his own pocket. Helen's trying to get him to sue for false arrest. Apparently motor insurance policies don't cover you for having your car impounded by the police for fingerprinting – I imagine it's somewhere in the small print. You know, I remember once, when this idiot fell off the edge of the pavement and – " He launched into a story intended to demonstrate the sadistic and cretinous nature of people who work for motor insurance companies, a favourite theme of his. I didn't listen; I was sure he'd changed the subject on purpose. I chased peas across the cooker top with a spoon. *I* wanted to be married. I'd been married for just about half of my life and I liked it. Being married meant knowing that the man in your life would always come home for you to say sorry to; it meant never having to paint your own guttering;

it meant always having someone there whose wrinkles were growing at the same pace as yours. I couldn't imagine facing a future that didn't include a proper, paid up husband.

I think I knew I was in for a bad day the moment I walked in the office and saw Mr Heslop standing by my desk looking at his watch. His face had a grey, taut appearance.

"As far as possible I want everything for this week's edition ready by four o'clock this afternoon. I'm seeing a specialist tomorrow."

"Oh dear, what is it?"

"They're going to have to do an endoscopy," he said tensely. "But we haven't got time for my personal problems. What's the latest on the Cottis Wood murder?"

"Ah! Well, for a start, it isn't one of the Face Murders. Don't look so disappointed! There's much more to it than meets the eye. I've got a theory concerning Rosemary Tindall's shoes, which I think – "

He held up an impatient hand. "We can do without the fashion angle, if you don't mind." His stomach emitted a growl, and he clutched at it in agony. "Write up the story the way we agreed, will you? And get on with it. Have you any idea how close it is to Christmas, and the amount of work we've got backed up?"

"Listen," I interrupted, desperately. "You remember that anonymous letter we received? The one we rang too late? Well, Rosemary Tindall sent it. Look what I found amongst her rubbish." I pulled the cut-up sheets of newspaper from my handbag and laid them on the desktop. One of them was a page from the *Hudderston Advertiser*, and the sight of its logo turned his expression even sourer.

"Now, look, I won't tell you again," he said, grimly. "We are writing a story about the brutal murder of an innocent young woman. The public don't want to read some kind of smear campaign. Unless there's likely to be an arrest before we go to press tomorrow I want your story written up and ready to go by four o'clock today."

He limped hastily back to his office and managed to get the door shut before he broke wind.

I groaned. Nobody seemed to want to listen to me.

I dialled the number of Hudderston Central and asked for Wayne's extension. He said with disarming gallantry that he was never too busy to talk to me, and listened patiently while I told him what Miss Corby had said, and gave him my opinion of Mrs Stubbs' evidence. He was issuing instructions to someone else away from the mouthpiece, but he kept returning to me and saying "go on", in an encouraging tone. When I'd finished there was a long silence, and then he said, "Well, that's very interesting, Chris. Especially the bit about the six o'clock news being on every night. We'll have to remember that."

"Oh!" I said, stung.

"I'm sorry," said Wayne. "Sarcasm is an art form here. The thing is, I'm going to have to explode your theory about the Tindall girl being killed on Monday night, because she was still very much alive on Tuesday morning. We naturally contacted her employers – er, Taylor Group – when we were trying to piece together her last day. Apparently she phoned them on Tuesday morning to say she wouldn't be going in as she had food poisoning. Must have tried to go to work on an egg, ha, ha."

"Oh," I said again, feeling a flush starting at the back of my neck. "I didn't think to check. I'm awfully sorry. Miss Corby was so *sure* about that shoe."

"That's all right," replied Wayne, pleasantly. "Your heart's in the right place. But let me tell you something about Cottis Wood – Give me that, that top sheet, Frank – That's the one. Cottis Wood is a regular tip. People only go there to dump or to hump. Listen to this, it's a list of things we found within fifty yards of the body. Four bicycle tyres, one shopping trolley, two prams, half a shopping trolley, one man's army boot size 10, one pair ladies' shoes size 8, lacking a sole – Jesus, how poetic – three car batteries, ten used condoms – one of them a French tickler, it says here – "

"Yes, I see," I said, scarlet from hairline to collarbone. "I'm really sorry to have wasted your time. Do you think you're likely to come up with anything new before we go to press tomorrow?"

He laughed. "In a word, no. We've asked the owner of

the car for a complete list of all the people who may have sat in it over the last month, and then we'll have to go round and fingerprint them all. The theory is, any fingerprints we find on the car which don't match with the people we've fingerprinted *could* belong to the murderer. It'll tie up my DCs for days."

"I thought you could do this sort of thing quickly with a computer."

"Well, you show me the computer which can knock on people's doors and explain to them what we want their fingerprints for, then stand back politely listening to their opinions on identity cards for football supporters, capital punishment, and any other bloody thing they feel like talking about, and I'll be very interested."

"Yes, I see. Well, thank you for updating me," I said. "I won't take up any more of your – "

"Actually," interrupted Wayne. "I was going to phone you anyway to thank you for the lunch." He hesitated. "I was wondering if you'd like to do it again some time." He waited for me to respond. I didn't. Wayne said, "Right. Well, I'll be in touch," and replaced his receiver.

It took a full two minutes for my blush to abate. Then I realised I hadn't mentioned the anonymous letter. In the circumstances this was probably just as well. I folded up the sheets of newspaper and put them away.

I wrote my story in three parts, and in the end I was quite pleased with it, despite the fact that it didn't contain the magical phrase "This reporter has discovered . . ." Anyway, there was always next week. Under the headline "The Quiet Wife who took a Short Walk to Death: Copycat killer strikes in Hudderston", I chronicled the discovery of the body and the police investigation to date. I said that Rosemary could be assumed to have met her death within minutes of leaving home on Tuesday evening, and in the second part of my story I detailed the police appeal for sightings of her that night. Then I completed the final part of the story, which was really Rosemary Tindall's obituary. She'd had a happy married life and had been a tireless worker for the Church, I wrote. It wasn't very exciting, but it was as near to the truth as I could get and wouldn't offend anybody, and that's what people have come to expect from the *Tipping Herald*. To complement the story I selected a photograph of Rosemary and Graham in the bulbfields, and one of Miss Corby standing at the gate to Cottis Wood.

Mr Heslop studied the layout in front of him.

"Yes," he said. "Not bad. One thing, though. Next time you take a photograph at a murder scene, *don't* let your witness smile. Look at that – even the bloody dog is grinning. It ruins the effect."

"Yes. Sorry."

He leaned back in his chair and gave me a friendly smile.

"You're our headline story this week. Well done."

"Thank you."

As he attempted to close my Rosemary Tindall folder a strip of paper from the *Hudderston Advertiser* slipped from its spine. He looked at it absently, then tucked it back inside.

"Now you can forget about this until they arrest someone. If they ever do. Then we can just re-work the original story. Good."

"Oh, but don't you think we ought to try and find out what Rosemary's anonymous letter was about?"

His frown returned. He didn't like being contradicted. "What do you propose to do? Employ the services of a medium? Let's get on to other things, shall we?" He produced a paper from his in-tray. "Did I tell you I want you to cover the opening of the new Dolphin Shopping Precinct? It'll be something I think you've really got the flair for." This was his way of telling me he couldn't get anyone else to work on a Saturday. "Well, as long as you're doing that you may as well take this on as well. Victor Taylor. Taylor Group are one of the firms involved in building the Dolphin, and they're contributing to some sort of celebration outing for pensioners." He scowled at the paper in his hand. "Bastards! They shell out a few quid towards a minibus and they get themselves in the editorial columns of my newspaper instead of having to pay for advertising space."

"Rosemary Tindall worked for Taylors," I remarked.

"Of course, you know who I blame," said Mr Heslop. "That Bob Geldof! He started the whole ball rolling. Now instead of buying double page ads these bastards plant trees in the park and stuff pensioners full of turkey lunches!"

"Well, I suppose as long as deserving causes are helped it's not such a bad thing."

"Not such a bad thing! You don't have to look at our advertising revenue graph! I hope you still think it isn't such a bad thing when I have to ask you to take a salary cut! Dear, oh, dear!" He muffled a belch. "Anyway, Victor Taylor thinks we ought to do a write-up on his family's connections with the area, or something. I've heard he's got political ambitions. He's been on to me twice, so I've made an appointment for you to go and see him on Friday. Do a nice hype job, just say what he wants you to say. Remember, nobody will actually read it except possibly his mother, and we might get a regular ad out of him in the future."

"Yes Mr Heslop," I said. "I'll do my best."

I took Julie with me that evening for our weekly "big shop". It was the first time for several weeks that I'd been able to do a "big shop", and I knew it would be very therapeutic. I glided gracefully between aisles of tinned dog food and breakfast cereal, lovingly eyeing the growing mountain of goods in my trolley.

"Mum," said Julie, thoughtfully. "Don't get me wrong. I know we had to leave Barrington Avenue, and I'm not sorry we had to move to a smaller house in a worse area." Which meant, of course, that she didn't really know any such thing and was extremely sorry.

"Oh," I said. "Good."

"But it's just – a couple of things. Have you washed your hair lately?"

"Why? Does it look awful?"

"No. It's the taps in the bathroom. The cold one runs all the time. It's terrible, Mum, you can't get the water right. I got my ears frozen off this morning and I told Pete and he just sort of looked blank."

I looked fondly at her beautiful blonde hair. "Your hair

looks lovely. I'll remind Pete. I expect he was in a hurry to get to work."

Julie chewed her lip thoughtfully, and then said in a rush. "And then there's the kitchen. It's small but it's not that small. If we just reorganised it I'm sure we could do an awful lot more with it. I mean, two of us could work in there at the same time. What I was thinking was – "

Before she could get any further with these extraordinary remarks we were interrupted by the sudden arrival of a familiar but unexpected figure. An unmistakably and stomach-churningly familiar figure.

Keith stood obstructing my way, a packet of crinkle cut chips in his hand.

"Fancy seeing you here," he remarked, with grim sarcasm. "Shopping for lover boy's supper, are we?"

I was rooted to the spot. If we had a scene in the frozen food section I'd have to change my supermarket.

I smiled nervously. "You look very well. Have you – have you been away somewhere, or something?"

"I'm fine. I look after myself," he snapped, adding, "You OK?"

Julie had made a strategic departure towards the soft drinks.

"Yes." I felt breathless. "Of course, I've been very busy. There's been a lot on at the paper, as well as the move. I'm working on a murder."

His eyes narrowed. "Oh, really? Why don't I help you? I'd love to see that boyfriend of yours with his throat cut."

I laughed, but both of us knew this wasn't meant to be funny.

"I'm working on something else now," I said nervously. "Do you remember Taylors? That row you had with them about the thermocouple? I'm going to interview Victor Taylor on Friday."

Keith sighed, and dropped the chips into his basket.

"Yes, well, he's the coming man, isn't he, Victor Taylor? A very clever bastard. I'd like to know how he's done it. Who'd've thought ten years ago that Taylor and Son would end up being members of the Colgate Club?"

"What's that?"

"The Colgate Club? Colgate – the ring of confidence, remember?" He'd always hated explaining things to me. He adopted his best patronising tone. "Chris, almost every major project round here involves RMP Developments, Sloane Homes, Kearns Miller & Kravitz the Architects, Butterleys Contractors – one or two of that lot anyway. And now Taylors seem to have got in on the act. They did the heat and vent at the new District Hospital, didn't they? Yes, the Colgate Club, that's what we call it at Hattons." Hattons was the firm of Civil Engineers for whom Keith worked. He snorted. "I should like to know how they got in on that lot."

"Probably just good workmanship and luck."

"Don't talk wet. I'll bet there's a golden handshake or two somewhere along the line." Keith had always believed that anyone who did well (i.e. better than him) did so by some form of diabolical trickery. "I just wish you'd let me join the Conservative Association. You put paid to all that for me when you went round delivering those bloody Liberal party leaflets!"

I picked up a packet of frozen sweetcorn and tested it for lumps, while trying to think of a way of changing the subject.

"You haven't replied to my solicitor's letters," I said eventually. He didn't answer.

"So you're all right then, are you?" I asked. "Has Barbara moved in with you yet?"

"I haven't made up my mind yet about Barbara."

I dropped the sweetcorn into my trolley.

"I've missed you," said Keith, suddenly. "Are you going to give me your phone number – or what?"

"My home phone number? Do you want to phone me?"

"Yes, I want to phone you. Of course I want to phone you."

"Well – why don't you give me *your* number? If you phone me, it might be – awkward."

He nodded. We exchanged phone numbers and addresses on the backs of our shopping lists. Julie had reappeared and stood looking on uncomfortably. In the mirror over the freezer cabinet I could see the lower halves of our bodies reflected – a tight knit little family group of lower body halves.

Julie and Keith chatted briefly about school and all the rain we'd been having recently.

"Well," said Keith, his very attractive blue eyes smiling at me. "I must be off or I won't get home in time for the football. I'm glad I saw you. Will you be in touch?"

"Yes," I said. "I'll be in touch."

8

It was sunny, it was Friday, and as I drove to keep my appointment with Victor Taylor I was feeling especially pleased with myself. Next to me on the passenger seat was this week's copy of the *Herald*, and *my* story on Rosemary Tindall filled almost the entire front page. Beneath the *Herald* lay a copy of the *Hudderston Advertiser*. They'd printed a small head shot of Rosemary, and one of those computerised maps nobody understands, to show the killer's supposed trail from Tucker Gardens via the Eldon Lodge car park to Cottis Wood. I can't think why they'd bothered with the map; probably just to prove to readers they had a computer which could do one. Their story was headed "Woman killed by crazed misogynist; Women's groups call for action", and shared the front page with an item about the record-breaking takings from a charity concert held at Hudderston Civic Hall, coincidentally on the same evening as the murder. *My* story was much better.

Taylor Group occupied a two storey office building just off the Hudderston by-pass. They'd been on this site since the war, but the original ramshackle converted house surrounded by sheds full of boiler parts and lengths of flue had long since been demolished. The "Works Entrance" was now discreetly to the rear, and the forecourt had been tastefully decorated with tubs of dwarf conifers. Well, perhaps not so tastefully: it depends whether or not you're turned on by the sight of a stunted tree grasping at life in a plastic pot. Anyway, there were no spaces in the car park, so I parked on double yellow lines in the street.

The girl in Reception showed me through to a large, airy room at the back of the building which had a picture window overlooking a river and fields. In the distance, the constant roar of traffic on the by-pass was audible as a background murmur through the double glazing. A carpeted staircase led to an upper floor, and to the left of the window was a doorway to a small, unlit office. A girl seated in front of some very streamlined looking office equipment motioned me towards the sofa. I sank into it. It was like going into a time warp – the smell of instant coffee, the muted ring of telephones, the distant mutter of keyboards. Just for a moment I was twenty again and waiting for a member of my parents' generation to decide whether or not I'd got what it took to tap out his words on a typewriter. I didn't like it – the being interviewed part that is – and I wasn't so sure about being twenty again, either.

I'd been waiting for about five minutes. The girl at the desk, who looked about nine and a half months' pregnant, kept flexing her back uncomfortably and casting glances in my direction. I leaned towards her, and said, "Are you sure you should still be working? Your ankles look a bit swollen."

"Oh, I'm all right," she said. "That's just how my legs are, I'm afraid. If they weren't maybe I'd've got to be Miss Hudderston and I'd be off making money somewhere." She laughed infectiously. Well, you'd never survive in an office without a sense of humour.

"Do you think Mr Taylor will be much longer?" I asked.

She shrugged. "I'm afraid he keeps everyone waiting. My husband says he does it deliberately to show how important he is. Still, I just hope he doesn't come out here." She nodded towards the empty desk. "That's Gail's. She's only been here two weeks and she hates it. She went for a job interview and hasn't come back. If he finds out he'll go *spare*." She hissed the words "job interview" in the obligatory stage whisper.

"In that case," I began, unable to resist it. "I'm the reporter who did the story on your colleague Rosemary. Do you think you could spare the time to answer a couple of questions? My name's Chris, by the way."

"I'm Carol," said Carol, looking very serious. "It's *awful*, isn't it? Everybody here's still in shock. That was her office." She nodded towards the empty room. "Rosemary had been here ages. She started when old Mr Walter was still in

87

charge, and then after he died she helped Mark Williams, our Accountant, set up the new office system. So she knew everything about everything. How they'll manage without her I don't know."

"Really? What was her official title?"

"Office Manager," said Carol. "Which sounds pretty posh, doesn't it? But mainly she was Mark's PA. He's terribly upset. But he's so stiff upper lip he tries not to show it."

"Yes," I said sympathetically. "Was she Victor Taylor's PA as well?"

Carol shook her head. "No. *Mrs* Victor usually does Mr Victor's work. Mind, he's above the day to day running of things, if you know what I mean. Mrs Victor's in the same club as me at the moment, though, so poor Rosemary did a few bits and pieces for him. I expect he's pretty cut up about it as well, but he's a cold fish."

At that moment the door to Reception opened and two men came in, obviously laughing at some private joke. They were both young and smart, the sort who liked to give out signals that they would one day have "Company Director" listed on their passport as their occupation, but who were not above casting surreptitious glances at the ankles and breast outlines of lowly office girls. These two were wearing close cut hair and floppy suits, as opposed to the floppy hair styles and close cut suits they used to affect in my day, but I recognised them anyway. The one carrying an umbrella and a stack of brochures dropped an untidily piled wire tray on Carol's desk.

"Tell your friend Williams, here are his bloody cheques, all countersigned and approved. I don't know how he does it. A bloody great pile always lands on my desk just as I'm going out," he remarked, still laughing at the private joke.

"Wouldn't be much point giving them to you after you'd gone, would there, Alan?" suggested Carol, but the two men behaved as though she hadn't spoken.

"I'm going to bring it up at the next Management Meeting," said Alan. "I shouldn't be countersigning cheques at all – I'm Marketing! Come on, Steve."

Steve and Alan departed.

"He *won't*," said Carol, contemptuously. "He won't bring

a thing up at the next Meeting. He'll just sit there and tremble over his monthly figures. People who rock the boat here find themselves out of it. Steven – my husband – says that's the problem the world over." She stared out of the window, thinking about this.

I glanced up the carpeted stairway. There was no sign of Victor Taylor.

"You're absolutely right," I agreed emphatically, as though impressed by her wisdom. "You really are. People should speak out more."

Carol smiled at me, flattered, and I sat up straight, preparing myself. Carol was not just a lowly employee, anxious, as most lowly employees are, to show off her inside knowledge of the Company, she was also quite obviously on the point of leaving.

"Carol," I said, very earnestly. "This is just between you and me, all right? Listen – I've got good reason to believe that a couple of weeks before her death Rosemary may have written an anonymous letter to the *Herald*." Carol's eyes opened wide. I hurried on, "Of course, it may have absolutely nothing to do with Taylor Group, but she said she knew something about the wrongdoings of a Hudderston businessman."

She stared at me incredulously for a moment, then laughed. "Well, there are lots of businessmen here who are guilty of wrongdoings! They all fiddle their expenses like crazy!"

I laughed obligingly. "Didn't Rosemary ever confide in you about anything here that worried her?"

Carol looked baffled. "Rosemary was ever so loyal to this place! I mean, it was her *life*. This place and dashing home to darling Graham. Besides, Mr Victor always makes us do everything by the book. Mr Walter was the one for cutting corners. If he could get away with fiddling an extra few quid on people's bills, he would. Oh, I'm not saying there isn't a big panic when the Safety Officer or a VAT Inspector turn up, but that's normal, isn't it? Mr Victor would chop off a few heads if there were any irregularities, I can tell you!"

Two lights flashed up on her switchboard, and she turned to answer them. I bit my lip. Maybe this had been a mistake.

My attention was caught by the open door of Rosemary's office. I stood up. "Do you mind if I take a look?" I mouthed at Carol, and when she didn't actually say "no", I made for the door.

The office was small, with just enough space for a desk, chair and filing cabinet. A narrow window looked out over the river. On top of the filing cabinet, and along the window sill, small pots of cacti clustered and jostled one another, like a tightly packed football crowd. A cork wallboard was covered with postcards depicting various parts of the world, all of them a lot warmer and more inviting than this office overlooking a cold Hudderston river bank. I pulled off one of the postcards and read it. "To all you slaves at Taylors," it said, and it was signed "Carol". I sat down at the desk. The word processor stared back at me accusingly, and I remembered why I'd been so unwilling to go on a word processor course to enable me to return to office work. These machines might edit out errors and save you hours of searching for blank bits on the Tippex, but they had no soul. There was nothing like coming into work in the morning to greet your old green Olympia, its keyboard shined by the grease from your fingertips, its insides clogged with broken fingernails, splashes of congealed yoghurt, mountains of rubbed out words, last month's bad dandruff attack, sweat, tears, and possibly the odd drop of blood. Nothing ever got trapped inside a word processor, except things you desperately wanted to get out – like Page 4 of the Board Meeting Minutes.

Carol stood at the door, looking worried.

"Mr Taylor's ready for you," she hissed.

Victor Taylor sat at his desk, which was occupied by a pristine onyx ash tray, a leather bound diary, and nothing else. He smiled as I entered.

"Mrs Martin, isn't it?" He offered me his hand. If I'd been here for a job interview I'd've been extremely intimidated by his urbane, perfectly manicured appearance, the gold cuff-links, and the bright, cold eyes. As it was *I* was supposed to be the one doing the interviewing.

"Would you like coffee – or tea?" he asked, and I shook my head, thinking of Carol. "Very well, then, Mrs Martin, perhaps we could just get on as I do have another meeting at four." So much for my being in charge.

"Right. I'll fill you in on the background story of Taylor Group. As you may know," he began, resting his elbows on the desk and clasping his hands. "My family have lived in Hudderston for generations. In fact, we had a genealogist look into our history for us and he was able to date us back to 1750 – of course, we were just lowly farmworkers in those days." He gave me a "man-of-the-people" smile. "However, that's beside the point. To get back to the present day: my father – who unfortunately passed away two years ago – started us off just before the war with nothing but a hacksaw and a pair of Stillson wrenches." I wrote this down, wondering how much it had been inspired by a Hovis commercial. "My father left school at fourteen. How he managed to scrape together the money for an apprenticeship I'll never know – working eighteen hours a day, I imagine – but he made it and qualified for his Master Plumber's Certificate." Victor Taylor gestured at the wall behind him. It hung there, not quite stained with blood.

"When the war started," he went on, "there was a good deal of work for the newly formed firm of Taylor & Son."

"What – repairing bomb damaged buildings and so on?"

He smiled indulgently. "Actually I don't think the Germans ever bothered to bomb Hudderston. No, I'm talking about the sort of routine plumbing work a community simply can't do without."

"He – your father was able to avoid being called up then, was he?"

He frowned. I hadn't meant to, but I think I'd hit a sore point. "He didn't *avoid* call-up. To his great distress he was pronounced medically unfit. I do assure you that keeping the home sewers running was every bit as important as shooting the guts out of enemy soldiers." I glanced up at him. He was deadly serious.

"Anyway," he continued. "After the war Taylors were ideally placed to contribute to the massive building programme that went into operation, and we soon developed our central heating expertise."

"So, really, you did quite well out of the war, didn't

you?" I suggested, without actually meaning to be provocative.

His frown deepened. "Look," he said. "If there's a hurricane, people cry out for roof repairers. I don't think it does to pare down everyone's motives too finely, do you? We all have our part to play. In any case, Taylor Group have come a long way since those days. We are now proud to have been associated with such projects as the Dolphin Precinct and the District Hospital, and we are shortly to begin work on the Abbey Farm housing estate." He sat back, smiling.

"In fact it's only during the last year that you've become involved in large projects, isn't it?" I said. "Before that you were mainly associated with small domestic work."

"Yes, indeed," he agreed. "As you probably know we sold our maintenance department two and a half years ago and reinvested in the industrial side of our business."

This didn't sound like the sort of thing people wanted to read about. I wouldn't, anyway.

"Actually," I said, "you sold off the part of the business your father had built up. Do you think he would have been pleased about that?"

"Of course he would. He would have been extremely proud. Progress is everything."

"Well, you certainly have progressed very fast. Lots of people have been surprised how quickly you've got involved in these big projects." Well, Keith and the staff at Hattons have, anyway. "Could you explain it?"

Victor Taylor inclined his handsome head to one side, displaying the grey streaks at his temple. "It's merely a question of having the right thing to offer at the right time, I do assure you," he remarked, with his indulgent smile.

"Good workmanship and luck?" I prompted.

"If you like," agreed Victor, absently. He flexed his wrist, glancing at his watch. Then he leaned forward and adopted his earnest tone.

"My father remained fit and active and involved in the firm to the end, but the welfare of those pensioners less well off than himself was always close to his heart. So I know he'd be particularly pleased that we're contributing towards making Christmas more memorable for some of the area's pensioners. We're taking them up to the West End to a show, you know, and then entertaining them to a slap-up dinner in the Dolphin Restaurant. Do you have details of that? I don't think a date's been fixed yet but when it is we'll let you know. I expect you'll be wanting to send a photographer along," he added, glancing again at his watch. He leaned back in his chair. "So, Mrs Martin, if you'd be good enough to write something to the effect that our continued involvement in the community is a fitting tribute to my father's memory – " He waved his hand vaguely, but I think he knew exactly what he wanted.

"Yes. Thank you for your time." I smiled and rose to my feet. From somewhere outside came a great clang, like the sound of a piece of heavy equipment being dropped, followed by a volley of shouts. Victor Taylor winced.

Halfway across the deep pile carpet, I turned.

"You must be deeply saddened by Rosemary Tindall's death," I said.

He glanced up. He'd already lifted his telephone receiver. "Yes, indeed," he said. "A dreadful tragedy. Yes – Hallo, Carol. Tell Mark Williams I want him in my office – That's his problem. Tell him he's got five minutes."

I closed the door to his office silently. I decided I didn't like Victor Taylor very much. I'd write what he wanted me to write, but I wasn't going to enjoy doing it. Mr Victor Taylor had succeeded in business by being ambitious and ruthless, qualities I found far from endearing, but they were surely not "wrongdoings" in anybody's book.

Carol smiled at me as I descended the stairs. She looked out of breath. "All right?" she queried. "Phew! I could do with Rosemary now. She always used to pop out and help when I was on my own."

"You two were pretty close then, were you?"

She shook her head. "Not really. Rosemary was the serious type. She didn't go in for gossiping."

I nodded. "Would it come as a surprise to you to know she was considering leaving here and working full time for the Church?"

Carol did a double take. "Really? Christ, I didn't know."

"I don't think her husband did, either," I said carefully. "Was everything all right in her marriage, as far as you knew?"

"*What*? Are you kidding? They were the original love-birds, those two. He was *always* on the phone to her, regular as clockwork, every afternoon at three, and – " She stopped talking and stared out at the fields for a moment. "What you said about her leaving, I wonder – "

"What?"

"Well, do you know, it's an odd thing. The last few weeks she was really uptight. She helped me out on the switchboard one afternoon and made a thorough mess of it. That wasn't like her. I asked her if there was anything wrong but she said there wasn't. Perhaps she was wrestling with her conscience about whether or not to leave here. As a matter of fact, when she phoned in sick last Tuesday I wasn't surprised at all."

"Weren't you? What did she actually say when she phoned?"

Carol shook her head. "I don't know, actually. I didn't take the call. It was my morning at ante-natal. They kept me waiting for two hours – God, you've no idea. It was absolute chaos when I got in here, what with Rosemary away as well and Gail only on her second day."

"So who did take the call?"

"I don't know, actually. Hang on, I can find out."

She began shuffling through a collection of untidy message pads. The door opened and Mark Williams walked in. I recognised him immediately by his expression – his nose was permanently wrinkled in distaste like that of a man whose finger has just gone through the toilet paper – and I think he recognised me too. He gave me a sharp look, and then turned his scowl on Carol.

"What are these cheques doing here?" he demanded. "I thought I'd told you before about leaving them lying around. Why didn't you bring them straight in?"

"Well, I'm sorry," said Carol, in an aggrieved tone. "But I have been very busy and I'm on my own this afternoon – Mr Victor's waiting for you."

"Really. And is this lady distracting you?" he asked,

nodding towards me. "Why do we have members of the Press hanging around our office? Does Mr Victor know she's here?"

"Certainly. She's here to interview him for the *Tipping Herald*!" retorted Carol, grandly.

"Oh." He looked at me and with a disgruntled snort walked slowly up the stairs to Victor Taylor's office, leaving behind his distinctive odour of wintergreen.

"Poor old devil," whispered Carol. "What with his rheumatism and that awful wife of his I don't suppose he has much of a life. I found out once he'd been going for job interviews, but nobody wants him because he's *too old*. Now Rosemary's gone he – "

I wasn't interested, and in any case I didn't care to hear of someone only a few years my senior being continually referred to as *old*, so I interrupted her.

"Look, I'd really like to speak to whoever took that message from Rosemary," I said.

"Oh. All right." She resumed scuffling through one of the pads. "Here we are," she said. "It was Gail."

Right on cue the door opened again and in strode a tall, dark girl whose expression was not dissimilar to Mark Williams'. She slumped in her chair, shrugging off a leather jacket and kicking her handbag under the desk.

"How did you get on?" hissed Carol, in a stage whisper.

"It was just as shitty as this place," Gail said, at full volume. Carol and I winced in unison.

"Gail, this lady's from the *Tipping Herald*," said Carol. "She wants to know about the message you took from Rosemary last week."

"Oh, really?" queried Gail, rudely.

I tried a smile of encouragement. Gail picked up the message pad and looked at it.

"Christ, that was ages ago," she said. "That was my second day in this piss-hole and the day I decided I was getting out. What do you want to know?"

"Well, I'd like to know exactly what she said."

Gail's expression turned even nastier. "Can't you read, or what? It says here 'Rosemary sick with food poisoning.

Not coming in. Tell Carol'." She tossed the pad back at me. "Satisfied?"

I stopped trying to smile. "Do you actually remember talking to her? Is that precisely what she said?"

Gail wrenched a packet of Kim's out of her pocket. "I don't know what she bloody said. She said she'd got the shits, I suppose. Got a light?"

"So you don't remember talking to her? No, I'm sorry I don't smoke. Are you absolutely sure it was Rosemary herself on the phone?"

"You're joking!" Gail struggled with a disposable petrol lighter. "You expect me to remember something that happened two weeks ago? Look, I wrote down the bloody message – I wrote down about twenty bloody messages – and that's all I know. What – are you going to give me a medal or something?"

I examined the message pad. "You've written down times on all the other messages," I said. "You haven't put a time against the message from Rosemary."

Gail ignored the remark, drawing deeply on her cigarette.

"You see," I said. "You might have been the last person to speak to Rosemary before she was killed."

For once, Gail agreed with me. "Yes, that's right, I was," she said. "That's what the detective said when he came round to interview us. Look – the message comes between the one I took at ten and the one I took at ten twenty-five. Is that what you want to know?"

"The police think Rosemary must have spent the day in bed," said Carol. "Best thing, isn't it, when you're not feeling well? They said they couldn't find anyone else who'd seen or spoken to her that day, apart from Gail. They wanted to know if we'd any idea where she might have been going in the evening, but of course we hadn't. She never chatted much about what she did outside the office. It's just such a shame, isn't it, that she was feeling well enough by the evening to go out? If only she'd stayed at home in bed – "

"Yes. But you see, the thing is, I'm wondering if it really *was* Rosemary on the phone. Could it have been

96

someone else phoning on her behalf – her husband perhaps?"

Gail shrugged.

"I don't think so," said Carol. "He was away on a course."

I looked again at the message. I placed it in front of Gail. "Do you see what you've written?" I said. "You've written 'Rosemary sick with food poisoning'. It's as if that's what someone *else* told you to say, not what she said. Do you see what I mean?" They both stared at me blankly, and in Gail's case, hostilely. I sighed. "My point is that the police believe you were the last person to speak to Rosemary, and maybe you weren't. Maybe you didn't speak to Rosemary at all – just to someone who claimed to be phoning on her behalf. Maybe – "

Victor Taylor's office door suddenly opened, and he emerged with Mark Williams. Both Gail and Carol immediately went into a flurry of activity over their word processors.

I hesitated for a moment, but I wasn't going to get anywhere with them anyway, so I whispered goodbye, and left.

A brisk wind had got up while I was ensconced in the warmth of Taylor Group's offices, and it sent swirls of leaves and waste paper scampering across the forecourt. In the car park, a few feet from the rear of a shiny new black Toyota Celica parked in the space marked "For V.T. only" a large, unidentifiable object made of galvanised metal (it was probably the guts of an industrial boiler) had fallen off the back of a lorry and demolished a dwarf conifer. Two men wearing overalls and desperate expressions were trying to shift it, using ropes. They saw me looking and one of them shouted, "Do you wanna give us a hand, missus?" I shook my head; what I'd actually been thinking was that this was the one and only time in my life I'd seen anything which had literally fallen off the back of a lorry.

I sat in the Mini and ran a quick editing pencil through the notes I'd made on Victor Taylor. Then I made another note for my Rosemary Tindall file, of the exact words contained in the message Gail had taken. I gave a little shiver of excitement. I just *knew* I'd been right about that shoe.

I re-read the message, and gazed at the photograph of Rosemary Tindall in the bulb fields. There were just two people in the world who knew that Rosemary hadn't made that call to Taylors on Tuesday morning – and one of them was her murderer.

9

As it was Friday, I knew Richard would contrive to be home from work early, and I decided to surprise him. His flat was over a video shop in a dilapidated Victorian terrace behind Hudderston's old bus station. Rather guiltily, I locked up the car with extra care, and waded through fish and chip wrappers and plastic bags splotched with a sticky white substance (which I tried to tell myself had nothing to do with glue sniffing), towards Richard's flat. It was just the sort of place one hoped other people's children would end up living in.

Through the lettering on the window of the shop ("Free Membership, litereally (sic) 100's of titles always in stock. VHS specialist"), I could see the proprietor eating chips and watching the early evening news. He wore baggy grey clothing and scratched his privates frequently. Richard said he kept an old World War Two revolver in the shop, because he'd been robbed twice and didn't like involving the police.

I climbed the steep stairs, circumnavigated a rusty bicycle on the landing and pressed a reluctant finger to the doorbell.

"Mum!" exclaimed Richard in surprise. "What're you doing here?" He had obviously only just arrived home, and was still wearing his suit. The trousers, I noticed, needed pressing.

"Well, we keep missing each other on the phone, and I haven't seen you for ages," I said. "Can I come in?"

He looked embarrassed.

"It's a bit of a mess," he said. I stumbled over a pile of dirty washing in the doorway and went into their tiny living-room. Slumped across the sofa, and looking like a younger and spottier version of the video shop owner, was Richard's flatmate, Barry. This resemblance wasn't surprising: they were uncle and nephew. Barry didn't look up.

"Well, how are things?" I asked, cheerfully. "Are you both managing all right?"

"Yes, Mum," agreed Richard, patting my arm soothingly.

"Why – are you offering us a loan?" suggested Barry, still without looking up.

Richard stepped forward hastily.

"Let me take your coat and things," he said. I gave him my coat and a carrier bag, which he put on the sofa beside Barry.

"That's for you," I said. "There are a few packets of soup and a chicken curry for you. I thought maybe you needed a few things for your larder."

Barry sat up suddenly. "Ooh, what have we here?" he asked, with mock excitement. "A goody bag! Let's have a look. Beef with spring vegetable – my fave!"

I took my breath in sharply but managed to hold back a response. Richard went into the kitchen and I watched him plug in the kettle for tea.

"I saw your Dad the other day, Richard," I said. "He seems very well."

"Good. I saw him last week in the pub."

Barry was removing everything from the carrier bag. He'd come across my notebook.

"Was there any special reason why you phoned me?" I asked.

"Well – " Richard looked sheepish. "I just wondered if we could use your washing machine occasionally. We have to queue for hours in the laundrette. I'd pay for electricity of course."

"Don't be silly. Of course you can use it. Just call round any time."

He hesitated. "Actually, I'd like to come when *he's* not there."

"Who? Oh. Why?"

Richard shrugged and wrestled with the kettle lead. "Doesn't matter. Let's not discuss it."

"Is this shorthand?" asked Barry. "Wow, it looks really clever."

Privately I wished Barry would disappear into the wood-work where he looked like he belonged.

"I think we *should* discuss it, actually," I persisted, un-happily, adding: "Pete will be your stepfather one day." Or at least I *hope* he will.

Richard flushed and shook his head angrily. "He won't. I'm twenty-one. He won't ever be anything to do with me."

"Yes, he will. However old you are, he'll still be – " I felt suddenly sad and tired. "Richard, please don't be like this. Let's at least talk this over."

"Dog called Off," quoted Barry, from my notebook. "You can't call a dog Off! That isn't even funny." He gave a high pitched giggle.

"Excuse me," I said, unable to stand it any longer. "But that's – "

I was interrupted by two loud thumps from the floor directly beneath my feet. I jumped.

"What's that?"

"Big rats," said Barry, giggling again. Richard laughed, too. They exchanged glances.

"Oh, I suppose *I'll* have to go," said Barry. He got up and slouched across the room, depositing the notebook in my hand. "Here you are, madam," he said, with false politeness. He had a large red spot to the left of his mouth, around which he had omitted to shave. I gave an involuntary shudder, which Richard must have noticed, because when Barry had gone, he said, "You see, *you* don't like *my* friends much either, do you?"

I pulled a face. "Well, I think you might have done better than this place, that's all."

"Oh, do you indeed?" He dug his hands deep into his pockets and pulled up his shoulders rigidly, a shrug of pain and anger. He fought with his finer feelings, but I think the pain won. "What choice did you give me, you and Dad? You sodded off in your own directions – you with *lover boy* – and it was to hell with me, wasn't it?"

I let my gaze drop to the packet of beef and spring vegetable soup.

"Oh, Mum, I'm sorry," Richard said, quickly. "Sorry, I shouldn't have said that. I know it's not your fault. You – "

Barry came back into the room, lifted a blanket from a box in the corner and extracted a video cassette. There was no picture on the cover, but the words "Killer Tarts in Black Leather" were printed unevenly along its spine.

"What's that?" I asked again, stupidly.

"Porno videos," said Barry. "Richard, why don't you let your Mum have a look – see if there's anything she fancies? I'm sure we can do her at a discount."

He left the flat and ran down the stairs.

Richard shrugged dismissively. "They're Barry's uncle's. It's safer for him to keep them up here because we're not supposed to be connected with the shop. It's OK. Nobody bothers about porno stuff these days."

"Who told you that? I don't think the Vice Squad would agree with you," I said. "What sort of stuff is it?"

"Oh, to hell with that," snapped Richard. "Why don't you try and sort yourself out, Mum? It's not too late. Dad hasn't divorced you yet. I was reading in a woman's magazine in the dentist the other day about women in their forties going through hormone changes. It's nothing to be ashamed of. Simon-at-work's Mum went all funny, too. She had some sort of therapy." My mouth dropped open. I think Richard took this for admiration at his insight into my problems.

"You know, Dad's right," he said. "It was the stupid job. Some women can take the extra stress of working, and some can't. If you give it up I know you and Dad could get back together – it's what *he* wants, you know."

My mouth was still open, and I tried to make it say something. It wouldn't.

Barry returned. "Another satisfied customer," he remarked, adding, with a smirk, "Well, not entirely, I suppose."

He slumped on to the sofa and turned on the television.

"Well," I said, letting out tension in a deep sigh. "What with the traffic and everything, maybe it would be best if I didn't stop for tea." I glanced meaningfully in Barry's direction, and Richard bit his lip. "I'll take all this washing for you, if you like, and do it over the weekend. You can pick it up when you like."

Richard checked that Barry wasn't looking, then gave me a hug. "Love you, Mum," he muttered.

He showed me downstairs.

"By the way," he said. "Did Julie tell you about that nice little earner I put her on to?"

"No, she didn't."

"Oh, well, I expect she will. Don't forget to give her my love."

"Nice little earner," I thought, as I negotiated my way through the garbage again; that wasn't Richard's phraseology.

I'd parked the Mini opposite a church. On the wall was a sign proclaiming in bold capitals "Train up a child in the way he should go: and when he is old he will not depart from it." Across this someone had scrawled in red spray paint the word, "Bollocks". A frustrated parent, probably.

I began my write-up on Victor Taylor with one eye on the notes of my conversation with him, and the other on my copy of Gail's phone message concerning Rosemary's alleged food poisoning. Actually, I thought ruefully, I could probably have done the Victor Taylor piece with both eyes closed. I opened it with the words "Mr Victor Taylor, Chairman of Taylor Group, and son of the late Walter Taylor, announced earlier this week that he was grateful for the opportunity of contributing . . .", and then my mind wandered back to Rosemary Tindall. I didn't want to phone Wayne again about the murder, and risk another dose of sarcasm, and besides – I switched off the typewriter, abandoning Victor Taylor. Besides, I hadn't actually found out anything, apart from the fact that there was a possibility Rosemary hadn't made that call to Taylors herself. I had a few vague suspicions concerning Graham Tindall, and I believed Rosemary had written an anonymous letter which no longer existed. What I needed was to find one person, just *one* person, who would back up my theory that Rosemary was something other than a model of innocent happiness. And it didn't look as if such a person existed.

I switched my typewriter back on, and wrote: "The Taylor family's first links with our area began in 1750, when – "

My telephone rang.

"Chris. Thought I should ring to congratulate you."

I closed my eyes, concentrating my memory on the familiar elements in the voice.

"Your piece on the Rosemary Tindall murder. Awfully good."

Of course, it was Fiona Lomax. "Oh, thank you," I said, surprised.

"Tell me, how did you manage to get an interview with the husband?" she asked.

My instinct prompted me to reply truthfully that I'd had nothing to do with arranging the interview, and that I hadn't particularly wanted to do it, but I'd worked in newspapers for almost a year, so I said quickly, "One has one's ways."

"Jolly well done. Nice piece. One thing, though – the headline, Chris. Quiet *wife*. Not really on, that, is it? Quiet *woman* would have been better. We mustn't perpetuate the image of women as appendages of men, must we, Chris?"

I was about to reply that the word "woman" didn't actually have the connotation I'd intended, but Fiona rushed on, "You covered that big corruption story in the summer, didn't you?"

"Yes, that's right."

"Hmmm. You were working in collaboration with what's-his-name, weren't you? The rather dishy one with the little sports car. Not that that detracts from your own achievements, of course. He's moved on now, hasn't he? Good thing. He caused a lot of grief round here last year. It turned out he was seeing both my PA *and* my photographer. And the thing was, even after they'd both found out about it he managed to keep this little ménage going for several months." She chuckled to herself. "We're our own worst enemies at times, aren't we, Chris?"

I hadn't known about the photographer.

"I live with him, actually," I said.

"Oh. Well, not to worry. We're all entitled to one blind spot! Reason I called, Chris, is that if you were ever thinking of making a career move, I'd like you to get in touch."

"Thank you." I put the thought of Pete and Fiona's

voluptuous blonde photographer out of my mind temporarily. "It's kind of you to phone. Er – tell me – when your people worked on the Tindall story, did you come across anyone who was close to her? Other than her husband, I mean."

Fiona had been about to put her phone down. "Sorry?" she prompted irritably. "No, we didn't. Nor did the police, as far as I know. Mrs Tindall's entire life was invested in her husband, apparently," she added, with a hint of disapproval.

"Oh. I just thought – " I was disappointed, and muttered, half to myself. "Maybe I spoke to the wrong person at Taylors. There must have been other women on the staff – in book-keeping, or – "

"Actually," Fiona interrupted. "I wouldn't pursue that line, Chris. We don't want to get away from the main issue here, do we?"

"Er – "

"Chris, the fact is that Rosemary Tindall was murdered for no other reason than that she was a *woman*. This is the point we've got to get across. Your piece was very good, but I don't see any further advantage in character analysis. Her loss *as a person* is tragic, but she was murdered *as a woman*. Don't forget that."

"Well, really, I don't suppose it matters much to her whether she was killed as a person or a woman. She's still – well, she's still – "

"Fine," replied Fiona, absently. "I've got a call on my other line, Chris. Do keep in touch." The phone clicked and abruptly went dead.

"Goodbye," I said, replacing the receiver.

I stared unseeingly at my piece on Victor Taylor for a few moments. If neither Fiona nor I had been able to find anyone in whom Rosemary had confided her problems, then perhaps it was because she'd had no problems to confide. Perhaps her only dilemma had been deciding whether to remain at Taylors or take up the Reverend Hollingsworth's job offer: writing anonymous letters to newspapers might have been a harmless, cranky hobby not worth talking to anyone about. I ripped out my copy of Gail's phone message, and was filing it with other items on the murder, when I suddenly remembered something. Of course, Rosemary had had one close friend. I reached for Yellow Pages. Rosemary had been prepared to spend weekends "shop-sitting" for her friend Tania, at a pet shop in Hudderston. I looked up Tropaquaria. It was listed as a "Specialist in Cold Water and Tropical Fish", and had an address in a back street off Hudderston High Street.

I made a note in my diary, and returned reluctantly to my piece on Victor Taylor.

Tropaquaria nestled uncomfortably between a Turf Accountant's and a dingy little shop selling reject bed linen which had been having a "Closing Down" sale for the last seven years. I could see a young woman in Tropaquaria's window, busily sticking lumps of cotton wool on to the glass in an effort to make her fish look festive. She had encircled the window with tinsel, and spray painted it with the outline of a spindly looking reindeer and a sleigh. The reindeer had a very grim expression. A bell rang as I opened the door, and the woman smiled at me above a display of plastic water weed.

"Be with you in a second," she said. "What do you think?"

"Well – " I was tempted to say that the reindeer looked as though he could do with an Alka Seltzer. "It reminds me a bit of one of those glass balls full of water you shake, and snow comes down over a Father Christmas."

"Oh, great!" She climbed down from the window. "That's exactly what it's meant to be. Only I'm not having a Father Christmas. I've got a polystyrene mermaid coming tomorrow."

"Ah. Look, I'm sorry to have got you out of your window, because I haven't actually come here to buy anything. I'm a reporter for the *Tipping Herald*."

"Oh." She was in her mid-twenties, and was dark and pretty. I detected a note of hostility in the "Oh".

"You may have seen my story on Rosemary Tindall in last week's *Herald*." No response. "I believe you were a close friend of hers and I just wondered if you'd mind if I asked you a few questions about her."

She frowned "Why? You've already done your story. Has there been some progress in finding the murderer?"

"Er, no, but we might be doing a follow up. Sometimes things happen in a case if you can just keep it in the public eye."

I glanced sideways and found myself staring into a large round eye ringed with gold and blue stripes. The eye regarded me unblinkingly, and then moved away in an effortless surge of rippling fins. The whole shop was filled with the sound of bubbling water.

I got out my notebook. "You're Tania, aren't you?" I queried. "Can you tell me how long you knew Rosemary?"

Tania stared angrily at her half completed window. She shook her head. "I don't see any point to this. If you don't want to buy anything I'd like you to leave my shop."

"Ah." I hesitated, then said boldly. "Don't you want to see the person who killed Rosemary brought to justice? Won't you feel just a little bit guilty if the murderer kills someone else?"

She laughed incredulously. "This is ridiculous! How is my telling you about what Rosemary did at school going to help the police find the murderer?"

I smiled. "So you went to school with her, did you? I didn't know that. And then you shared a flat with her? Where was that? You must have known her when she first met Graham – "

Tania slapped her hand angrily against a large polythene sack labelled "ornamental shale". "You're not interested in finding Rosemary's murderer, you're only interested in muck-raking! If you don't get out of my shop, I'm going to call the police!" She took a step towards the door, with the clear intention of ushering me out of it.

Pete always said that if ever anyone accuses you of muck-raking, you may be sure that if you stick your rake in a little bit further, you will find some muck.

I closed my notebook. "All right," I said. "If you won't spare me five minutes to talk about Rosemary, and give my paper an excuse for reminding the public of her death, I suppose we'll have to forget it."

She looked abashed, but opened the door anyway. "Listen," she said. "The fact is that Rosemary and I used to be close friends, but we weren't any longer. She got married, and I didn't, and we drifted apart. It often happens. I hadn't even spoken to her for months."

I took a reluctant step towards the door, and then the full impact of this statement hit me.

"But you must have!" I said. "You must have spoken to her at least twice – when you asked her to look after the shop for you, and when you rang to cancel the arrangement."

The shop doorbell rang suddenly and unexpectedly, making us both jump. Tania closed the door.

"Oh, of course," she said, reddening slightly. "I'd forgotten about that."

"When did you ring her to tell her not to come at the weekend? Was it on the Monday, or the Tuesday? Did you ring her at her office?"

She gripped the doorhandle, her blush spreading down her neck.

"Yes, at her office."

I nodded, my heart pumping. I knew I was on to something, but I didn't quite know what. "You must have rung her on the Tuesday, then," I suggested, helpfully.

"I think it was," she agreed, smiling gratefully.

"Well, that's very interesting, Tania, because Rosemary wasn't *in* her office at all on Tuesday. According to the staff at Taylors, she was at home sick."

Tania groaned. "Oh *God*! I've never been any good at lying to people. Oh, what's the point! It's not even my problem. All right, we made the whole thing up – I never did ask Rosemary to look after the shop, and I never rang her to cancel it. I hadn't spoken to Rosemary for months and I don't know anything about her personal life, so you've come to the wrong person, haven't you? All right? Now you know."

I frowned, baffled. "But *why*? Why did you make it up?"

She sighed, and peered into a tank of small, almost transparent fish with enormous mouths that clung lasciviously to the side of the glass. "It was Graham's idea. He didn't want anyone to know that he and Rosemary had split up."

"They'd *split up*? Why? When?"

Tania walked past me towards the counter. She leaned against it, shaking her head. "Oh God, this is awful. This is precisely what Graham wanted to avoid. If I tell you, will you promise not to print it? It's got absolutely nothing to do with her murder. I wish I'd never got involved in it."

I said, "You're not really in a position to bargain, not after lying to the police."

Tania groaned again. "All right. I'll tell you the whole story." She glanced at the shop door, as though hoping it would open and admit a saviour. "Graham was always nuts about Rosemary. When we were kids he used to hang around outside her house, and he'd follow Rosemary and me to discos. We spent most of our time trying to lose him. He was OK, but if you don't fancy someone, you just don't."

"And Rosemary didn't?"

"No. She went out with him a few times – out of pity, I think – but she said he irritated her. Being so faithful, probably – like a dog. Rosemary had this habit of falling for the wrong kind of men – lame ducks, misfits. You know, the sort who stand on their own at parties and pretend to be drunk because they've got such awful personality problems no one wants to get involved with them."

This was news to me. I'd thought it was only women who worried about having personality problems.

Tania hesitated, looking at her hands. "Well, she had a lot of bad experiences, like we all do, and then there was this guy where she was working. He was married, but he said he was planning to leave his wife – the usual story," she added with a meaningful look. "This time Rosemary really got hurt. She swore off men for life – but then back came good old Graham."

"So she married him on the rebound?"

"Yes. Definitely. I warned her she'd be sorry, but then she got very involved with the Church." Tania shrugged. "She started trying to save lost souls instead of rotten men,

I suppose. I don't know. Anyhow, that's when we rather lost touch."

"I see. And you said she and Graham had split up?"

"Yes, apparently. According to Graham she told him the Sunday before she died. She said she just couldn't go on with the marriage any longer. Look, that's all I know," said Tania, holding up a hand. "That's what Graham told me and like I said, I hadn't seen Rosemary for ages."

"So what was this story about the shop-sitting for, then?"

She was getting hostile again. She stared at me contemptuously.

"To explain why Graham didn't report her missing earlier, of course! He got back from his course and she was gone, just like she'd said she'd be. He said he thought she might have come to stay with me. Anyway, on the Sunday morning he heard on the radio that a body had been found, and he thought it sounded like Rosemary – so he rang me. Afterwards, when he'd identified the body he *begged* me to help. He said it was bad enough Rosemary being dead, he just couldn't face having to tell people about all their problems as well."

I shook my head. "That's what he told you – and you believed him?"

"What do you mean?"

"I think it's obvious." The fish with the golden eye had been joined by a companion. They nuzzled towards my ear with full, pulsing lips. "Graham was obsessed with Rosemary," I said, moving away from the fish. "He'd spent most of his adult life waiting for her – and waiting on her – phoning her at work, cooking with her. He couldn't bear to see her walk out on him. Graham killed Rosemary himself, and attempted to make it look like one of the Face Murders. And if he'd had the courage to report her missing straight away instead of involving you, he'd very probably have got away with it."

Tania stared at me for a moment, and then laughed. "I don't believe this," she said. "If it wasn't so pathetic – if *you* weren't so pathetic – I'd call the police. You'd better not print any of this! My God, I know there's a shortage of good quality school leavers these days but it's coming to something when a person like you can get into journalism."

The rush and bubble of the aquaria now seemed to be coming from inside my head. Pete had said never argue; he said when people started insulting you, the time had come to leave – preferably before you got hit. I decided he had a point.

"Thank you," I said. "Thank you for your time."

I drove back to the *Herald* building at an average of ten miles per hour over the legal speed limit, not even attempting to evaluate the information I'd just been given. I'd got to work all this out carefully. I ran to my desk and dialled the number of Hudderston Central police station.

"Well, what can I do for you this time?" asked Wayne, amicably.

"Oh – well – I was just reviewing the Cottis Wood murder for this week's edition, and I wondered if there'd been any developments."

"Did you? You must be psychic – the forensic report on the car has just landed on my desk. Let's cut out the crap and give you the interesting bits. You all right, love? You sound out of breath."

"I've been – running," I gasped.

"Oh. Didn't know you were into athletics. Right, well, as expected we found a quantity of mud from the Cottis Wood area in the wheel arches of the car, and in the carpeting under the driver's seat. The odd thing is, they haven't come up with anything to prove the victim was ever in the car. Not so much as a hair from her head."

I nodded to myself happily. This was just as I'd expected, because of course according to my "Monday" theory of the killing Rosemary's body had never been inside John's Granada.

"And there are a lot of fingerprints which we haven't yet managed to identify. It's not very exciting, routine police work, is it?" suggested Wayne. "How are you going to make headlines out of that?"

"I'm not," I said, adding, "I know most routine police work must be awfully boring – just like routine newspaper

111

work. What I wondered, was – you remember when we had that very nice lunch together? Well, you said something about checking Graham Tindall's movements for the Tuesday – the day of the murder. Would you mind running through it again for me, please?"

"Sure." He couldn't resist adding, "Why? Are you doing a survey of news bulletin times throughout the country? Graham Tindall was in a hotel in Shepton Mallet on the evening of Tuesday, 10th November. He was in the Conference Room, attending a lecture on computer viruses which seriously overran its time. He – let's see – he left when the discussion broke up at six twenty, and he apparently went out for a stroll. He didn't join the rest of his yuppy friends in the restaurant. Is that really what you want to know? What are you up to?"

"I'm not up to anything," I said, innocently. "Just putting together my own file on the murder. Oh – my other phone's ringing. Thanks for your help. I'll give you a ring some time. Bye!" I put the phone down hastily. I was beginning to get good at this.

On the wall outside Mr Heslop's office was a map of Southern England. I studied it carefully, measuring the distance between Shepton Mallet and Hudderston with a broken pencil. I tried to work out the scale, and gave up. It didn't matter. Wayne had said it took two to three hours to drive from Hudderston to Shepton Mallet. That meant Graham Tindall could have left his hotel at half past six and been in Hudderston by nine – just. It was close, especially considering the make of car he drove. I grimaced. Well, it didn't matter if it was close, it was possible. I went back to my desk, biting my lip in excitement. With the information Tania had given me this afternoon I was sure I could piece together what had happened. Graham Tindall hadn't gone straight from work to Shepton Mallet on Monday night. Instead, he'd returned home to Tucker Hill Road. He'd probably killed Rosemary in a fit of anger – or despair – and I didn't know exactly when or where but then he'd hidden her body in Cottis Wood. The following day he came up with the idea of making the murder look like the work of the Face Murderer, and when his lecture finished he drove back to Hudderston. I'd no idea how he'd managed to obtain a shotgun, but this seemed a minor detail. On his way to the wood he'd stopped at the Eldon Lodge and borrowed John's car, probably reasoning – quite rightly – that the gunshot would attract attention, and that his bright yellow 2CV was too readily identifiable.

Well, the theory was neither complete nor perfect, but it was good. Too good to be ignored, anyway, and too good to hand over to someone else – Wayne for instance. I wondered what I should do. I stared at the spot where Pete's desk had once stood, and my stomach turned momentarily liquid. Of course, Pete would know what to do. He always had an answer for everything.

I tucked all my notes on Rosemary Tindall into my shopping bag, along with the washing powder and the new sink plug I'd picked up at lunchtime, and decided to do nothing until I'd spoken to Pete.

10

Sunlight filtering through the worn patch in the bedroom curtains startled me out of a bad dream. At least, I thought it was a bad dream, only it wasn't. I sat up. I was still wearing my clothes, it was seven a.m. and Pete's half of the bed remained pristine and untrammelled. Immediately the gnawing headache and the gnawing fear I'd fallen asleep with reasserted themselves. The duty officer at Tipping police station had sounded irritable, and resigned to dealing with hysterical women when I'd phoned him at five past midnight. He said an adult who'd only been missing from home for five hours was scarcely a priority police matter, and had I tried the hospitals? When I explained that Pete could have had an accident anywhere between Tipping and London, he asked nastily whether or not the missing person was in the habit of drinking and driving, and I quickly replaced the receiver without giving my name and address. The less said about Pete's drinking habits the better, especially to the police.

I sent Julie off to school as usual, making soothing noises about "reasonable explanations", etc, but she didn't seem very concerned. She'd got a French test later, and anyway, it was other people's relatives whose cars skidded into the paths of oncoming lorries.

I got into work late, not sure whether or not to be relieved that no grave faced policeman had turned up on my doorstep. I took off my coat, crossed all my fingers and toes, and rang Pete's number at the paper.

"Yes?" he said.

"Oh, Pete! Oh my God! What happened?" The flood of relief sent a wave of pain coursing through my temples.

There was a moment's silence. "What are you talking about, darling?" he asked, puzzled. "Have I missed something?"

"*Missed* something? I'm talking about last night – What happened to you? Are you all right?"

"Yes, I'm fine, darling, thanks."

Just for an instant I thought I must be losing my grip. Just for an instant I considered apologising. Then I lost my temper. I shouted at him about how I'd waited and waited and phoned the police station, about how much sleep I'd lost, and about how he'd better have a very good explanation for putting me to so much misery. When I'd finished I got the impression there was no one on the end of the line.

"Hallo?" I queried.

"Jesus," said Pete. "What's up with you? I told you I was meeting some of the guys last night and might not be back."

"No, you didn't."

"Yes, I did. I told you at breakfast."

"You don't have breakfast!"

"All right, I shouted it through the bathroom door. Christ, Chris, I've got a bloody awful headache, I don't need this."

"Where did you sleep?"

"What do you mean, where did I sleep?"

I didn't bother to answer this.

"I slept on Joe's sofa."

"Who's Joe?" I went through a list of Pete's various drinking buddies and couldn't come up with anyone called Joe. This time Pete didn't bother to answer.

"Look," I said, grimly. "You didn't tell me you were going to be away last night. I'd've remembered if you had. You didn't take any overnight things with you, not even a toothbrush!"

"I'll be right with you, darling," Pete said, away from the mouthpiece. "Now, listen, Chris, you're not my bloody mother. If you're so worried about my teeth you can put your mind at rest – I keep a toothbrush in my desk, and a change of underwear. What's the big deal, for Christ's sake?"

"What do you mean, what's the big deal? Are we living together, or what? There was something important I wanted to talk to you about last night. Are you just going to go off for the night when you feel like it without bothering to tell me? How would you like it if I – ?"

"Chris," interrupted Pete. "Shut up. You are overreacting. Is there something you wish to say which is so important it can't wait until tonight?" I was speechless. "In that case, darling, I am going to put down this phone." And so saying, he did.

I spent the rest of the day alternately smouldering and fuming, and sometimes doing both at once. By the end of the afternoon I'd got a red-hot iron rod of righteous indignation for a spine and I was ready to cope with anything. I didn't need Pete; I'd solved the Rosemary Tindall murder case all by myself and there was nothing on the face of the earth apart from changing the Hoover band that I couldn't handle. I phoned Julie to say I'd be late home as there was a murderer I had to bring to justice, and to take something out of the freezer. (I didn't actually mention the murder: that would have been going too far.)

It was dark, and wind-borne raindrops spattered the windscreen as I parked in Tucker Hill Road. It was much like it must have been on the night of the 9th November. I locked up the Mini carefully and slowly and walked up the path beneath the grasping branches of the monkey puzzle tree. I was already beginning to feel a little less certain and a little less righteous.

Graham Tindall opened his front door and peered at me. He hadn't shaved that day, and the bristles on his chin glinted gold in the conservatory light.

"Can we come in, Mr Tindall?" I asked, instinctively seeking the safety of imaginary numbers. He gazed beyond me, baffled, and stepped aside. He stood opposite me in the cold, pale glare of a solitary light bulb and stared at me. He looked guilty and nervous and frightened.

"What do you want?" he asked, plunging his hands into his pockets.

"Well, we could start with the truth," I suggested, because this sort of approach usually works on television.

"What truth? What do you mean?" asked Graham, whose tastes in television probably differed substantially from mine.

I gritted my teeth. "I spoke to Tania yesterday. Didn't she tell you? You got her to lie to the police and she's very upset about it."

He looked as though I'd hit him in the stomach. His pale eyes bulged.

"I was only trying to make things better," he protested. "I didn't know what to do."

This was such an inadequate response that it took the wind out of my sails. "Look," I began, appealingly. "You may as well admit it. I'm sure it was really an accident. The longer you go on with this pretence the worse it will be. I do understand, honestly."

His hands were in his pockets, clenched. He started to remove them. Just for a moment I felt a twinge of fear, and I stepped backwards. Out of the corners of both eyes I could see only blackness beyond the glass walls of the conservatory.

"I'm trying to help you," I said. "You can phone the police yourself, or I can do it for you. I've got the number – where's your phone?"

"My phone," whispered Graham, hoarsely, his hands still half out of his pockets.

"Yes." I took another step backwards, watching his hands. I cleared my throat. "You killed Rosemary on Monday, 9th November. You didn't go straight down to Shepton Mallet like you said you did. The staff at the hotel remember how muddy you were when you arrived. You killed Rosemary and dumped her body in the wood. You rang Taylors office on Tuesday morning and told them Rosemary was in bed with food poisoning. Where did you get the shotgun from, Mr Tindall? Is it still in the house? You'll have left fingerprints on the Granada. You don't really want to get away with this anyway, do you? How can you go on with it on your conscience?" I ended desperately. He was staring at me in growing disbelief.

Suddenly, I just knew I'd got it all wrong.

"I can't believe this," said Graham, still in a whisper. "I always thought Tania was jealous of us – she kept Rosemary and me apart for ages, you know – but I didn't think she'd make all this up. I thought she'd want to help for Rosemary's sake."

Oh God, I thought, why did I do this?

"Would you like to explain yourself, Mr Tindall?" I

117

suggested, trying to sound as though I was still in control.

"There's nothing to explain. I mean – I don't know what Tania's told you. All I asked her to do was to tell the police if they checked with her that I'd been expecting Rosemary to spend the weekend at her flat. Where was the harm in that? I knew they'd wonder why I'd taken so long to report her missing – I just didn't want people to think Rosemary and I weren't happy together."

"You *weren't* happy together. You were splitting up."

"Yes, I know, but – " He took his hands out of his pockets and held them out towards me in a gesture of supplication. "It would only have been temporary. She'd've come to her senses. I told you, we were made for each other. This other thing was all over anyway, but if I'd told the police they'd've wanted to know the man's name, and the whole awful story would have been dragged out."

I started. "What man? Are you trying to tell me Rosemary was involved with someone else?"

Graham hesitated. "Would you like to come inside?" he asked, indicating the dark hallway of the house.

"No, thank you. What man?"

"I don't know what man. I don't want to talk about it. What does it matter now anyway?" He leaned heavily against the doorpost. "Please go away."

"I can't. I won't. I want to know about this man Rosemary was having an affair with. He may be the one who killed her."

Graham had closed his eyes despairingly. Now he opened them and looked at me. "That's nonsense. Rosemary stopped seeing him months ago, she told me. And anyway, she was killed by a total stranger. The police said the murderer probably watched some documentary on television a few weeks ago, and – Please go away."

We were getting nowhere, fast.

"Mr Tindall, I'm sorry if I jumped to the wrong conclusion, but making up all that nonsense about shop-sitting and not living in one another's pockets was very stupid. Will you please just tell me the whole story or I won't leave."

He hesitated. "Will you come inside, then?" His hand

moved to the light switch. Light flooded the bungalow's hallway, showing up the layer of dust on the woodblock flooring, criss-crossed by Graham's footprints. A pile of untouched newspapers and mail had built up in a corner.

"All right," I agreed, doubtfully. I followed my instincts into the hall and sat down on the cane sofa. Graham sat down next to me. He pulled a handkerchief from his pocket and blew his nose.

"I suppose you're right," he said. "I suppose I knew I'd have to tell the truth eventually. That last Sunday, when Rosemary came back from Church, she told me she was leaving me. She said she'd fallen in love with someone else, and though the affair hadn't worked out she seemed to think she shouldn't go on with our marriage. Well, I don't understand that, do you?" he demanded, turning to me. "*I* still loved her. Why didn't she want to stay with me?"

I shook my head. When I didn't answer, he continued. "I'd've done *anything* for her. I've never even looked at any other woman. I'm telling you, I forgave *her*, but that morning when she told me, if I'd known who the bastard was – " He clenched his fists and stared at the white patches forming on his knuckles. Even when he got angry he didn't look like much of a threat to anyone. I'd been too ready to jump to conclusions, but I said:

"Is that why she wouldn't tell you who her lover was?"

Graham winced. "Don't use that word, lover. *I* was the one who loved her," he said, bitterly.

"Did you try to stop her going?" I asked.

"Of course I did, but she'd made up her mind. She said God wanted her to *atone* for everything – she said that several times. She said she didn't know exactly what she was going to do, but that when I got back from the course she'd be gone. She said she didn't want any money from the house, or anything. She'd just take a suitcase full of clothes and the few hundred pounds in her post office savings account. That's what finally alerted me to the fact that there was something wrong. I really thought she'd have gone to Tania's – that bitch would've been glad to see us separated – but then I realised that all her clothes were still in the wardrobe. I heard it on the news, you see, on Sunday morning, about a body being found that sounded like Rosemary. God, I knew Tania never liked me much, but I thought she'd help. I thought she'd do it for Rosemary's sake."

I cleared my throat. "Actually," I said. "Tania did do her best to help. It was me – I put two and two together and came up with five. You see, I've got a theory that your wife was murdered on the Monday evening, not the Tuesday, and at the hotel in Shepton Mallet they said you arrived very late on the Monday, and that you were soaking wet when you got there. They said you didn't eat in the restaurant on Tuesday, and I thought – "

"I didn't eat in the restaurant any night!" interrupted Graham. "I hardly ate at all. And I was wet and muddy when I arrived on the Monday because I'd been sitting on a gate in a field in the rain, trying to think what to do."

"Look, Mr Tindall," I interrupted. "I jumped to a very wrong conclusion and I apologise. But I'm sure you can see it's important we find out who Rosemary's – friend was. I mean, he may have nothing to do with her death, but there are other things. Did you know for instance that your wife had written to my paper anonymously offering us information about a local businessman?"

He looked startled. "Who? What information?"

I grimaced. "I'm afraid I don't know. Anyway, you must have *some* idea – even just a very wild guess – who her lover was."

Graham frowned angrily at the offending word, but said, "All right. There is something. The police gave me back her handbag this morning, and there was a name and address in it I didn't recognise. I looked it up in the phone book, but it wasn't listed." He hesitated. "I can get it for you, but I don't want this to end up in the paper. I don't want it all raked over and splashed about in the *Sun* and the *News of the World*."

I could have told him that his wife's death was already old news, and that her life hadn't been important enough to warrant this kind of attention by the national press, but I hardly thought that would be comforting. I said, "I'm sorry Mr Tindall, but we must get at the truth."

Graham Tindall got up and fetched a brown paper parcel.

It had been opened and carefully re-wrapped. He parted the sellotape again and pulled out a black patent leather handbag. The contents of the bag were in no particular order – keys, purse and till receipts all jumbled up with crumpled panty shields and lipsticks. I guessed the police had listed the items and then scooped them back into the bag from a desk top.

Graham extracted a tightly folded sheet of paper, which turned out to be a bank deposit statement made out to a Mr A.L. Demarco of 88 Walworth Road, Hudderston. At the end of December last year Mr Demarco had had the sum of £8,304 in his account. At first it just seemed odd that Rosemary would be in possession of this man's bank statement, whoever he was, but when I refolded it and held it up to Rosemary's purse it fitted perfectly against the hidden zipped compartment, which even bore the outlines of its sharp folds. I found a second sheet of paper, folded in exactly the same way – a bill for a meal eaten by two persons at the Old Barn Restaurant last May.

"I see what you mean," I said. "It looks very much like she kept these in her purse as souvenirs of a love – of a friendship." I thought wryly of the receipt for a night's stay at a bed and breakfast hotel on the South Coast, which had lain in my purse for twenty-one years (and which just might have been indirectly responsible for Richard's existence).

I opened Rosemary's purse and tipped the contents into my lap – a few coins, a paper clip, and a small pink card bearing the name Milly Molly Mandy and a phone number. It looked like a hairdresser's business card. I tucked it back inside the purse, and stood up.

"Mr Tindall, I'm afraid you will probably be hearing more from the police about this," I said. "I'd like to take these documents with me so I can tell them what I've found out."

He nodded. He didn't follow me to the door. He sat on the cane sofa with Rosemary's handbag – and then he called to me when I got to the step.

"Do you think – do you think Rosemary would have come back to me eventually?" he said. And because I didn't know – or maybe because I didn't think she would have – I retreated down the path without answering.

Of course, on my way back to Tipping I couldn't resist a detour by way of Walworth Road. It wasn't a very salubrious street. All the houses were old and mostly divided up to provide offices for small firms of insurance brokers, or clinics for chiropodists and homeopaths. No. 88 had been split into eight flats. I studied the names on the doorbells. There was no mention of a Mr Demarco. The front door was open, so I stepped into the dim hallway. It smelt as I imagine a United Nations cafeteria must do, of garlic and pizza, vinegar, chips and vindaloo. Through thin partition walls the cadences of sitar music vied with Chuck Berry. On the table next to the door lay a jumble of junk mail, free newssheets, and long buff window envelopes, most with the addresses printed in red. It looked like the sorting office on a bad day. Some of this mail had been collected into piles for the addressees, and some of it looked as if it had been there for months. I couldn't see anything addressed to Mr Demarco.

I was still contemplating the letters when the door of Flat 3 opened and a youth in fashionably torn jeans emerged, carrying a large bag of dirty washing. When I asked him if he could tell me anything about a Mr Demarco, he looked me up and down suspiciously, as though I might be from a debt collection agency, or worse. He'd lived in the house for eight months, he said, and had never come across anyone called Demarco living there. He thought Mr Demarco must have moved on. He suggested I ask the landlady, Mrs Kaussmann, who lived in Flat 1, and he rang her bell vigorously for me. I waited in the hall until the Chuck Berry number had finished, by which time it was obvious that Mrs Kaussmann was not in residence. I decided to give up on Mr Demarco for the day.

Pete and Julie were sitting in the living-room with their legs on the coffee table when I got home.

"Here he is, Mum!" exclaimed Julie, brightly. "I told you he'd turn up all right. Are you going to give him a good telling off?" She patted his hand playfully. "Don't worry, her bark's awful, but she's a soft old thing really."

Pete attempted to smile at me. I ignored him and marched grimly upstairs to the bedroom. To my surprise, the bed had been neatly made and the sweater and jeans I usually wore at home were evenly folded and laid across my pillow. Pete followed me into the bedroom and closed the door.

"All right," he said. "I admit it. I didn't tell you I was going to spend last night in town, primarily because I didn't know. I should've phoned you but I didn't. I suppose I forgot."

"About me?" I took off my jacket and threw it on the bed.

He looked uncomfortable. "Don't be silly. How could I forget about you?"

"Well, you did, didn't you? If you must know I was very worried about you. I thought something awful had happened to you."

"Did you? Does that mean you still love me?" he asked, sitting on the edge of the bed and stretching a hand out towards me.

"Of course I love you." I decided to ignore the hand. I'd forgotten that being in love made you feel so vulnerable, and I wished I wasn't. I was too old for all this. I pulled off my top and began tugging at my skirt zip.

"Well." He was trying to read my expression. "Are we going to have a row about this, or are we going to make up and forget about it? It's up to you. You're calling the shots on this one."

"Am I? Why?"

"Because according to you, darling, despite the grievous verbal damage you did to my ear this morning, *you're* the injured party." He smiled disarmingly, and poked his tongue out at me. "Go on, I've said I'm sorry. Let's kiss and make up."

I hesitated, then leaned over the bed and touched his lips with my mouth. I didn't want to row with him. Rowing with Keith had been therapeutic: the rows always followed exactly the same course and ended up with us both feeling a lot better. With Pete, I wasn't sure where they might lead.

Pete caught me in a long lingering kiss that made my toes curl up.

"All right," I conceded, stepping back and out of my skirt. "I forgive you. After all, it's a long time since you had anyone to go home to. You just didn't think." I pulled off my slip. "We've never really had a proper row, have we? I think we ought to keep it like that."

"Go on," said Pete.

"Go on what?"

He smiled. "Undressing. It's nice."

My knees began to dissolve like jelly cubes in warm water. I reached for my sweater, smiling awkwardly. *Kissing* and forgiving was one thing: reminding him of the devastating effect he had on the parts of me not normally on display was quite another.

"We must make a definite policy of talking things out," I said. "I'm sorry I shouted at you this morning. I was upset." He got up from the bed and stood in front of me. My eyes were on a level with his throat, and I studied the small brown mole on his Adam's apple and realised that I passionately wanted to kiss it. "I missed having you in bed with me, and I didn't know where you were," I murmured, resisting the impulse. "You could have been hurt, or ill – or" He unfastened my bra, let it fall to the floor and cupped my breasts in his hands as though weighing them. "Well, really, you might – " His finger and thumb began exquisitely teasing my left nipple. I swallowed down an ecstatic response. "I tried to phone the police but they wouldn't help – "

Suddenly he frowned and bent closer to examine my left nipple: it had gone as hard as a peach stone.

"Did you know, Chris, that you have a very common female complaint?" he whispered, undoing his trouser belt.

"*What*?"

He smiled. "You're beautiful. You've got skin like white satin and a tummy as inviting as a swansdown pillow after a hard day's night – but do you love me even half as much as I love you?" He pushed me on to the bed and forced my legs apart, running a fingertip slowly along the curve of my stomach beneath my pants' elastic.

"Stop it! Don't tease me!" I begged, pulling feverishly at his trousers. "You're cruel – you know how much I love you. What female complaint have I got?"

He lowered himself on to me. "Silly," he whispered. "You just talk too bloody much!"

*

I was fishing over the end of the bed to retrieve our clothes, when my stomach emitted a loud growl of protest.

"I've been too worried to eat," I explained, smiling at him fondly as I struggled to free his underpants from his trouser leg.

"Good," said Pete. Downstairs, the phone was ringing. "Your daughter and I had a meal ready for you at half past six – Where *were* you this evening, by the way?"

"Oh, following up the Tindall murder case," I said, and told him all about my meetings with Tania and Graham and how I now suspected that the murder might be a crime of passion.

Pete said nothing for a moment. Then his expression changed to a frown of incredulity. "Am I understanding this right?" he asked. "You worked out that this guy had brutally murdered his wife and then called at his house – by yourself, on a dark night – to ask him if he'd like to make a comment on it?"

"Yes. Well, no, not exactly."

"Do you realise." He threw a balled up sock at me. "Do you realise that if you'd been right about Graham Tindall you could at this very moment be lying in a ditch with bits of your face in the next field?" He pulled on his trousers and made for the door, sockless.

"Is that all you can say?" I asked, hurt. "Aren't you impressed at how far I got with this case all by myself?"

"Christ!" He was furious. He looked like Keith had the first time I scratched the car. "What's the matter with you? Haven't you got any sense at all? I wouldn't have believed you could be so stupid!" He slammed the door and ran downstairs, still doing up his shirt.

I pulled on sweater and jeans and ran after him, but was arrested in mid-pursuit by the sight of Julie doing exercises against the hall wall while engaged in a phone conversation.

"We can do it easily," she said, excitedly. "I'll use Mum's food processor for the pastry . . . And how about getting some of that posh lettuce from Sainsbury's? . . ." She spotted my look of amazement. "Got to go now," she said. "Talk to you later."

"What are you up to?" I asked. "What's all this about posh lettuce?"

"Oh, you know, that floppy pink stuff that tastes like dandelions."

"Well, I wish you wouldn't call it that. People will think we don't use it except on special occasions."

"We don't," protested Julie, innocently, adding, "And could we borrow your food processor? You mostly give us things from packets now anyway, so you wouldn't miss it. Stephanie and I have got a chance to go for this catering job. It'd only be occasional work but the money's fantastic."

I frowned miserably; it was the remark about eating things out of packets that hurt. Julie misunderstood the look.

"Oh, I just knew you'd say no! Pete and I have washed up and made you a great dinner and you haven't even said thank you."

"Thank you," I said, surprised. "But that's not *catering*, is it? Don't you think this is a bit much for you to take on? What about school?"

"What's school got to do with it? This would just be at weekends. It's this woman Richard knows. She does catering for parties and weddings and with Christmas coming up she's *desperate*."

She must be, I thought, wryly. "Our kitchen's very tiny, Julie," I said, doubtfully.

Julie muttered something under her breath which was probably quite rude, but I was feeling too guilty about the packets and the size of the kitchen – not to mention my current lack of underwear – to take her up on it. I took the coward's way out.

"We'll talk about it later," I said.

DI Carver's office was small, and lit by a single fluorescent tube. His cork wallboard had so many notices pinned to it it looked as if the slightest breeze might cause an avalanche of paper. He leaned forward in his chair, appearing to listen intently to my every word. When I'd finished he glanced at Wayne and something close to a smile flickered across his thin lips.

"As a point of interest, Mrs Martin," he said, "why do

you think the fact that Mrs Tindall was in possession of Mr Demarco's bank statement indicates she was having an affair with him? Would you give your bank statement to a lady you were having an affair with, Wayne?"

Wayne laughed. "I certainly wouldn't. My bank statement would damp down anybody's passion."

"It's not just because she possessed it," I said. "It's because she was carrying it in her purse with the restaurant bill. You know, as a souvenir."

The door opened, and a young constable with acne put his head round it.

"Sorry, sir, but it's important," he said.

"Another point," went on DI Carver, frowning at the constable. "We looked for Mr Demarco when we first came across his name in the victim's handbag. It was our only clue to her identity. No one living at that address in Walworth Road remembers him, the landlady – who is in her eighties and stone deaf – doesn't keep proper rent records, let alone forwarding addresses, and he's not on Hudderston's current electoral roll. So whatever her relationship may have been with him, we came to the conclusion that it was in the past. What is it, Huckins?" he added, to the young constable, absently handing the statement back to me.

"It's *Mrs* Carver, sir. The Council planning officer says that if you don't submit new drawings by midday today your application will have to wait another six weeks – "

"*Christ almighty!*" exclaimed DI Carver, angrily. "These people are bloody extortionists! There's nothing wrong with the position of my stopcock! Get my surveyor on the phone."

"Yes, sir," replied Huckins, departing.

"I might add, Mrs Martin," continued DI Carver, returning to his mild conversational tone, "that I'm a bit surprised by your attitude. For years you women have been complaining about police insensitivity in rape cases. We're told it's not supposed to matter if a woman has previously had intercourse with the whole of Aldershot Football Club plus reserves. If she says no to the ref, then it's rape."

"If she had intercourse with the whole of Aldershot's team before matches, it could go a long way to explaining their bloody awful performance on the pitch," suggested Wayne.

Inspector Carver threw him a disgusted glance. "Mrs Tindall was murdered by a psychopath – to put it simply," he added, with a condescending smile. "Her lifestyle is of little interest to us. Nor should it be to you." His phone rang.

"But Rosemary Tindall wasn't raped! She – "

"Good morning," said DI Carver, into his telephone. "One moment." He covered the mouthpiece with his hand. "I'm not qualified to give you a lecture on the relationship between sex and violence in the abnormal male," he said, managing to imply by his tone that he was. "But I think we can safely class Mrs Tindall's death as a sex crime. Good morning. It's Carver, here. Look, they insist it's no go on the downstairs toilet. That planning officer – who'd better have his car tax and insurance up to date – is insisting I re-do my waterworks – "

"Well, what about the anonymous letter Rosemary wrote to the *Herald*, and the fact that she may not have made that call to Taylors on the Tuesday morning – ?" I interrupted, desperately.

Inspector Carver placed his hand across the mouthpiece yet again, and regarded me with distaste. He managed to twist his mouth into a smile. "I think I'd be right in saying that one of your favourite television programmes is Cagney and Lacey, wouldn't I?" he remarked.

Wayne showed me out.

"I'm sorry about DI Carver, love," he said. "He's having a bad morning. Apart from his extension he's just had a right bollocking from the Super about overtime. He'll give me one later about something else, and then I'll round up as many DCs as I can lay my hands on and give them one for sloppy paperwork. Or something. Horton's law of the ever-increasing bollocking: What starts at the top gets bigger as it goes on down the line. Come tonight there'll be a few poor sods brought in drunk and disorderly who'll really get the shit kicked out of them – and all thanks to the Super."

I tried to keep up with him along the corridor.

"I just can't see why you're not interested in the fact that Graham Tindall lied about his relationship with his wife. Or that she had a lover."

Wayne halted in front of the coffee machine. He leaned on it and it swayed backwards, oozing brown liquid from its drip tray. "Want a coffee?" he asked. I shook my head. "Look, if *my* old lady fell in the alligator tank at London Zoo this afternoon I'd say what a tragedy it was and how much I'd loved her. But she won't – she's alive and well and busy making sure there isn't any money left in our joint account. So I'll carry on slagging her off. You married?"

"Separated."

The word "separated" had its usual strange, aphrodisiac effect. Wayne smiled, then gave the coffee machine a hefty kick.

"You see your problem," he said, "is that you're trying to make a mystery out of a perfectly straightforward case."

"If it's so straightforward how come you haven't made an arrest yet?"

He grinned. "I said it was straightforward, I didn't say it would be easy to solve. Tell you what, as a special favour, if you can turn up the original of that anonymous letter I'll send it to forensics, see what they come up with."

I groaned. "You know I haven't got it any longer."

He spread his hands in a "there-you-are-what-did-I-tell-you" gesture. I turned to walk away.

"You just don't give up, do you?" he called after me. "Do you know what I'm looking for at the moment? A woman who won't give up on me!"

I carried on walking, permitting myself a smile. If there was one thing I liked about Detective Sergeant Wayne Horton, it was that he always left me feeling that I knew a certain amount more than he did. About ten years more than he did.

11

I suppose I knew that morning as I drove back to the
Herald building along Tipping High Street, which was now
festooned with plastic Father Christmasses and stark red light
bulbs, that this was the point at which any sensible person
would have shrugged and called it a day on the Tindall story.
Looking back, I think I wish now that I had. But I didn't. It
was like having your best bead necklace break as you walk
down the garden, and finding ninety per cent of the beads.
I'd got to find the rest of the beads, even if it meant having
to re-plant the odd rose bed or two.

I sat down at my desk and rang Carol at Taylors. She
was the only person I'd spoken to so far on the Tindall story
who'd seemed even mildly anxious to help, and she was as
good a starting point as any in my search for Mr Demarco.
She said no, no one of that name had actually been on
the staff of Taylors, but it definitely sounded familiar. She
offered to go through Rosemary's address book and check
out the postcards on her wallboard. I asked her if she'd like
to phone me outside working hours with the information,
and she suggested that we meet somewhere *anonymous* to
talk it over.

We finally agreed on a rendezvous at the Grand Opening
of the Dolphin shopping precinct, but after I put the phone
down I had second thoughts about it. I'd got this awful feeling
Carol might turn up wearing sunglasses and a false beard.

That Saturday morning I was woken at eight thirty by the
phone ringing downstairs. I was in the middle of a dream
about Keith. He was standing in my old kitchen with
Rosemary Tindall, and he was shouting at her. I couldn't
actually see Rosemary's face, but I knew it was her, and I also
knew that he was having an affair with her. Or had been. He

kept shouting something about her having broken his chain saw, and that he was going to have to fix it. Or her. Yes, I think he was going to fix her. And then the fire alarm bell sounded in the distance and I knew someone was coming to save her. I sat up, feeling sweaty and very disturbed. Keith had never had a chainsaw and he'd never threatened to fix anybody. Not only that, Rosemary wasn't his type (he liked women who wore lots of red lipstick and had hips like sofa cushions). I sat up and shook my head to clear it.

The phone was still ringing and I gave Pete's dark head a quick kiss and stumbled downstairs to answer it. I suppose because I'd been dreaming about Keith I got it into my head that it would be him on the phone, and I ran my hands through my hair and smoothed down my eyebrows.

"Oh hallo. Is that *Chris*?" enquired a tentative female voice.

"Yes." My heart sank a little. "Who is this?"

"I'm Jennifer Saunders. I live at No. 2 Cottis Villas."

I was cross with myself for being disappointed it wasn't Keith. "Yes," I prompted, irritably.

"Well, I wonder if you'd like to come and talk to me."

Keith wouldn't be ringing me; he was waiting for me to ring him. "Why?"

"About that – *murder*."

To hell with Keith. "Ah. Did you say Mrs Saunders? I don't know you, do I? Cottis Villas. Is that one of the cottages opposite the wood?"

"Yes. But I'm not *Mrs* Saunders. I'm *Miss* Saunders."

"And what did you want to talk about?"

"Well – I can't say, really."

She fell so silent I thought for a moment we'd been cut off. "Hallo?" I said.

"Hallo?" said Miss Saunders.

"Look, it's very early in the morning," I protested. "Is it anything important?"

"I've been up all night," said Miss Saunders.

"Ah." Miss Corby must have given her my phone number, I decided, but I wasn't at all sure I wanted to speak to her. I said, "Look, I've got a note of your address. I'll pop in and see you next time I'm in the area. All right?"

131

"Yes," she agreed, doubtfully.

I put the phone down and stared at the awful brown squares on the hall wallpaper. I would really have liked that to have been Keith on the phone. I didn't know why, but I knew that that deep dark pit at the bottom of my stomach was disappointment.

I took Julie with me to the Grand Opening of the Dolphin shopping precinct. It was a cold, sunny morning and half of Tipping seemed to be packed into the concrete and glass square that had once been the site of a very popular, if dilapidated, public house. I didn't like it much, but I expect the design looked awfully good on some architect's drawing board. On the wall behind a girl in a mini skirt giving away gas filled balloons, was a gold embossed board listing firms involved in the design and construction of the Dolphin. Taylor Group's name was halfway down the list. I showed my Press badge to a group of very officious looking officials, and Julie and I took up a position just outside the area that had been roped off for the Famous Comedian who was to open the proceedings.

"What a rip off!" remarked Julie, sagely, and I made notes which included such phrases as "excited throng", and "gazing in admiration at their surroundings", and other similar expressions I thought Mr Heslop would like. Of course, I knew perfectly well that in a few months' time we'd be doing a piece entitled "Dolphin given the flipper down by shoppers", and listing all kinds of defects, but you have to play the game or it isn't worth the bother of going. We waited in obedient anticipation for about ten minutes beyond the advertised starting time, and Julie repeated the words "Rip off" and "Gross" several times in relation to the new shops and their plastic and polystyrene setting. I'd noticed that her tendency to disgust at the world in general seemed to increase according to how much Clearasil she was getting through. Finally her eye settled on a bridal boutique. She gazed long and hard at a white satin and fur creation in the window.

"I suppose you and Pete won't be going in for all that non-sense, will you?" she remarked, casually dismissing about a thousand pounds' worth of designer styling.

"I don't know about it being nonsense, but at our age marriage is quite a different prospect. We may decide not to actually get married at all," I said carefully, listening to the words as I uttered them and wondering how I felt about them.

"Oh." She stared at me incredulously for a moment. Her mouth opened to form a question, but she couldn't make up her mind about it. Finally she said. "I needn't save up for a wedding present then, I suppose. Oh. But anyway, I still *desperately* need some cash. You *will* let me do the catering job, won't you, Mum? We went to see this woman, and she said it would only – "

At that moment a sudden current of excitement began to stir the crowd. A ragged corridor opened up along which a convoy of green uniformed officials and men in dark suits proceeded towards the roped off area. Somewhere amongst them, according to the rumours flying back and forth, was the Famous Comedian. We shuffled out of their way. The Famous Comedian – who, as everyone said, was a lot shorter than he appeared on TV – made straight for the microphone and launched into a re-hash of jokes he'd used on last Saturday's show. He managed to insert the name of Tipping into some of them, and only slipped up once when he referred to "the lovely old market place local people are so proud of". His researcher must have confused us with one of the Chipping something-or-others, because we've never had a market place in Tipping. Everyone applauded politely anyway. I ran my eye over the little knot of men in dark suits and noted down those I recognised. There were Tipping's Mayor, a couple of local Councillors, and several over made-up ladies wearing large hats. I wrote down "accompanied by their wives". Representing those responsible for providing Tipping with the Dolphin, and deferred to several times by the Mayor in his speech, were the Chairman of RMP Developments, and one of the partners in the firm of Kravitz, Miller & Kearns, Architects. Messrs Maurice Prestage of RMP, and Dudley Kravitz of KMK were old friends. They wore suits probably bought from the same expensive tailor's, styled their silver hair in the same distinguished style, and appeared

133

to be married to wives carved from the same unyielding substance.

There was a much repeated titbit of juicy gossip doing the rounds of the County's Press which concerned Dudley Kravitz and Maurice Prestage. It went like this: Two years ago while returning late one night from the opening of one of their latest projects in London, they were involved in a freak accident on the Hudderston by-pass. Their car apparently hit the central reservation and over-turned and they were left semi-conscious and dangling from the safety straps for half an hour until a police patrol car came to their rescue. Pictures of the crashed car went on every front page, and Messrs Kravitz and Prestage recounted how they'd been travelling at the regulation speed along the by-pass with no other vehicle in sight, when . . . What did not get on to the front page, because the original police report mysteriously vanished without trace, was that Messrs Kravitz and Prestage had not been alone in the car. Occupying the back seat – so the glorious technicolour version of this story went – were three young ladies clad in suspenders, fake fur coats, and nothing else but goose pimples. Where the fivesome might have been going, and for what purpose, had set many an imagination running on overtime.

The opening ceremony was completed to a burst of applause and a general stampede in the direction of the Famous Comedian. Julie and I hung on to the ropes and resisted being carried along with the tide. I wondered how I was going to find Carol.

"It would really only be occasional work," went on Julie, as though there'd been no break in our conversation. "I'd need a couple of hours and the use of the kitchen on a Friday night, for example. You'd hardly notice it, Mum. How many quiches do you think we could get in our oven at one time?"

I was checking over my notes. I said, "Er – " absent-mindedly, and then caught sight of Carol seated on the edge of the ornamental goldfish pool in the centre of the square. She was waving frantically at me. At her feet a boy of about two lay slumped with his mouth open, a gas balloon bobbing languidly from its mooring on his coat button.

"My nephew," said Carol, looking at him fondly. "He pegged out and so did I. He's good practice for me." She patted the parapet next to her and swept a lolly stick into the pool so I could sit down.

"Well," she said briskly. "I did everything you asked. I went all through Rosemary's office, I checked her postcards and I went through her address book."

"Did you find out who Mr Demarco is?" I asked, excitedly.

"No, but I've definitely established that he wasn't a stationery rep or anyone Rosemary had contact with through Taylors," she announced confidently, as though this was a major breakthrough.

I was disappointed. "But you are sure the name is connected with Taylors?"

"Oh. Well. To be honest, I don't really know. I mean, it's one of those names, isn't it, that sort of sounds familiar? I mean I'm sure I've seen it or heard it somewhere, but – well." She shrugged. "Who is he, anyway? Is he the businessman Rosemary wrote a letter to the *Herald* about?"

I hesitated. "I don't really know. Actually, I think Rosemary may have been having an affair with him."

Carol's eyes almost bulged to match her stomach. "*No*! Really! Well, I never – little Miss Butter-wouldn't-melt-in-her-mouth! That Graham did seem an awful wimp, I suppose, but honestly, you'd never have guessed." Julie, sensing our discussion had something to do with sex, sat down next to me.

"Of course," went on Carol. "Christians are really weird about sex. You can tell them you've done something absolutely awful – like bashing up a car in a car park and driving off – and they'll forgive you, but if you say you've had a one-night stand with a gorgeous bloke and got pregnant, they treat you as though you're a creature from another planet!" I misunderstood Carol's remark and looked in horror at her stomach.

"Oh, no, not me," said Carol. "No such luck!" She laughed. "Only joking. Steve's OK. He's a bit of a bore, but having a kiddy will put us right."

I smiled weakly. The trouble with being over forty is

that you can see other people's problems coming a mile off.

Julie grinned.

"Oh well," I said. "Never mind."

"Mr Victor liked the story you did about him," said Carol. "We all had a good giggle over it, especially the bit about Mr Walter being happy to see money being donated to pensioners. Mr Walter was as mean as Old Nick! He and Mr Victor used to have big rows about it. Mr Victor used to say you'd got to invest in goodwill if you wanted to get on, and Mr Walter said, '*Stuff* goodwill – we just want to make a few bob!'"

I made a face. I considered defending the story, but decided it wasn't worth it.

I said, "Well, thanks Carol. I'll keep in touch if anything comes up."

"Oh, don't go! Look, I brought you this." Carol's nephew suddenly opened his eyes, squeaked, saw the balloon, and staggered to his feet. "Darren, come here! Look, it's Rosemary's shorthand book. You remember what I said about her being upset and uptight for the last few weeks before she died? Well, you look at that."

Julie was retreating in horror at the sight of Darren's sticky fingers.

I opened the book and glanced through it. At the beginning all the entries were neat – 95 per cent pure Pitman's – but as I flipped forward through the entries for September, a change took place. Rosemary's outlines became ragged – strokes elongated, vowels sliced through the page. It all fitted into my theory that Rosemary had been at some crisis point in her life – perhaps connected with her failed love affair, perhaps not. I was about to return the book to Carol when a date caught my eye: 9th November, the day I believed she'd died. Ringed round in red with the date were the words "follow form", written in shorthand, and the rest of the page was blank.

"Rosemary didn't have any interest in horse-racing, did she?" I asked, surprised.

Carol laughed. "That says 'Folly Farm'. It's a house belonging to Mr Victor. Mr Walter bought it to retire to, but he could never get round to retiring. I think it's got a couple of fields attached to it and he fancied himself as a gentleman farmer. It's in Polepit Lane." She thought for a moment. "I expect Mr Victor asked Rosemary to send a couple of men up there to check over the heating or something – I told you she'd been doing some overtime for him. You know, it makes me sick, a beautiful big house like that being left empty when there are people sleeping on the streets. Do you know what Steven says? *He* says – "

Fortunately, at that moment Darren made a sudden bid to join the goldfish in the pool. Julie, Carol and I leapt up and headed him off like goalkeepers in an FA Cup Final, to a ripple of applause from several women nearby. Darren then burst into screams that must have gone off the decibel register.

"Oh God," muttered Julie, who seemed to possess a natural abhorrence for small children.

"We'll be off," I said, when Carol had got her breath back.

I thanked Carol enthusiastically for all her efforts, and patted Darren on the head. As an afterthought I gave him a bar of chocolate I had in my handbag, and he and Carol departed as happily as if they'd actually given me some information worth having, and I'd actually paid them for it.

When we got back to the car, Julie said, "All right, Mum, so what's your final word?"

"On what?"

"The catering job."

I had a feeling our harmonious relationship was about to take a knock.

"Well, to be honest, I'm not really wild about you trying to cater for parties in our tiny kitchen. It's not that I mind you trying to earn some money. In fact I think it's quite a good idea. Look, the paper's full of ads for temporary pre-Christmas jobs. Why don't you – "

"Je – *sus*!" she interrupted, provocatively copying Pete. She didn't actually like cooking, but this was the job she'd been offered and she didn't see why she should be put off it by me. She huffed and puffed angrily, reached into her pocket, and flung something on my lap. I flinched. "*You* have this, then. You don't want me to do anything for myself, do you? You want to run my whole life!"

Lying in my lap was a little pink card. I turned it over. It said "Milly Molly Mandy", and there was a phone number.

"Where did you get this?" I asked.

"I told you. Richard gave it to me. The woman we went to see is a friend of his flatmate's uncle. I think she's a customer of the video shop, or something."

This information rolled around inside my head like a silver ball in a pocket maze, continually running into barriers.

"And you say they're caterers?"

"Yes."

"How odd."

"Why? There's nothing odd about catering. Our home economics teacher says there are some very good careers in catering. Of course, I'll never find out if I like it if you don't let me do it. You're always saying I ought to think about the future, and – "

She launched into a revised version of things I was always saying. I turned on the ignition, and while trying to negotiate my way through a seriously double parked street, did my best to re-state my case on most of them. The little pink Milly Molly Mandy card lay ignored beneath my feet.

Of course, I was disappointed that Carol hadn't been able to point me in the direction of Mr Demarco, but there had to be other ways of tracking him down. On Monday I began by ringing his bank. They kept me holding on for a long time, and finally said that although they wouldn't be prepared to release a customer's address, they might in certain circumstances forward correspondence to him. They suggested I address a letter to him, care of the bank. I thanked them and hung up dejectedly. The police had already tried both Mrs Kaussmann and the electoral roll, without success, so I would have to think of something else. I looked at the bill from the Old Barn Restaurant. It was over six months old. It hardly seemed likely that the staff would be able to recall anything about either Rosemary or

Mr Demarco after so long, and anyway, Mr Heslop would never pass my expenses claim for a meal there.

I got out Rosemary's file and turned over a few sheets of paper. My fingers stopped at the typed sheet detailing my conversation with the Reverend Hollingsworth. Why not? Rosemary's life had revolved around her job, her husband, and her Church – why shouldn't she have found a soulmate amongst the Reverend Hollingsworth's flock? I rang him immediately, and asked guardedly if he knew of a family named Demarco. He considered carefully. No, he said, he knew a Degorski and two Dempsters, but no Demarco. All hope endeth here.

By the end of the day I'd failed to come up with any new and inspired ideas for tracing Mr Demarco, and I collected the brown paper bag from under my desk, put on my coat, and tucked my notes on the Tindall murder despondently into my bottom drawer. The newsroom was already half in darkness and I was the last to leave. I groped my way towards the back stairs.

The *Herald*'s car park is at the rear of the building, and is lit by a single lamp which illuminates only those cars parked immediately beneath it. I found my car keys before opening the outer door. A sharp, cold wind hit me and I shivered as I walked across the bleak blackness of the car park. In my right hand I kept a firm hold on the spanner and washers I'd bought in preparation for tackling the bathroom tap. Pete had had a go at it on Sunday, but his idea of mending a tap was apparently to ram a piece of cork forcefully up its spout. I think I chuckled out loud, walking across the car park, as I thought about this.

I reached the Mini, all by itself, next to the dustbins. I moved towards it with the key. And then a hand fastened itself on my right shoulder.

12

"For God's sake, Keith!" I gasped. "What are you trying to do to me? How would *you* like to have someone creep up on you like that?"

"How can I be creeping up on you?" he retorted, sulkily. "You're my wife. What am I supposed to do? You promised you'd ring me and you didn't. I can't phone *you* at home in case *he* answers, and I'm not going near the *Herald*. They all know who I am and they laugh at me behind my back."

"I'm sure they don't. Laugh at you, I mean," I said. Or know you actually.

He hugged himself and breathed clouds of steam into the cold night air.

"Can't we go somewhere and talk?" he pleaded.

"Oh, Keith, Julie's waiting for me. I'm already late."

"Please, Chris. I only want to talk."

"Look," I said. "If you promise – just five minutes – I know Julie would be glad to see you. You can follow me to my place." Almost as soon as I'd said it, I wished I hadn't.

His face broke into a broad grin. "Five minutes." He nodded, ecstatically. "Five minutes."

Our hall looked even smaller with Keith standing in it. Julie was in the kitchen, eating an enormous bowl of Honey Smacks, and when she saw her father her expression went through just about all the emotions known to a teenager.

"What's happened?" she demanded.

Keith smiled innocently. "How're things? I've come specially to see you. When's your next Open Evening?"

"Why – are you going to come?" she asked, amazed.

"Of course. Here, I've got something for you." He reached into his pocket and produced four audio cassettes. "I hope

140

you haven't got any of these. I thought they were your favourites."

She took the cassettes and looked at them. I immediately recognised the first as being identical to one I'd tripped over this morning on the stairs, but she said, "I haven't got any of them. Thanks, Dad." She gave him a kiss on the cheek and stood up, abandoning the Honey Smacks. He watched her as she went upstairs with a look of bewilderment on his face, as though she wasn't quite the way he remembered her.

"She's grown up, hasn't she?" he remarked, wistfully.

"It's only been six weeks."

He took a deep breath and began peering from room to room.

"We haven't got it sorted out yet," I remarked, defensively.

Keith shrugged. He stood with his hands on his hips. "Do you remember how long it took us to get Barrington Avenue sorted out? Do you remember all those Sundays we spent in the kitchen with you handing me screwdrivers and things? You were a great help, even when you were so pregnant you could hardly bend down." He tapped the wall, as though checking the plaster, and sighed. "It was bloody good, wasn't it, Barrington Avenue? Everything we always wanted."

"Yes," I agreed, because it was true. We stared in silence at the wallpaper.

"You look as if you're keeping very fit," I said.

He nodded. "I do weight training once a week. You can't afford to let yourself go at our age. I've been trying to get Richard to come along with me but he keeps saying he's too busy."

I frowned. "I'm a bit worried about Richard, actually. I don't like his flatmate."

Keith had stepped inside the living-room for a tour of inspection. He rounded on me grimly. "Well, I don't like yours much either, but there's sod all I can do about it."

I winced. He picked up one of Pete's Dire Straits LPs, then dropped it back on to the sofa. He turned his attention to the hi-fi speakers on the wall.

"So that's where they went," he muttered. "I thought

Richard had got them." He placed a finger on the nearest speaker, which immediately rocked away from its fixings. "Good God!" he exclaimed. "He hasn't even used rawlplugs! He'd better not have bloody damaged either of them."

"Those speakers were mine anyway," I protested. "That's why I took them. You gave them to me as an anniversary present." As though anyone could forget being given a pair of speakers for an anniversary present.

"Don't be silly. We all used to listen to them. And I don't remember agreeing to your taking that tiled coffee table either. I *made* that. What else have you got that I don't know about?"

I drew myself up stiffly. "If you came here to discuss the furniture then I suggest you go home and get your clipboard," I said. "I seem to remember we never did finish counting the clothespegs."

We stared at each other, separated by the stark rectangle of the coffee table. I dropped my gaze first.

"Sorry," said Keith. "Look, it's not the furniture, is it? I mean, Christ, twenty years – twenty-two really. We can't divide that up. Stop wasting money on solicitors' letters, will you? This is between us. What do you want a divorce for anyway? You're not seriously intending to marry that little creep, are you?" He looked as though he wanted to say a lot more, but couldn't put it together. Finally he said, "I don't want a divorce, Chris."

"*What?* But you were the one – you'd been seeing that Barbara for years – you were the one who put our house on the market!"

He nodded. "I know. But if you want the truth, I didn't really expect anyone to walk in and offer us the asking price that very afternoon. I was bluffing, Chris."

A groan started deep in my stomach and gathered painful momentum as it made its way through my chest and finally filled my head. I had to bite my fingers to stop it coming out.

"What's that?" asked Keith, looking at my hands.

"What?"

"That thing you're holding."

142

I stared stupidly at the paper bag containing the spanner and washers.

"Oh – we've got a leaky tap. Pete hasn't unpacked his tools yet."

He snorted derisively. "Give it to me. I'll do it."

"No, you won't."

"Yes, I will. Where's the mains?" He marched purposefully into the kitchen. "Oh, and you'd better watch me, because next time I might not be around."

I glanced with horror at the kitchen clock. Pete might be home at any minute, but somehow it seemed quicker to let him do it than to argue. Or maybe I just wanted to get the wretched tap fixed.

Keith re-washered the bathroom tap and dried his hands on my towel, leaving an oily stain. I watched and pretended I'd taken it all in.

"We haven't really talked," he said suddenly, screwing up my towel and tossing it into the washbasin.

"There isn't time. Honestly, you'll have to go."

"When then?"

"Oh, Keith, I can't."

"*When?* You want to as much as I do. Stop pissing about. We've got to get ourselves sorted out."

Ourselves . . . "All right. Let's make it Friday." Between now and Friday I'd have time to decide whether or not I really wanted to go ahead with it, and if so, what excuse I could give Pete.

He smiled. "Where?".

"Oh, I don't know. Please go now! All right – how about the Old Barn Restaurant at eight?"

He looked pleasantly surprised. "Fine. The Old Barn Restaurant, Friday at eight."

The following evening I got home from work early. I thought of Keith again as I entered the hall and looked at the doorway where he'd stood reminding me what fun we'd had decorating Barrington Avenue. I almost tripped over something in the corner, and the image of Keith vanished. What I'd stumbled against was a bulging sack of washing with a note pinned to it, which said "Thanks, Mum. Love R." (I wouldn't have minded, but the sack turned out to contain several pairs of nasty looking nylon underpants I was sure belonged to Barry.) There were two more notes next to the telephone, both in Julie's handwriting. One said, "Pete rang and he's sorry but he's got stuck on something and you're not to wait up", and the other said, "Am in my room with Angie who has a *terrible emotional problem*. Do not disturb. Have eaten." I went into the kitchen, imagining Pete superglued to a barstool and the awful blonde streaked Angie up in my daughter's room describing some sexual practice I'd probably never even heard of. I'd never liked Angie, and had hoped that Julie would see the light about her before Angie got them both into some sort of unimaginable trouble.

"Oh, God!" I said aloud, confronted by the state of the kitchen. Angie's terrible emotional problem had not prevented her from eating a hearty meal of baked beans and fried bacon, a good deal of which was now adhering firmly to the cooker top. I groaned and sank down on to a stool. This was too much, as if I didn't have enough problems. Things seemed to be closing in on me like Hallowe'en witches round a cauldron. If Julie couldn't at least clean up after her culinary efforts she could stay permanently out of my kitchen. I started towards her door with a few choice words on my lips, and then stopped, remembering our last discussion on the subject of catering – the Milly Molly Mandy card.

It was still there, under the driver's seat of the Mini. What possible link could there be between Rosemary Tindall and a firm of caterers known to Barry's uncle? It was probably just another dead end, but in my opinion Barry's uncle had the words "criminal element" striped through him like seaside rock, and that alone made it fascinating. I cast a stealthy glance up the stairs towards the strip of light beneath Julie's door. She'd conceded defeat over the catering job, and this might be a lead. I began dialling the number. Ask any friend of Barry or his uncle for help and I'd got a feeling you'd end up reaching deep into your pocket for unmarked fivers. I decided to try subterfuge instead.

Milly Molly Mandy's phone was answered promptly by a woman with a brisk, deep voice. The voice had overtones of

Lauren Bacall, hair sweeping across one eye, and the kind of cold, superior manner that would freeze a suggestive comment to an icicle on a man's lips. It came as rather a surprise.

"I believe you're looking for someone to help out with cooking," I said, speaking quietly so that Julie wouldn't hear.

"Yes, that's right," agreed the voice, patiently. "What sort of experience have you had?"

"Oh. Well, I've fed my family for twenty years and done dinner parties for eight, that sort of thing."

"Hmmm. Could you speak up? I can hardly hear you."

"Sorry. I've got a touch of laryngitis," I hissed, as loudly as I dared.

"I see. Well, I'm not interested in people who are going to be ill and let me down."

"Oh, I wouldn't. I always soldier on. And it's not contagious or anything. Could I possibly call and see you tonight so we could discuss the job?"

She paused. "Actually tonight would be good. I'm not doing anything tonight."

I shouted upstairs to Julie that I was going out, ate a sandwich off the bread board, and set off for the address she'd given me on the Greenmeadows estate. The Greenmeadows estate was one of our area's neutral zones, occupied in equal numbers by first time buyers on their way up, and retired couples on their way down. "Milly Molly Mandy" presumably hoped she was on her way up. Her house was an end-of-terrace with a contractor's board in the front garden and a trench dug across her lawn that wouldn't have looked out of place at Ypres.

The Lauren Bacall voice said "Good evening", but when experienced in the flesh was actually much harsher than the original. Its owner was thirtyish, elegant and naturally blonde, and would have been extremely attractive if her nose had been two inches shorter and minus the 'U' bend.

"I'm Camilla Douglas," she said. "Do come in."

"Camilla," I repeated. "Oh, I see – you're Milly."

"Yes. I'm Milly, my partner is Mandy, and there isn't a Molly. We met up when we both moved into houses on the estate at the same time, and the name just seemed to suggest itself."

She seated herself elegantly on a sofa, and waved me towards an armchair. She retrieved a burning cigarette from an ashtray.

"Now," she said, sucking in smoke. "You say you've not had any professional experience?"

"No, I haven't. Does that matter? As a matter of fact I was once thinking of doing a Cordon Bleu course and starting up on my own." This at least was true; only the realisation that cooking for a living would tie me even closer to the kitchen had stopped me.

Camilla pursed her lips. "You and everyone else who's ever picked up a saucepan," she remarked, icily. "That's what makes it so hard for those of us who are serious. There's a lot more to catering than having heard of Robert Carrier and knowing which way the accents go on your menus. Believe me, there's some very tough competition out there."

I tried to look sympathetic. "What sort of functions do you cater for?"

"All sorts. Whatever we can get. We're busy at the moment because of the run-up to Christmas, and to make matters worse I've got to move out of this house while it's underpinned, which means I shan't have my usual cooking facilities. The point is that we are really only talking about a temporary job for you. Would you still be interested?"

"Oh, yes." Somehow, I couldn't imagine this woman being a friend of Barry's uncle.

She tipped her ash carefully on to a delicate glass ash tray.

"And how did you get to hear about us? I haven't advertised for help yet."

I was ready for this. "Rosemary told me. Rosemary Tindall – you know, Mr Demarco's friend." I waited. I expected her to say, "Oh, dear, didn't you know? I'm afraid Rosemary was – "

She frowned. "I don't know either a Demarco or a Rosemary. Still, not to worry. Let me show you some of our menus, and see if you think you could cope."

She handed me a plastic wallet containing several neatly printed sheets of paper. I frowned over them in puzzlement. Clearly she did not know Rosemary at all, not even as a murder victim.

"These are nicely done," I remarked. "Do you have a word processor?"

She glanced at the machine in the corner. "One needs every aid to survive these days," she said. "I tried my hand at the antiques game before this and got my fingers badly burnt. What you have to realise is that it's not enough simply to enjoy doing something and half-heartedly charge people for doing it. You've got to pull out all the stops if you want to succeed."

"And you really want to succeed, do you?" I smiled, but Camilla ignored the remark grimly.

I pretended to study the menus, while glancing as covertly as possible around the room. There were no family photos on the mantelpiece, no roller skates hidden messily behind sofa cushions.

"You're on your own, are you?" I suggested.

"If you mean am I married, the answer is no, not any longer." She was clearly irritated by the question. "What do you think of that lot?"

"Er – " Something was nagging at me. There was something missing from this tastefully furnished room, something I'd expected to be here and wasn't. Unfortunately I wasn't sure what it was. There were books, a living flame coal effect gas fire, the Amstrad, a small portable television –

"Of course!" I exclaimed, in spite of myself. "You haven't got a video!"

Camilla's nose appeared to lengthen as her brows moved downward into an angry frown.

"I *beg* your pardon?"

"You haven't got a video," I repeated, more timidly this time.

"Of course I haven't got a video. I don't spend much time looking at television. May I ask what this has to do with my menus?"

"Oh, I'm sorry. It's just that – well, I thought I'd seen you before in a video shop in Hudderston." She glared at

147

me with suppressed fury. "Sorry. I must be mistaken. Well, I'm sure there's not much here I couldn't manage. Would you like me to run up a few dishes so you can see what I can do?"

She drew deeply on the cigarette and tapped it angrily against the ash tray.

"You seem very much better," she remarked suddenly. "Your laryngitis. You seem to have recovered."

"Oh. Yes. Like I said, it comes and goes." A blush was spreading upwards from my neck. I'd made a mistake in trying to pull the wool over this woman's eyes, and I was particularly glad I wasn't going to have to work for her.

"Write your name and phone number here," she said, handing me a notepad. "I'll give you a trial. I have to keep up my reputation."

I stared at the pad in consternation for a moment, and then wrote down Chris Schiavo, and my old phone number. Hopefully, she would never find me. Julie would be sure to draw the wrong conclusions if she did.

As I rose to leave I gave it one last shot. "I'm really surprised you didn't know Rosemary. Rosemary Tindall. She certainly knew you people. She gave me your card. Now let me think – Rosemary worked for Taylor Group and helped out at St Mary's Church – " Somewhere, I seemed to have struck a chord: Camilla's nose twitched, but she remained stony faced. Perhaps I was mistaken. "She was splitting up from her husband, you know. Of course, I haven't seen her for a couple of weeks – "

"Mrs Schiavo, I do have rather a lot to do," interrupted Camilla, coldly. "I don't wish to speculate with you about your friend's personal life."

"No." I had a brainwave. "Perhaps it was your partner Mandy Rosemary knew. Like I said, Rosemary was getting divorced so she might have wanted some extra work herself. Perhaps Mandy had offered her a job."

Camilla laughed shortly. "Mandy has many talents, but interviewing prospective staff and handling the business side of things are not among them. If I may say so, Mrs Schiavo, you seem rather more interested in idle chatter than in discussing the needs of my business. I don't think that augurs particularly well for our future relationship."

"Oh no, of course," I muttered, allowing myself to be ushered out. "I'm sorry. I hope I'll hear from you soon."

I offered her my hand but she ignored it.

As I picked my way across her devastated lawn, I heard her shout, "I don't think we need look too far to discover the cause of your laryngitis attacks!"

I jumped into the Mini and slammed the door. I'd made an awful hash of that. It would have been so much simpler and less embarrassing if I'd just asked her how and why she knew Rosemary. Still, I would have received the same response. She clearly didn't know her, and not only that, she seemed to have no connection with Barry's uncle either. In her drive was parked a white Metro which bore a ribbon and champagne glass motif, and Camilla's phone number inscribed in pink and gold. It was stylish and elegant, and not the hallmark of a woman whose friends wore nylon underpants and owned video shops in derelict back streets. Julie must have been mistaken about how Richard had come by Camilla's card.

I drove slowly home to Tipping. Perhaps I was approaching the enigma of Rosemary's personal life from the wrong angle. The letter to the *Herald*, Mr Demarco's bank statement, Camilla's business card, the restaurant bill – these were no more than pieces of paper with writing on them. What could anyone learn about me from a few pieces of paper with writing on them? That I'd got married, that I was seeking a divorce, that I paid for my petrol by Access? These were details, these had nothing to do with what went on inside *me*. The traffic lights ahead turned to amber. I could have gone through, but I stopped, thinking about Rosemary. She'd married a man on the rebound from an unhappy love affair; she'd filled the void in her life by working, and by espousing the Church; and finally she'd fallen in love with someone else. Inevitably, perhaps. But what sort of person had she fallen for? She was serious-minded, totally unfrivolous, and according to Tania had a penchant for men with terrible personality problems. And then it hit me, just as the lights changed. I jerked forward, almost stalling. People with personality problems naturally gravitated towards employment in the psychiatric services, but there was another obvious starting point for them. They could become – or seek to become – writers. What better way of getting things off your chest was there, than by inflicting your thoughts on the world through the medium of print (or at least on that small section of the world not intimidated by the price of hardbacks)? I raced a learner moped rider to the bend excitedly. Rosemary had attended regular classes in Creative Writing at Burymead County Secondary School – and that had been where she'd met her lover.

By the time I arrived at Burymead School on Wednesday evening, I had built up an Identikit picture of Rosemary Tindall's lover. He would be in his late twenties and have a pinched embittered look about his face. Most of his life would have been spent in establishments like Mrs Kaussmann's, surrounded by dog-eared manuscripts secured with string, terse rejection slips and the pervasive odour of Pernod. He probably had a beard and wore leaky shoes, patched denim jeans, and corduroy jackets with holes in the pockets. Of course Mr Demarco also had a bank deposit account containing over eight thousand pounds, which didn't exactly fit my picture, but no doubt there was a simple explanation for this.

The girl in Enquiries directed me to Room E134. I marched boldly into the class with only a perfunctory knock. About twenty people were sitting in a semi-circle, and one of them was reading something in a faltering voice. The man at the head of the class (who to my intense excitement was wearing a green corduroy jacket) looked me up and down and remarked, "Word Processing. Room E137, two doors along on your left. Carry on, Alison."

Alison cleared her throat nervously ". . . on the beach, where limpid pools left behind by the receding tide were cold and wet under my bare feet. I looked at Daniel, excited by the touch of his rough uniform against my – " She stopped and stared at me. They were all staring at me. I stared back at them.

"One moment, Alison," said the class teacher, frowning at me. "Was there something else you wanted?"

I gazed around the room. The Creative Writing Class wasn't exactly what I'd expected. Most of its members were women, all were middle-aged, and the only beard amongst them was on Alison.

"Well," I began, dismayed. "I'm a reporter for the *Tipping Herald*, and I'm doing a story on Rosemary Tindall."

There was a murmur of interest from the class. The teacher looked at his watch.

"Do you want to finish sharing that with us, Alison?" he asked.

"No!" squeaked Alison, sitting down abruptly and dropping several pencils.

"It's very nearly coffee time anyway," said the teacher. "I suggest we break now and I'll have a chat with this lady. Will somebody bring me back a lemon tea? Thank you, Thérèse."

He seated himself on the edge of his desk and folded his arms. He was dark and dishy and I had to stop myself from trying to fluff up my hair.

"Well, I've been doing a story on Rosemary Tindall," I began again, "and I understood she attended your classes for some time." I produced my notebook with what I hoped was an impressively professional flourish. "Might I have your name and your general impression of Rosemary?"

"Reilly. Ken." He placed a hand on my arm. "Have they got someone yet?"

"I'm afraid not."

The classroom had emptied out, and footsteps and muted conversation echoed back from the corridor.

"Senseless, senseless," muttered Ken Reilly. "That's about all one can say about it. And what would the *Tipping Herald* like to know about Rosemary Tindall? Ah, thank you, Humphrey, I hope it was some help," he added, to a student who'd just placed a copy of John Osborne's *Look Back in Anger* in front of him.

"Perhaps you could tell me what she wrote about," I suggested.

"Nothing."

"What – *existentialism*, you mean?" I queried, glad that all those wet Saturday afternoons reading the *Reader's Digest* had finally paid off.

"No, I mean she didn't write about anything, as a rule," he explained patiently. "In the early days she produced some rather promising poetry, but her contributions to the class were patchy, to say the least. I hope you're not going to ask me to let you have some of her work, because I don't really feel free to give it to you. Even if her husband gave his permission, I'm not sure it would – "

"No, no," I interrupted. "In point of fact I'm more interested in her relationship with another member of your class. Mr Demarco is the name I've been given."

A flicker of understanding crossed Ken Reilly's face. "I see. There's no one of that name in my class," he said, sharply.

"Are you sure? My information is that Mr Demarco moved to a new address about six months ago, so he could have been in your class for the last school year."

"No, he couldn't. I've never had anyone of that name in my class."

The class was beginning to reassemble. One of Ken Reilly's students handed him his tea, and he placed it on the desk.

I tried to smile my way back into his favour. "Look, Rosemary came here regularly for more than a year. She must have formed an attachment to someone."

Ken Reilly chuckled unpleasantly. "My dear, I hold these classes with two purposes in mind. One is to help people to express themselves creatively, and the other is to further the understanding of literature. I do not run a Lonely Hearts Club. If that's what people want then they'd do better to peruse the personal ads in your paper."

"Oh. Yes, of course. Well, I suppose you get all sorts here," I said, breezily. "I suppose people come to your class in the hope that they'll be discovered as the new Ernest Hemingway, or Margaret Drabble – or whatever."

"Really? Is that what you think? Well, well." He made a neat stack of the books on his desk. "I'll tell you what they come here for. They come because they'd like to be able to communicate their thoughts on the human condition to other human beings, and to see more clearly through the eyes of others. They come because they need to be able to verbalise their experiences. Would that be too much for the *Tipping Herald* to comprehend? It would certainly be too much for them to spell correctly."

I scowled at him. Jokes about newspapers not being able to spell were the lowest of the low.

"Thank you very much, Mr Reilly," I said, snapping my notebook shut.

In the doorway I was accosted by a small grey-haired woman with a nervous tic in her right eye.

"I do envy you, working on a newspaper," she said. "It's what I always wanted to do, but the children got in the way. Poor Rosemary. I've still got her pen. She dashed off before I could give it back to her – in the middle of class."

"Did she?" I thought about this. "Would that have been the Wednesday before her murder? Let's see – the first Wednesday in November?"

"Yes. I think it must have been."

"You wouldn't happen to know if she was waiting for a telephone call that night?"

The woman's eye blinked rapidly. "She was, as a matter of fact. How did you know? She didn't come to coffee with us. Instead she walked off down towards the payphone."

I glanced at my watch. It was five past eight. I smiled wryly. "Oh dear, and the call never came," I said, shaking my head.

She looked baffled. "Didn't it? I thought it did, actually. She came back into class, white as a sheet, picked up her things and left. I thought she'd had bad news. Of course that's why I didn't get the chance to give her back her pen."

"Jean," interrupted Ken Reilly, frowning at me. "Could we take our places now, please?"

"I'll have to go," said Jean. "We're going to do a play reading."

"All right – but can I just ask you. Mr Reilly – " I turned my back on Mr Reilly. "Mr Reilly said Rosemary wasn't particularly friendly with anyone in the class, but I can't help wondering if there was anyone – any *man*, that is, who – "

"Oh no," interrupted Jean, shaking her head and winking vigorously. "She wasn't like that. Do you know, I shouldn't say this, but some of them here – all they want to write about is sex." Ken Reilly had taken a step towards us. "Well, anyway," went on Jean, hastily. "Rosemary's husband used to meet her after every class and take her out for a meal."

"Did he?"

"Yes. She'd go into the Ladies and spend ten minutes re-doing her makeup. She was such a pretty girl, too. Her husband used to wait outside by the cycle sheds. They had a regular table booked at the Old Barn Restaurant apparently, and – "

Ken Reilly's green corduroy clad arm descended on Jean's shoulder.

"We mustn't detain the lady from the *Tipping Herald*, must we? We may be keeping her from a traffic accident," he added, with particularly nasty ambiguity.

"Did she tell you it was her husband she was meeting?" I asked.

"No," said Jean, and suddenly the obvious conclusion struck her too. "Oh," she said, "I never thought of that," and she allowed herself to be led off by Ken Reilly.

I walked away from the Creative Writing class dejectedly, another brilliant theory having just bitten the dust of a County Education department corridor. It had been a good theory, too, and for a moment I'd almost believed Ken Reilly might have fitted my Identikit picture of Rosemary Tindall's lover. In fact, I thought maliciously, it would have given me a great deal of satisfaction to have pointed the long arm of the law in his direction.

Still, if nothing else I'd discovered that Rosemary and Mr Demarco were regulars at the Old Barn Restaurant. It would certainly be worth pursuing this – my one and only remaining lead on the mystery.

13

The sound of Texan accents and nervous violins wafted from the living-room. I peered round the door, expecting to see Julie sprawled on the sofa amid school text books and heated rollers. Instead, I found Pete. He had his feet up on Keith's tiled coffee table and was asleep under a copy of *What Car?* magazine.

"Well! This is a surprise!" I exclaimed, as *What Car?* slid from his face, bounced off the chair arm and landed tent-like over his drink.

He opened an eye and looked at me. "Don't be sarcastic. It doesn't suit you."

"I didn't mean to be. It's just that you're hardly ever here at this time of the evening."

"Is that your main complaint?"

"What do you mean? I haven't complained about anything, have I?"

He rubbed his eyes and stretched, looking for the drink. "Living with me hasn't exactly lived up to your expectations, has it?" he remarked.

I uncovered the drink and handed it to him, ducking the question.

"You haven't answered my question."

I sat down next to him on the sofa. I wasn't ready for this conversation. He took my chin in his hand and shook it gently.

"Come on, give. I want to know if what is wrong with me is terminal in your eyes."

I laughed. "There's nothing wrong with you. We've only been together for a couple of weeks. Why should there be anything wrong?" Except that in some way I can't define you aren't what I thought you were, and the sunset I imagined we'd walked off into doesn't look so rosy any more. Actually,

155

that's not fair, because you are exactly what I thought you were, it's just that what I really wanted was someone who'd always know precisely what to do on Christmas morning when the cooker fuse blew, and who'd be sitting at the dinner table with his knife and fork poised every night at seven. Someone just like Keith, in fact.

Pete said, "I'd do anything for you, you know. I'll have the dentist change all my amalgam fillings for those white ones, if you like."

"Don't be silly. I love your teeth the way they are."

He stroked my neck with his fingertips, and undid the top button of my blouse.

"I'll have a demon manicurist pull out all my cuticles."

"Don't! Just – say you'll marry me."

"Ouch! Now you've gone too far. Why don't we stick to what we're good at, darling?" He undid the second button of my blouse, and sought the curve of my breast with his fingertip. "We don't want to end up in court screaming at each other, do we – or worse, boring each other to death."

"It doesn't have to be like that. It isn't always – "

"Yes, it is. The minute that bloody wedding bell clangs it's seconds out, round one, and off you go for life – or until someone else puts you asunder. This way is better."

A crescendo of music and J.R.'s face in freeze-frame distracted our glance to the television.

"Before I forget," said Pete. "A woman phoned for you."

"Oh God, not Camilla!"

"She said her name was Saunders. She said it was important." He undid the third button of my blouse.

"She said she wanted you to get in touch with her urgently, and you'd know what it was about." He buried his face in my cleavage. "*I* want to get in touch with you urgently, and I know you know what it's about." He moved his hand slowly over my stomach, finding the little bits of me that were waiting to be found. I moaned and snuggled against him, feeling happy again.

"It isn't me, you know," he said, suddenly, stopping at one of the best bits. "It isn't me who's having problems with this

156

relationship. *I'm* not the one who's putting all her energies into looking for the murderer of a woman she doesn't know from Adam. *I'm* not the one who can't decide where her loyalties lie."

"What do you mean? What loyalties?"

"Work it out," said Pete, adding edgily, "When you have a spare moment."

I pulled into the muddy layby at Cottis Wood just after eleven the following morning, and sat in the car for a moment, sorting out my notes. I'd no idea what to expect of Jennifer Saunders. I was combing my hair in the rear view mirror when a dark blue Sierra estate briefly attempted to park behind me, then suddenly reversed, swerved back on to the road, and swept past me at high speed. I caught a glimpse of the driver's face, and it was John Redfern. Stunned, I dropped the comb. The Sierra stopped on the grass verge about twenty-five yards further on. I was sure of two things: it *was* John, and he'd seen me.

Ignoring the quickening patter of rain, I wrenched my keys from the ignition, leapt from the car and ran after the Sierra. The driver's door opened as I approached.

"Hallo, Chris," said John, looking startled and unmistakably guilty. "I thought it was you. I wasn't sure."

"Just detouring through Hudderston to drop in on someone you know?" I suggested, in a tone I hoped was sharp and incisive.

He eyed me warily. "Come and sit inside," he said. "Out of the rain. Look, I suppose you think it was pretty odd, my spending the night in Hudderston and not mentioning it when we last met. The fact is, I try not to talk shop at weekends – not always easy, actually – and the whole thing was best forgotten about anyway."

"Why?"

"Well, I expect you know about my car being nicked. I mean, that hotel's the pits anyway. I shan't go there again." He chuckled over-enthusiastically. "Talk about Fawlty Towers! And then of course coming down in the morning and finding someone had borrowed the car – Christ! Definitely best forgotten about. Anyway, how're you two?"

"Oh, fine. I hear you're thinking of suing Hudderston police for false arrest."

"Ah. Well, on balance we decided it would be best not to. The legal position's a bit tricky, and I didn't really feel up to a prolonged battle. What's a few hundred quid, anyway?" He winked. When he smiled his face lit up. It was the sort of face you'd be tempted to trust.

"How're the children?" I asked.

"Getting excited about Christmas. Well, the boys are. Catherine seems to think she's too old for it, but that hasn't stopped her writing out a present list as long as your arm. Tell you what, why don't you give Helen a ring and have a chat about what we're all going to get the kids? Pete tends to forget how much they grow up from year to year." He smiled again. "Not his fault, of course. He – er – he hasn't said any more about having the kids over at Christmas, has he?"

I shook my head.

"Ah, well," he said.

"He doesn't forget them," I protested, defensively. "He's got a lot on his plate with the new job and everything."

John grinned. "I'm sure you'll soon put him on the right road, Chris. I'm a firm believer in the reforming power of love."

"*Are* you," I remarked, meaningfully.

"Yes. There's nothing like it. I don't know where I'd be if it wasn't for Helen." He was smiling an awful lot, like salesmen do just before they get you to sign on the dotted line for ten thousand pounds' worth of double glazing. But then he was a salesman, and *I* certainly wasn't buying. I knew too much.

"I'd better be off," I said. "I've got to see someone."

"Yes. God, look at that." Rain was pouring down the windscreen as though practising for the monsoon season. "There's an umbrella somewhere under your seat. Have a grope round."

I leaned forward and my fingers found something hard beneath the seat.

"John," I said. "If you don't mind me asking – what *are* you doing in Cottis Wood? It's not exactly on the way to anywhere, is it?"

"No." He laughed again. "This is going to sound silly. It's like I said, I was just passing by on my way to Kingston and I thought I'd take a detour to have a look at this wretched place. You know, the cause of all my misery the other weekend."

"And what do you think of it?"

He glanced over his shoulder disinterestedly. "It's grim, isn't it? Any luck with that umbrella?"

My fingers closed over a cold, hard object, and I pulled it triumphantly into view. It was a two foot length of copper piping. I stared at it in amazement.

John laughed. "I often carry one of these around with me," he said, taking it from me and gripping it threateningly like a club. "As an awful warning."

He thrust the end of the pipe towards me. "You see the inside? All furred up with limescale. That's what you get if you don't have a Zircon water softener fitted in your home, and I can tell from your shocked look that you don't have one." Of course, that hadn't been what I was thinking at all. For a moment I'd been thinking something quite different. He unbuckled his seat belt and leaned over the back seat. "What's the matter – don't tell me you've never noticed what goes on inside your kettle. Here's the umbrella. I'll walk you back to your car."

When I was safely back in the Mini I watched him striding off in the rain, hidden by the umbrella. The awful phrase "returning to the scene of the crime" snaked its way across my mind, like one of those advertising slogans you see being towed by small planes, but I treated it with the contempt it deserved.

The door of No. 2 Cottis Villas was opened by a woman in her late forties who had let all the colour drain out of her face and hair. She looked like one of those old grey dishcloths that loaf about on the side of your sink.

"Chris Martin," I repeated. "From the *Herald*. You phoned me twice."

"Aha. Gwen used to think I might be losing my upper register. She wanted me to go for a checkup."

"I'm sorry?"

"The doorbell. How many times did you press it? I'm all right with the phone for some reason. How many times did you ring the bell?" she smiled, revealing a large gap in her front teeth.

"No, no, it's all right. I've only just arrived," I protested, my heart sinking.

"Of course, I never really get to know any of them," said Jennifer. "That's the trouble. Gwen's moved on now."

I followed her into her tiny dark hall. "Er – who's Gwen?"

"I'm not a priority. They only send an Assistant Social Worker now, and between you and me, I don't think she knows what she's doing – not even as much as Gwen. How can someone like that understand what I've been through?" A flash of pain suddenly illuminated her face, making her seem younger. She banished it with a tremulous smile. "Tea or coffee?"

"Oh no, thank you." Guiltily I recoiled from her toothlessness and the slightly musty odour of unwashed clothes. "I'm in a bit of a hurry to get back to the office."

"No hurry, no worry," muttered Jennifer, bafflingly. "When I worked in advertising it was all rush and bustle. I still miss it, of course." She opened a door. "You don't believe I worked for a top agency, do you? I thought up the Puddlewell Bears."

"Oh. Yes," I nodded sagely, as though I knew what she was talking about.

"Well, sit down, sit down. Sit in Gwen's chair."

I took a step towards the chair and heard the door close behind me. Jennifer's footsteps receded across the hall and another door opened and closed. Silence, apart from a ticking clock. Staring at me from the shelves of a glass cabinet were twenty pairs of glazed eyes belonging to an assortment of china dogs, and the faces of a dozen or so toddlers captured in brass and silver frames. Looking closer at the pictures I saw that they weren't photographs at all, but appeared to have been carefully cut from the pages of magazines and newspapers.

Jennifer entered suddenly with a tray, closing the door with her foot. "I hope the biscuits are all right," she said, doubtfully.

I helped myself from the tray. Jennifer seated herself opposite me and began swaying gently to the rhythm of the clock.

"Did you have something you wanted to tell me about the murder?" I prompted.

"Oh, yes." She stared vaguely at a point beyond my left shoulder. "Wasn't it awful?"

"You did say it was urgent."

Jennifer selected a custard cream from the plate and studied it with interest. She bit into it, and her tongue came out and delicately scooped up a morsel of cream which had fallen back on to her finger.

"Look," I began, exasperated.

"I saw this black car out there," she said, suddenly.

"It wasn't black. It was maroon," I said. "The police know about it. Somebody got the number."

"No, it was black. The murderer came in a black car. Like a Porsche."

I frowned. "Just a minute, *when* are we talking about? *When* did you see this black car?"

"Then. You know, the night of the murder."

"Yes, but – " I got up and looked out of her window. "Are you telling me there were *two* cars out there that night? Is that what you're saying?"

She looked confused. "Two cars?" she repeated. "I'm telling you – I saw a black one."

I stared at her. "Look, let's get this straight, shall we? You heard the big bang, the night everybody thinks Rosemary Tindall was murdered, and you looked out of your window and you saw *two* cars out there, is that what you're saying?" I stared across the rainswept road. Water cascaded down the sides of the Mini, parked in the layby. Beyond it, from Jennifer's window it was possible to see some distance round the bend. It would have been possible for anyone at this window to see further round the bend than any of the other witnesses were in a position to do. Had another car been there, Jennifer could have seen it.

"Come here," I said. She put down the custard cream and came obediently, like an old, well-trained dog. "Will you describe to me exactly what you saw?"

161

She hesitated, then stabbed a finger quickly in the direction of the bend. "A black car there," she said.

"And?"

"And what?"

She sucked at the gap in her teeth. "There wasn't another car," she said. "Why would people want to come here?"

"Well – " My brain suddenly went into overdrive. "Look, you must be talking about the Monday night. The night *before* the shot. You looked out of your window for some reason and you saw the black car. What else did you see? Did you see the driver? Did you see the man carrying the body? Do you remember any part of the number?"

She backed away, alarmed. "I couldn't see it very well," she said, doubtfully. "I just heard the shot and I looked and there was the car. A black car like a Porsche."

My heart sank. Clearly Jennifer Saunders had no idea when she'd seen the black car. It *couldn't* have been on the Tuesday, because if it was the Tuesday she'd've described two cars – a black one and a maroon one. She'd probably seen the black car some other night, and confused the two events in her mind. It might have been on the Monday, and it might not. And anyway, even people who drove around in Porsches had old batteries to dump, and other men's wives to –

"I see," I said, crisply. "Well, I'm glad you told me about this. And thank you for the coffee. I really must get back now."

"Are you going to tell the police for me?" she asked.

I hesitated. "I'll mention it," I said.

"Good," said Jennifer Saunders, with a relieved sigh. "Then I've done my bit. I'll wait to see they've got this man. I wouldn't want him to go out and do it again to someone else so I'd have that on my conscience. I've got enough on my conscience as it is."

She looked like a person about to launch into the long version of their life history. I stepped purposefully towards the door and she showed me out reluctantly, going through the door closing routine again.

On her front doorstep I was assailed by a nagging doubt.

"You seem very convinced that the car you saw had

something to do with the murder," I said. "Can I ask why?"

"Oh, I am! I just know."

"So why haven't you told the police about it? Why did you contact me? Surely the police must have asked you if you saw anything when the body was first discovered."

"Your name was on the story in the paper. Someone said you were the best person to talk to – as I don't talk to the police," she added, darkly.

"Why don't you talk to the police?"

"Well, I don't have to, do I? There's no law, is there? I don't like them. They're always nasty and they're so sarcastic about everything – 'Oh *did* you, Miss Saunders? Well, well,' they say – " She did a passable imitation of someone who sounded a lot like DS Horton.

I smiled sympathetically, and decided the matter was best dropped. "All right," I said, "I'll pass the information on for you."

I got back in my car, screwed up the note detailing Jennifer's name and address, and pushed it into my over-stuffed ash tray. I did it very reluctantly. Jennifer Saunders obviously believed that the car she'd seen had had something to do with the murder, but as she couldn't come up with a single tangible reason for this belief, and as her statement contradicted that of every other witness the police had spoken to, it was clearly best discounted. She'd had a strange effect on me anyway; talking to her was like trying to communicate with someone through a thick but invisible screen.

It was cold in the car. I started the engine and got away from Cottis Wood as fast as I could.

The bar of the Old Barn Restaurant hummed with muted conversation and laughter. Keith was late. I couldn't believe I'd put myself through the trauma of lying to Pete about visiting an old school friend, only for him not to show up. Not only that, I'd carefully reserved Table No. 12, the table Rosemary and her companion had used on May 6th, and if Keith didn't arrive soon I wasn't sure how long they'd hold it. It was Friday night, and there was already a queue of hopefuls who'd turned up without reservations. The Old Barn was the kind of place where everybody who hoped to make an impression on someone else's wife went for an evening of Epicurean delight.

Keith appeared suddenly through a side entrance. He smelled strongly of aftershave, and I could tell from the gleaming pallor of his chin that he'd treated himself to an early evening shave. When he lived with me, he only used to do that if he had a tryst with Barbara.

We were shown to Table 12, which turned out to be in a discreet corner beneath the cosy glow of a wall lamp. Keith looked pleasantly surprised when I said I'd booked it specially. I was about to confide in him the reason but he took the words right out of my mouth by remarking on how pretty I looked.

"Don't be silly," I said, blushing. "A person can't look pretty at my age. The best you can try for is attractive."

"All right. Have it your way. Attractive, then. I'm surprised lover boy let you out tonight. Did he know who you were meeting?"

"Of course he did," I lied, fiddling with my napkin.

Keith grinned, and stretched contentedly. "I've really missed this, you know, being able to sit across a table and talk to you in the evenings."

I was unable to hide my astonishment. Apart from grunting at me to pass the salt, and spitting venom at news items on TV concerning the Labour Party, Keith's dinner-time conversation had been fairly limited.

"Well, all right, I wasn't exactly the perfect husband, was I? But it was partly your fault, you know. You never said anything. You just sat there looking aggrieved. You used to get this sort of pinched up, nobody-loves-me look on your face and if I wanted to do anything to you it was slap you."

"Well, thank you very much! Was I really that bad?"

He moved a rose vase out of the way and reached for my hand. "Go on, admit it, we were both to blame. Do you know when I miss you most? In the mornings when you're not there to make sure I eat up my muesli."

I laughed. "And do you still eat it?"

"Yes," he said. "I think of you and then I eat it."

The waiter appeared at that moment with the menus. I made a point of giving him a friendly smile, but he looked straight through it, and said, "Good evening, Mr Martin."

"Oh – I didn't know you'd been here before," I said, remembering his frequently repeated comment that he wouldn't pay a bill with a zero on the end of it for something I could cook almost as well at home.

He looked embarrassed. "Came here a couple of times with Barbara," he muttered.

We made our selections, without consulting one another, from the middle of the price range, and Keith gave our order to the waiter. When the waiter had departed – after stonewalling another of my smiles – I said:

"Now let's talk about the divorce."

Keith gave an odd laugh. "What's to talk about? If you want it you can have it." He began rearranging his place setting.

I was taken aback. "But you haven't been answering my solicitor's letters. I need your consent."

"Do you? Didn't need my consent to jump into bed with Romeo, did you?"

I blushed. "Can't we stop this? All these recriminations? You were unfaithful, I was unfaithful. I forgive you. I suppose you can't forgive me. We've already split up everything we had. Can't we just get the divorce over and get on with our lives?"

"I didn't say I didn't forgive you," said Keith.

There was silence. The waiter put a basket of French bread in front of us and I studied the rough, scaly crusts.

"All right then, I forgive you. There, I've said it," said Keith. "It's up to you. If you *really* want the divorce – if you *really* want us to part for ever. Is that what you want?"

I touched my hand to my throat, suddenly dry mouthed.

"I don't know," I croaked, reaching for the water. Forgiveness is a powerful gift: accept it, and you can be in someone's debt for ever. "Do you mean it?"

He filled my water glass with a flourish, and patted my hand. "You think about it," he said, looking very serious. "Just think about it." He closed his fingers over my hand

and lifted it. It was my left hand. On the third finger the pale mark of my wedding ring still showed. He brought my hand to his mouth, holding my gaze, and when I didn't resist he pressed his lips softly against my knuckle.

"Here's to us, Chris," he said, raising his wine glass. "To the past – and to the future."

Of course, next to the French bread this toast was just about the corniest thing around, and I shouldn't have let him get away with it. But it's an odd thing: a remark that would have you in stitches over baked beans on the kitchen breakfast bar takes on a whole new meaning when uttered over gleaming cutlery someone else is going to have to wash up. I should have told Keith then and there that I wanted to marry Pete, and that there was no chance of my backing down over the divorce. I should have said I didn't care one way or the other about his forgiveness, and that I'd only booked this table with its romantic ambience because I was hot on the trail of someone else's lover, but I didn't – primarily because not all of that was true. Actually, not much of it was true, and I really liked having him like me again.

The waiter stood by, smiling, with the coffee pot in his hand.

"Refill, sir?" he enquired. "I hope you've both enjoyed your meals?"

"Yes, we have," said Keith. "May we have the bill, please? I have to get this lady home before the witching hour."

The waiter chuckled appreciatively at this little joke. "Certainly, sir."

"Er – just a minute." I reached for my handbag. "Excuse me for asking, but is this normally your table?"

"Yes, madam, it is."

"In that case, would you mind taking a look at this," I began, producing the much folded bill. Keith's hand was frozen in the act of reaching for his wallet. "I know it's a lot to ask, but I wonder if you can possibly remember anything about this couple. I believe they used to come here regularly."

He took the bill and studied it. Immediately his expression

changed from deference to furtiveness. "Oh, come on," he said, and his accent was slipping as well. "If I said they had two bottles of red wine, then they did. I mean, anybody can make a mistake. It's a bit late to complain about it now."

"It's not the wine I'm interested in," I said. "This couple used to eat here every Wednesday after nine. They may not have always sat at this table, of course, but I'm sure you must remember them. Here, I've got a picture of the woman." I handed him a photograph of Rosemary Tindall.

His expression brightened immediately. "Oh, her, yes, I know her! She used to come here regular – and she was the one who got herself murdered, wasn't she? I saw it in the *Advertiser*!"

I leaned forward excitedly. "It's her companion I'm interested in. I believe his name was Demarco, but I'm having difficulty tracking down his address. Would you happen to know where he worked, or anything else about him that might help?"

Keith was staring at me, rigid with disapproval. The waiter looked suspicious. He turned to Keith for help, narrowed his eyes, and said, "*Why?*"

"Well, I'm a reporter for the *Tipping Herald*, and – "

"Oh, *Christ*!" interrupted Keith.

"What d'you think I am, a walking phone book?" demanded the waiter. "I don't know his name or nothing about him!"

"You knew Mr *Martin's* name."

"Yeah, well, he's been coming here for years."

Keith closed his eyes.

"Look, the bloke who came in with that woman," said the waiter, suddenly thinking of his tip. "He was an older bloke – you know, older than her. About – " He looked at Keith, then thought better of it. "Middle-aged," he said. "That's all I know. Unfriendly sort of bloke. Never tipped or nothing."

"Which is why you sometimes charged him for bottles of wine he hadn't had," I suggested, smiling sweetly. The Manager was watching our conversation with increasing concern. I gave him a long, hard look and began assuming the expression of someone who is about to complain bitterly about bad service.

"I think you'd better tell me everything you remember about him," I said.

"Look," the waiter began, in a wheedling tone. "He was just an ordinary bloke, fiftyish, going bald – too old for the likes of her, in my opinion. I haven't seen them lately. They used to come here and hold hands and he looked like he never enjoyed anything in his life, know what I mean? What she saw in him I don't know. The last time they was here they looked like they was having a row. That would be – what? – two months ago." He spread his hands appealingly. "That's all I can tell you. Honest."

I shook my head in disappointment. It was hopeless.

The waiter made a great display of adding up our bill and crossing things out. He handed it to Keith. He'd started to walk away when a thought occurred to him.

"One thing I remember about this bloke," he said. "You know I said he was old? Well, he smelt of that stuff – you know – My gran used to use it for her back. It's a sort of rub. God, what do you call it – "

"Wintergreen!" I exclaimed. "Was it wintergreen?"

"Yes, that's right. That's the stuff. All right, madam?" he added, returning to his former manner. "Hope to see you again soon, madam."

"You bitch," said Keith, through clenched teeth, when he'd gone.

I wasn't listening. "Wintergreen," I repeated. "But that means it was *Mark Williams* she was meeting. Mark Williams was Rosemary's lover."

"You conniving bloody bitch," went on Keith. "You brought me here to humiliate me. Showing off about your damn job. You haven't changed a bit, have you?"

"What's the matter? What have I done?"

"Don't give me that, you bitch." He threw his Access card on to the table. "You didn't come here to see me. You came here to play at being a reporter! How could you do this to me?"

"Keith, I didn't. It was a coincidence – "

"Bollocks!"

"Let me pay half," I said. "I want to pay my share."

"Oh, yes!" he exclaimed grimly. "You would, wouldn't

you? That's what this is all about isn't it? You and your bloody feminism! I left you sitting at home for years while I went out to earn our living – sitting there watching *Pebble Mill at One* and all the rest of that feminist propaganda. You lapped it up, and when it suited you to get up off your backside and go out and do something it was me who got shafted, wasn't it?" He seized the bill and the Access card. "Well, I'm not giving you the satisfaction!"

He stormed to the cash desk without giving me a second glance.

Our waiter and about a dozen or so spectators stared at me with open mouthed curiosity. I duly blushed, stared back, and left.

14

I woke Pete at half past eight on Sunday morning with a cup of strong coffee. I lay down on the bed next to him and tickled his neck.

"What?"

"I've got you some coffee. Can I talk to you?"

He opened an eye. "You've got your clothes on. What time is it?"

I decided it would be wise not to answer this. He'd stayed up until two the previous night watching one of those films where detectives with guns crash cars through people's windows for no particular reason.

"I've made a breakthrough on the Rosemary Tindall murder." He closed his eye. "I've discovered she was having an affair with someone at work."

"You've woken me up at the crack of dawn to tell me this," he said, into the pillow.

"I want you to come with me to talk to him about her," I said. "Yesterday, when you were getting your exhaust fixed I found his address. I rang up all the M. Williams in the phone book and asked for Mr Mark Williams, and when I got him I said I was ringing on behalf of a double glazing company. He put the phone down at once." Pete didn't move. "Well, I didn't want to alert him that we were coming. I thought if we called when he wasn't expecting us we'd be more likely to catch him with his guard down. It's *Sunday* morning – people are relaxed. They're at their most vulnerable."

"People aren't relaxed. I'm not bloody relaxed."

"If we go within the next hour or so his wife will probably be busy de-slugging an organic cabbage for lunch. She might even be at church. Look, if he had an affair with Rosemary over a long period of time he'll know things about her nobody else does – about the anonymous letter for instance."

He groaned. "Why don't you go downstairs and ring your friend at Hudderston Central and tell him all about it?"

"Because he's not interested. Nobody's interested in finding out about Rosemary's personal life except me."

He opened his eye again and looked at me. "Have you ever asked yourself why that might be? Leave the poor sod alone, for Christ's sake." He closed his eye and settled his head more comfortably on the pillow.

I prodded my fingernail into his neck. "He might have killed her, Pete. *He* could have been the one who gave the message to Gail about Rosemary having food poisoning. He might have killed her to stop his wife finding out about the affair."

Pete gave a prolonged groan and wrapped the pillow round his face. He muttered something about not caring if Mark Williams was the Boston Strangler, and turned his back on me.

"All right," I said, to the hump of his body in the bed. "If that's your attitude – don't blame me if I come back with my face shot off."

The Williams' house was situated at the end of a long private road in the southern, exclusive part of Hudderston. These were the sort of houses that had swimming pools and double garages and belonged to people who thought the poll tax was an awfully good thing. I parked the Mini with its rusty side facing the open road, and started up the gravel drive of "High Trees". The property had a gloomy, dilapidated feel to it. Overgrown Douglas firs clustered around its boundaries like a gaggle of ragged witches, and the door to the garage was propped open by a crumbling brick. Inside I could see Mark Williams' black Renault GTA with its "Nuclear Power No Thanks" sticker. It was probably just a coincidence, but I couldn't help thinking that the Renault looked at a quick glance rather like a Porsche.

A teenage boy sat on the porch steps. He was clad in black leather and surrounded by what looked like bits of motorbikes and an array of tools. The porch steps themselves were splattered with oily stains, and the oak front door had clearly long forgotten what a tin of varnish looked like.

"Er, excuse me, is Mr Williams at home?" I enquired, politely.

The boy peered into a tin can full of nuts and bolts. He produced a bent piece of black metal and stared at it, apparently oblivious to my presence.

"Mum! Dad!" he shouted, without looking up.

After a few moments during which I tried, and failed, to think of something to say which might be of mutual interest, the front door was opened by a woman. Her blonde hair was combed unflatteringly away from her face in a style fashionable in the fifties, and she was wearing a voluminous kaftan style garment.

"Oh, the Christian Aid envelope," she said, with resignation.

"No, actually I'm Press, and I wondered if I – "

"Oh, how simply marvellous!" She emerged on to the porch, and I noticed that she was wearing wellington boots encrusted with mud and straw. "I should have realised. I spotted straight off you weren't Special Branch. I'll get my coat. Gosh, how did you find me?"

I was temporarily winded and couldn't think of an answer.

"Are you with *The Sunday Times*? We always take that. Oh dear." She looked at my legs. "How could they send you like that?"

I looked down at my legs, wondering what was wrong with them.

"What size are you?" she demanded. "We'll see what we've got."

"Mrs Williams," I said. "I think there's been some misunderstanding. I've come to see your husband."

"My – " She looked aghast. "Why? What do you want to talk to *him* for? Haven't you come about the list?"

"What list?"

"The 'Founding Fifteen – Artists against Animal Abuse' – isn't that what you're here about? My goodness, now *I'm* going to be the one who's given the game away. Never mind. You see, what we believe is this – "

I jumped into her pause for breath. "Mrs Williams, I'm

from the *Tipping Herald*, and I'm doing a story on Rosemary Tindall's death. I've already spoken to your husband briefly, but what I'd like is – "

She gave a high, tinkling laugh. She produced a glass from behind her back and took a sip from it. It looked like gin and tonic.

"Oh dear, oh dear," she said. "Life never fails to amaze me. Rosemary Tindall. You find the murder of one incredibly insignificant human being more important than the daily mutilation and slaughter of hundreds of animals, do you?"

"I – er – haven't actually thought about it. I've been sent here on the Tindall story," I said, seeking refuge in the tried and tested "only following orders" routine.

She smiled, appearing to make up her mind about something. "Interesting," she said. "Interesting. Such a pity Jerry's not here. He'd soon put you straight. Anyway, I'm sure my husband would *love* to talk to you about Rosemary Tindall. Come in and I'll get him."

Her son scowled at her, throwing out his arms protectively to shield the tools spread across the steps.

"Oh, don't worry, darling," she said. "We'll go round the back. He's such a good boy," she added, making a measured leap over his socket set. "Follow me."

She led me along a weed-strewn path that skirted the house, stepping over mounds of cotoneaster branches that had broken from their moorings on the wall. We emerged on to a patio littered with a strange assortment of items – empty dog food cans, bales of straw, old exhaust pipes, a motor bike wheel, and soggy burst-open sacks of cat litter. Some of the items had been there so long they had weeds growing out of them. I stared at the garden in disbelief. It looked like a Third World shanty town. Old rusted caravans and badly constructed wooden huts vied for space on the lawn, and as we approached their occupants gave vent to a barrage of unearthly wails and screeches.

"What's going on?" I asked, horrified by the noise, and the stench that hung over the scene like a fog. "What animals have you got? Are they all right?"

"Of course they're all right," she snapped. "I've liberated them from pain and suffering. Have you been talking to my neighbours? Well, good, because they're an interfering bunch of busybodies with no sense of priorities. You tell your editor to send you back with a photographer. I can pose with the goat, but some of the monkeys will have your fingers off as soon as look at you."

She opened French windows into a small room that appeared at first sight to be a study, except that a single bed stood in the corner, heaped with blankets and clothing. Mrs Williams strode across the Persian rug that carpeted the room. It appeared to bear the marks of her muddy boots crossing and re-crossing it, and everything in the room was covered in a year-thick layer of dust and fingermarks.

"My husband's room," said Mrs Williams. "I'll get him. *Mark*!" she shouted shrilly. "Mark! A lady to see you." She shut the French windows, putting her shoulder to one of them to make it fit properly.

Mark Williams came downstairs, shrinking from contact with the banister. His permanent expression of distaste was heightened, and certainly didn't diminish when he looked at me.

"This lady wants to talk to you about Rosemary," said Mrs Williams, in an oddly smug tone. She sat down on the edge of the bed and folded her arms. "Sit down, sit down," she suggested, gesturing towards a chair heaped with newspapers.

"Petra," said Mark, fastening his shirtsleeves with long, precise fingers. "Will you please take those boots off."

"I'm just going out."

"Get them off. Get them off my carpet." Angry white blotches began to form on his cheeks. "I want those boots out of here."

Petra smiled insolently and rose to her feet.

"Well, I'll be back," she said, almost skittishly. "I've got to feed my animals and I'm not disturbing Daniel again." She raised her glass to me and waltzed out of the room, drinking.

Mark Williams adjusted his shirtsleeves fastidiously, and closed the door behind her.

"I don't like having my Sunday mornings disrupted," he said. "My wife has let you in on some whim but as far as

I'm concerned you are not welcome in this house. I don't wish to discuss Rosemary Tindall." He went to the corner of the room and produced a vacuum cleaner. He plugged it in, jabbed it into life with his foot, and meticulously vacuumed along the line of Petra's bootprints. When he'd finished he turned and stared at me pointedly, as though surprised I was still present.

I decided to surprise him still further.

"Would you care to comment on the fact that you had a long and passionate relationship with Mrs Tindall?"

He didn't blink. Slowly and carefully he wound up the Hoover flex.

"No, I wouldn't," he said. I was undaunted.

"Did you know she was planning to leave her husband? Do you know where she was going on the night she died? Was she planning to meet you?"

The door opened, and Petra entered, carrying a bucket of milk and a glass of gin and tonic. She set the bucket down on the carpet, spilling a little of the milk. I groaned inwardly. Mark had for a moment looked shaken and I thought I was going to get somewhere with him.

"Well, well, I'm surprised my husband isn't just dying to show off about his little dalliance!" exclaimed Petra. "It was his mid-life crisis, you see. He's forty-eight, so he left it a bit late, but then that's typical of him. Everything too little and too late." She gulped her drink and stood back to watch the beads of milk sink slowly into her husband's carpet.

"Will you shut up, for God's sake!" snapped Mark, angrily.

"Why? Don't tell me you've gone all coy! I'll spell it out for the lady, shall I? My husband was having an affair with that silly Tindall girl – knocking her off, giving it one – isn't that what they call it these days? It went on for months – oh, I had my suspicions. All those Wednesday evening squash games, *him*! Mind, he came back *exhausted*, that's true enough." She giggled hysterically. "He even brought her here, you know. One Monday, after I'd come back from a meeting with Jerry, I walked into this room and there was this *awful* smell of cheap perfume. I knew. Oh, I knew all right. And when I'd had enough of it I tugged on his leash and back he came."

I sneezed, suddenly and catastrophically.

"Bless you," said Petra, sounding increasingly drunk.

"Get out," said Mark, to Petra. "Go and have one of your antidepressants or valiums or whatever you take these days."

"I don't need anything, darling. I'm having simply the best time."

"Mrs Williams," I said. "Are you telling me you didn't object to your husband's affair?"

"Why should I? Honestly, who needs *him*? Besides, I knew he'd come running back. He'd never leave me – or more precisely he'd never leave Daddy's money. He just loves driving around in a car that cost more than Victor Taylor's and living in this *beautiful* house." She waved her hand vaguely in the direction of the peeling wallpaper. "He needs me and my Daddy. He always has and he always will. That little tart got what she deserved – and I'm not sorry."

"And do you think your husband gave it to her?" I asked, sharply.

Petra stared at me. "Do you mean, do I think he killed her?" She dissolved into delighted giggles. "Him? He couldn't kill a fly waving a white flag! Of course he didn't kill her. Why ever would he want to do that?"

"Well, perhaps you wouldn't mind telling me where he was on the night she died," I suggested, reaching in my pocket for a crumpled tissue.

"How the hell would I know?" asked Petra. "Who cares?" She picked up her bucket and was about to leave.

"Since you've gone this far with it, Petra," said Mark, through clenched teeth. "You may as well complete your performance by telling this – lady, where I was the night Rosemary Tindall was murdered." She looked blank and sulky. Mark took a step towards her. "You know perfectly well where I was. That was the night that idiot Jerry came round and sat here all evening finishing off my best brandy."

"Oh yes," agreed Petra. "And you were unspeakably rude. Of course I remember that. I'm sorry, my love," she added, to me, "I'm afraid I can't give you the rope to hang him with."

I blew my nose and stepped forward to detain Petra.

"You've just told me where your husband was on the night of Tuesday, 10th November, isn't that right?"

Petra thought about it, then nodded. I looked from one Williams to the other. "But that wasn't the night Rosemary died," I said. "That's just what the murderer wanted people to think. Rosemary was actually killed some time during the evening of Monday, November 9th."

Petra looked baffled. She shrugged, then said, "Oh, gosh, I remember that night! That was the night poor dear Jerry didn't turn up to take me to my meeting and I thought something terrible had happened to him. He drinks and drives, you know, but then he's an artist – it's the pressure, poor lamb. Anyway, I was waiting in by the phone. Mark was working in his study. I asked Mark to phone round the hospitals for me, but of course he wouldn't. He's jealous of Jerry. Youth and talent, that's what he's jealous of. Two things you'll never have, will you darling?" She took another large gulp of the drink, spilling some of it down her chin. "So I don't think we can very well send the men with the handcuffs for him – do you?" she added, with a giggle, and flounced from the room, as though defending her husband against murder accusations was a common, if rather tiresome, occurrence.

In her wake, Mark Williams and I stood and stared at one another. He was shaking slightly.

"Satisfied? Did you enjoy that? I hope you will print a nice little story in your paper about my affair with Rosemary Tindall. I really do. I should like to see my wife faced with that!" He wrenched open the French window which Petra had just jammed closed behind her. "Now will you please leave?"

I coughed and cleared my throat. "Mr Williams," I said, "as I told you, I've been looking into Rosemary Tindall's story and I've found out several very interesting things about her murder. Firstly, I don't think she was killed by a copycat Face Murderer, I think she was killed by someone who wanted it to look that way. I think she was killed on the Monday, not the Tuesday, and that her murderer phoned Taylors claiming she had food poisoning, so – "

"What nonsense!" he snorted. "I don't want to hear any of this. It's got nothing to do with me."

"You had an affair with her. You worked with her for a long time. Don't you want to see her murderer brought to justice?"

He was almost apoplectic with anger. He shook the door, bringing in a draught of cold air. "Get out," he said. "Get out or I'll call your editor and get you sacked. You can't waltz in here making accusations! You've already heard all about my affair – it was just a two-bit fling, anyway. If Rosemary was planning on leaving her husband it had got nothing to do with me. Maybe she'd met someone else. I don't know and I don't care."

"Did she ever mention anyone to you called Demarco?"

He stopped shaking the door handle. "Where did you get that name from?"

"Why? Do you know him?"

"No, I don't. Look, Rosemary and I stopped seeing each other – apart from in the office – two months ago. If she'd got anyone else in her life I didn't know about it."

"All right." I hadn't believed him when he'd said his relationship with Rosemary was a two-bit affair, and I didn't believe that the two of them could have carried on working together as if nothing had happened. Rosemary didn't seem like that sort of person. But if he didn't want to help find her killer then there was nothing I could do about it. I moved towards the door.

"Oh, one last thing," I said. "Did you know Rosemary had written an anonymous letter to the *Tipping Herald*?"

Mark Williams had stepped back delightedly to let me pass. He froze, one foot in the air. "What?"

"She'd written a – "

"Yes. I heard what you said. What nonsense! How on earth did you dream all this up?"

"Then you didn't know what it was about?"

"Of course I don't! I don't believe she wrote it. And I've got a good mind to write to the *Herald* myself to complain about your behaviour. Get off my property or I'll call the police!"

"Thank you, Mr Williams," I said, tight-lipped. "I won't trouble you any more."

I parked the Mini in our drive, noting that our downstairs curtains were still drawn.

"Mum!" Richard appeared behind me, clutching a bunch of pink carnations. "I was waiting down the road. Where've you been?"

"Out." I reached up and kissed him. "Have you been waiting long? You could have gone in, I'm sure someone's up."

"It's OK. Have you been to see Dad by any chance? I spoke to him on the phone yesterday and he said he wanted to talk to you about Friday, whatever that means."

Actually, I wanted to talk to Keith about Friday, too.

"Well, he knows my number," I said stiffly. "Come on in."

He hung back. "I just wanted my washing, if it's ready. We're running out of underwear. Here, these are for you, to say sorry."

I smiled. "I don't mind doing *your* washing," I said, pointedly.

He studied a leaf adhering to the toe of his trainer. "It's not about the washing. It's that business with Julie. I honestly didn't know."

"What? What didn't you know?"

"Well, about the porno stuff. Anyway, not to worry. All's well that ends well. Could I – er – just have my stuff? I promised Barry I'd only be half an hour."

I sneezed again, all over the carnations. "Please come inside. I think I've got a cold coming. What's all this about pornographic films?"

He rubbed the leaf off his shoe on to the back of his jeans, and mumbled something incoherent.

"Look, if you and Barry have let Julie get hold of one of these *disgusting* videos I'll never forgive you. She's only fifteen, for God's sake!"

"No, Mum, it's nothing like that! It was just that stupid catering thing – I didn't know the sort of parties they were involved with. I thought you'd found out. I thought that was why you wouldn't let Julie do the job."

"I still don't know what you're talking about. I did check out Milly Molly Mandy, as a matter of fact. They seemed to be a perfectly ordinary firm of caterers. The reason I stopped Julie doing the job was because our kitchen is so small. Of course, you haven't seen it."

He shrugged. "Oh, well, maybe I got it wrong. No, actually, I don't think I did. Apparently a few months ago there was a mix-up with some cassettes, and Barry had to go out to this farmhouse in the back of beyond to deliver the correct ones. He said he could hardly believe his eyes. There were topless girls, old guys lying around being fed grapes – " He broke off, laughing.

"What's this got to do with Milly Molly Mandy?"

"Oh, well, they were the people who organised the party. That's how Barry's uncle met this woman. She was hired to arrange a party – over a year ago, I think it was – and she wanted some really hot videos. Barry's uncle imports them specially, from the Continent. Most of our home-produced stuff is rubbish, apparently. Anyway, I didn't know all this or I wouldn't have mentioned the job to Julie."

"Richard, that's not the point! I could ring that Barry's neck! *He* must've – anyway, where is this farmhouse? Did Barry tell you its name?"

"Yes. It was kind of appropriate – it was Folly Farm. Barry said there were lots of important people there. Look, could I just have my washing? My vindaloo will have gone cold by the time I get back."

I unlocked the front door and reached inside for the bag of washing. Pete was just coming downstairs smelling of soap and aftershave. Richard backed away at the sight of him.

"Here you are," I said. "Wouldn't you just like to come in and see the place?"

Richard nodded sulkily to Pete, like a little boy being made to shake hands with the kid who's just cracked his best conker. "Another time," he said, "if that's all right."

It wasn't, but I didn't say so.

15

Mr Heslop called me into his office first thing on Monday for a conference. He pulled his calendar off the wall and showed it to me.

"What's this?" he demanded, stabbing it with his finger.

"Isn't it a calendar?"

He snorted impatiently. "It's Christmas," he said. "An ancient pagan winter festival hijacked by the Christians and currently an annual celebration of the power of creative retailing." He selected a pill from one of the bottles on his desk and swallowed it. "It has to be the biggest and most successful hype job of all time, and one day if there's ever a movement towards truth and plain speaking it'll re-christened 'Rip-offmas'. In the meantime what are *you* going to do about it?"

"Well, I – "

"You see by now any reporter worth his salt should have been able to come up with at least one 'Lonely widow to wed postman who delivered her first Christmas card' story. What have *you* got?"

"Ah. Well, I've had a bit of a breakthrough on the Rosemary Tindall case. You remember the anonymous letter she sent us? Well, I think I know what it was about. I think I know how Victor Taylor got himself into the Colgate Club so quickly." I waited for him to catch up.

"This doesn't sound very Christmassy," he remarked, suspiciously. "What the hell's the Colgate Club?"

"It's the name my husband's firm have given to the small group of companies who carve up all the big local contracts. Well, my soon to be ex-husband, actually," I added, thinking about this. His eyes glazed over. "It's got to do with parties and naked girls and pornographic films," I added, quickly. His eyebrows shot up to where his hairline

181

used to be. "Don't you remember that story about Maurice Prestage of RMP Developments and the Soho girls? Well, I haven't got down to any details yet, but I know for a fact that Victor Taylor gives these parties at an out of the way farmhouse and that he has some very important guests. I'm sure it'll turn out that – " I didn't like the look on his face. "Well, I thought you'd be pleased," I said, desperately. "Considering what you said about Victor Taylor and Bob Geldof."

"Victor Taylor and Bob Geldof? You know, you don't look well. I hope you're not going to crack up on me just as my stomach is about to erupt. Does your GP do Saturday morning appointments?"

"Mr Heslop, I'm perfectly well apart from this cold. But I've never handled anything like this. What shall I do with it?"

He took off his glasses and polished them slowly. "Perhaps I haven't made myself clear," he said, through clenched teeth. "This is the festive season. We are after snow bunnies, not bunny girls." He looked particularly pleased with this last remark. "Now I want you to drop whatever else you are working on and concentrate your efforts on Christmas. Look." He leaned forward, interlacing his fingers and studying them earnestly. "You are a woman, and Christmas is all about women and children and families. This is right up your street. You let me have your notes on this other nonsense and I'll hand them over to someone who can cope. Have you got them with you?"

"No," I lied.

"All right, then. Any time will do." He handed me a Press release from a department store, headed "Great Christmas Bonanza". "There you are – get stuck into this."

"Couldn't I just pop out to Folly Farm and see what sort of place it is?" I asked.

"What would be the point of that? We don't do a farming section," replied Mr Heslop. "Now get out there and remember – *think Christmas*."

I went slowly up and down Polepit Lane, searching for Folly Farm. Finally I spotted a gateway signposted "Access to

Wintershall House and Folly Farm only. No picnicking or turning". It was handpainted in shaky black lettering on a white board, and had "Trespassers will be shot" written between the lines. I got out of the car and dragged the heavy gate open, noting the worn groove it had made in the tarmac. Next to the gate was a single lamp post, tied to which were the forlorn remains of balloons put out as markers for a children's party. They looked as if they'd been there for years. I got back into the car and bounced slowly down the uneven track, glancing at Wintershall House as I passed. A woman in green wellington boots and a waxed jacket stared at me suspiciously, almost wobbling off the stepladder on which she was balanced with an armful of Christmas lights. I half lifted my hand in greeting; maybe she'd think she knew me. Just around the bend the road terminated at another gateway, and this time there was nothing subtle about the "Trespassers will be shot" notice. It was heavily underlined by barbed wire, a padlocked gate, and a notice warning "Guard Dogs always on patrol". I whistled softly, but no guard dogs appeared. I climbed gingerly up the bank opposite the gate for a better view of the house, but I couldn't see very much. A group of outbuildings clustered round a tarmacked yard, and the farmhouse was squarely built and unattractive. A picture postcard farmhouse, with oak beams and honeysuckle scaling the walls, it was not.

I made a few notes of my general impression of the place, and was about to leave when I spotted the woman from Wintershall House plodding towards me in her wellies.

"Not got the keys?" she asked, nodding towards the gate.

"Er, no. Have you?" I asked, quickly and boldly.

"Sorry. It's about time they got their act together if you ask me."

"Who?"

"The agents of course. The other woman came over a month ago. Not exactly getting their fingers out, are they? And considering the commission they charge. Which agents are they, by the way?"

I made a rapid assessment of the situation.

"Actually I heard about this place through a friend. I thought I'd come out and take a look."

She glanced at the rust holes on the Mini, and at me.

"Acting for someone else, are you?" she asked.

"Yes."

"Well, of course, it's none of my business," she said, obviously convinced that it was. "But Folly Farm is our only neighbour, so of course we are concerned." I nodded sympathetically. "I just hope the wrong kind of people don't get to hear of it. Friends of ours got some ghastly religious sect moving in next door and they had to put up with chanting and bell-ringing all day – or of course someone might want it for a *garden centre*," she said, clasping her hands to her face in horror. "All those Sierra estates in and out all the time with roof racks and hordes of children strapped in the back. Absolutely ghastly. Anyway." She walked over and rattled the gate. "My husband says he'll see to it they don't get planning permission." She peered into the Mini suspiciously, as though it might contain sacks of illicit peat.

"Is it not being used as a farm any more?" I asked.

"Goodness, no. They sold off the last bit of land to Prewetts Farm a couple of years ago, and then they just let it stand empty. We'll be glad when the whole business is settled."

"But it's definitely on the market, is it?"

"Well, isn't it?" she challenged.

I looked back at the farm. "I understand they do quite a bit of entertaining here," I said.

She looked surprised and even more suspicious. "How did you know? Private family parties, so we were told." She shook her head disapprovingly. "Cars coming in and out at all hours. We bought this house to try and get away from that sort of thing. We used to live in Wimbledon," she added, by way of explanation.

I said, "It's really a pity you don't have a key. I would have loved to have a look round. You said the house was empty. Who looks after it?"

She shrugged. "The owner. A Mr Taylor. He's something

184

to do with plumbing, I believe. We've lived here for three years but we've hardly ever clapped eyes on him. The only time he ever comes here is when he has these family get-togethers, about once a month." She shrugged again. "I suppose one shouldn't complain. I do so love the country, and the peace, and the birds singing – That's why I've been keeping my eye on things since the other woman called last month and we got wind of the fact they might be selling."

I had a sudden inspiration. I reached into the car for my handbag, rummaged through it, and found the photograph of Rosemary Tindall. I held it out to her.

"Was *this* the woman who came to view Folly Farm?"

Mystified, she produced a pair of spectacles and studied the photograph. She shook her head.

"No, it wasn't. I say, I've never known prospective property buyers to go around carrying photographs of each other. What's going on?"

I was disappointed. "Are you *sure* it isn't her?"

"Yes, positive. The woman I spoke to had red hair. She was rather like you, actually, except that she was very elegant."

I've always noticed that people who wear green wellies are rather short on tact. I still wasn't entirely convinced she didn't have a key.

"Before they hold these parties," I said, "somebody must call to arrange things. Who lets them in?"

"Well, *I* don't know. I think they have a firm of caterers to take care of the arrangements."

"Do these caterers drive little white Metros with a ribbon and champagne glass motif?"

"What? Goodness, what *are* all these questions? I don't know what caterers they use! Why are you so interested in their catering arrangements?" She narrowed her eyes. "Tell me who you represent."

I backed towards the car, smiling disarmingly.

"Do you think you'd mind doing something for me?" I said. "Next time they're holding a party at the farm, do you think you could give me a ring? I'll give you my number."

She put her hands on her hips. "I don't want your number. I just want to know what you're up to." I opened the car door and got inside. "All right, listen," she said, desperately. "I happen to know they're holding another party on Friday. I know, because they always ask us to leave the gate at the top of the lane open. We don't, of course. Now will you please tell me what is going on? Is someone planning to open a *restaurant* in the farm?" The full horror of this idea dawned on her after she'd said it. Her eyes bulged at me behind the spectacles.

I slammed my door and turned down the window. "I think I can safely say," I said, "that there are no plans afoot to turn Folly Farm into a restaurant. You've been very helpful."

When I got back to the office there was a note on my desk asking me to ring Mr Martin. I ignored it, and instead phoned Carol at Taylors.

"Did you know Victor Taylor had put Folly Farm on the market?" I asked.

She sounded surprised. "No. You'd think he'd wait for house prices to start going up again, wouldn't you? If they ever do. My Steven reckons the bottom's fallen out of property for good. He says it's the beginning of the decline of the capitalist system in this country, because – "

"Really. You don't remember Mr Victor asking you to put him through to any estate agents – or anybody ringing up for him who might have been an estate agent?"

"What, somebody who sounded like the sort of person I wouldn't want my little sister to marry, you mean? No. But honestly, he never tells us what he's up to. We could come in one day and find he'd sold us to the Japanese and it wouldn't surprise us. *Hey!*" A distinct note of relish crept into Carol's tone. "Do tell me – did you ever find out who Rosemary's lover was?"

I bit my lip. I was beginning to wish I'd never involved myself in Rosemary's personal life; her choice of lover had been a definite disappointment. "No, I didn't," I said, blowing my nose to rid it of the imagined scent of winter-green.

I said goodbye to Carol and put the phone down. She was right. It *was* an odd time to sell a house unless you had to. Not only that, but it was a remarkable estate agent who not only failed to provide keys to a property but also chose not to accompany you personally armed with more fiction than goes into the average TV blockbuster mini-series. Somebody had certainly slipped up somewhere.

Pete played around with the spaghetti on his plate, not eating very much, while I told him of my suspicions concerning Victor Taylor's parties at Folly Farm.

"Not bad," he said. "'Company Chairman in Champagne Sex Romp with Hot Hotpot Girls'. Hardly new, but new to Hudderston, I suppose. What evidence have you got?"

I wished he'd hurry up and eat the spaghetti before it got cold. I'd made the sauce myself, for once, using fresh tomatoes. "Well, actually, none. Apart from very strong suspicions. Victor Taylor's got on in the local business world remarkably fast, he got his first big contract from Maurice Prestage of RMP Developments, Barry said there were topless girls at a Folly Farm party, and of course – "

"Of course we all know the story about Prestage and Kravitz and their idea of a fun evening's entertainment. You don't have to tell me. I heard it all from Dave at Hudderston Central, and he got it straight from the traffic patrol that went to the scene." He struggled manfully to swallow a mushroom.

"Don't you like that? I thought spaghetti bolognese was your favourite."

"It is, but I've been feeling sick since lunchtime. Sorry, darling."

"It's because you drink too much on an empty stomach," I said, crossly. I took away the half-eaten meal and said even more crossly, "Actually it's just because you drink too much. Don't you realise what you're doing to your liver?"

He scowled angrily. "Stop trying to mother me," he muttered. "Do you want to follow up this story, or not?"

"Yes. But Mr Heslop says I'm to hand it over to someone who knows what they're doing."

"Oh, sod him!" He got up and extracted a beer from the fridge. "Listen, first you need to track down one or two of the girls and get them to cooperate. They will. If they're prepared to sell their bodies then someone else's reputation is no big deal. Just be friendly and sympathetic and keep patting your cheque book. Or if all else fails try scaring the shit out of them – most women have got a boyfriend or a mother or a kid they don't want to know what they're doing."

I looked at him appealingly. "I don't think I could do that sort of thing."

"Of course you could. But don't for Christ's sake part with any money. Remember, if people like Prestage and Kravitz are involved, then you've got a story – but if it's just a couple of Victor's mates in dirty anoraks from the local, no one will give a toss. And see if you can find out if he's holding another of these little do's in the near future, because if he is and you're going to put a story together then it'll come down in the end to keeping the place under surveillance, I'm afraid."

"I already know when the next party is. It's on Friday."

He looked impressed. "I told you you could do it. If it pans out I'll help you with the surveillance bit. We'll hang about in the bushes pretending to be a courting couple, or something."

"It'll be like old times."

"Old times, eh," he murmured. "And here's me thinking present times couldn't be better."

"I've also got a strong suspicion that Victor Taylor killed Rosemary Tindall because of all this," I said. "I think this was the wrongdoing she wrote to the *Herald* about, and I think when we didn't respond to the letter she confronted him about it and he killed her to shut her up."

Pete smiled. "That's a pretty big leap of the imagination, Chris. Personally, if *I* was hiring girls for the sort of orgy you describe – "

"Which you wouldn't, of course, because you've never had to pay for it in your life," I interrupted, still angry about the spaghetti and the drinking, and now about being contradicted.

"Don't be silly. Everything has to be paid for. No, but if I was, and someone found out about it, it wouldn't be the end of the world. It would be very embarrassing and I expect I'd have to change my hairdresser, and not go out without dark glasses for a while, but I don't think I'd kill anybody over it."

I thought about this. "No," I agreed. "*You* wouldn't. But then, you're not Victor Taylor. You haven't waited years and years to get control of your father's company – you haven't gone to an awful lot of trouble to influence important people – you haven't got political ambitions. *You* haven't invested – "

"Yes, yes." He touched one hand painfully to his head, and the other to my lips, to silence them. "But let's not go off half-cocked, shall we? Let's find out first whether this whole thing is the figment of an over fertile imagination. I'm going upstairs to have some Andrews' and lie down for half an hour."

"Are you sure you're all right?" I asked, alarmed. "You don't look all right. I really wish you'd think about – well, you know – cutting down – "

He closed his hand over my mouth again before I could complete the sentence. "Don't you worry, darling," he said. "I know exactly how much I can take."

It was obviously out of the question for me to make another approach to Camilla Douglas, and particularly not on the subject of her involvement with the parties at Folly Farm – but there was still Mandy. I got out my street map of Hudderston. The Greenmeadows estate didn't look very big, and I clearly remembered Camilla saying she'd met Mandy when they both moved into houses on the estate at the same time. So it would surely be quite a simple matter to tour the area and spot Mandy's distinctive white Metro.

I cruised round Greenmeadows for half an hour one morning with only one eye on the road, wondering why roads always seem so much longer in the tarmac than they do on the map. Mandy could be out, her car could be garaged. I was on the point of giving up when I spotted a post office van parked in a layby. I drew up behind him and got out of the car, leaving the engine running.

"Excuse me," I said, tapping on his window. "I'm trying to trace someone who lives on the estate."

The postman, who was eating a sandwich, stuck a thumbnail between his teeth and pulled out a piece of meat. He wound down his window.

"Do what, love?"

I gave him a helpless feminine smile. "Sorry to disturb you. I'm looking for a friend of mine. Her name's Mandy and she's got a white Metro, and the Metro's got a champagne glass and a pink ribbon painted on it. I thought you might know where she lives."

He looked me up and down.

"What's her dress size?" he asked, insolently.

I was almost on the point of coming up with a retort about public servants and the appalling quality of the first class letter service, when out of the corner of my eye I saw the rear of a white Metro rounding the bend at speed. I ran back to the Mini, leapt in, and did a dramatic U-turn seconds ahead of a head-on crash with a bus. The look on the postman's face was reward enough for this heroism.

But I wasn't fast enough for the Metro. Ahead of me the longest, straightest road on the Greenmeadow estate stretched towards a distant horizon, and there wasn't a white car in sight. And of course, I might have risked my no claims bonus for the wrong white car anyway. Face it, I thought, you've got no choice but to have another go at Camilla. And then I suddenly spotted the glint of sunlight on the rear door of a white car in a garage. A woman ran out of the garage, hesitated, looked at the up and over doors, shrugged and stumbled towards the house. She was wearing skintight denims and a teeshirt that exposed her midriff, and the sort of high heels that have no mercy on your calf muscles. I couldn't see whether or not the Metro bore the champagne glass motif. I parked behind a row of Renault 5s and Fiats, and walked up the garden path.

"Mandy?" I queried, as the front door opened.

She put down a toddler and brushed a fashionably wild lock of hair from her face.

"Yes."

We stared at one another uncertainly, and then before I could launch into my prepared and probably hopelessly inadequate speech about following up a tip-off from an informer, she said, "Oh, you can't be with Mother and Toddlers, so you must be the woman Camilla told me about. Oh God, I have got my knickers in a twist this morning! Come in."

I stepped into the hall. Mandy's living-room was knee deep in bean bags, toddlers, and women climbing over one another to extricate foreign objects from children's mouths.

"Have I come at a bad time?" I asked, hesitantly.

"No. It's me," said Mandy. "Here you are, girls." She tossed the carrier bag towards what looked like a vacant bean bag, but which turned out to be a very pregnant mother.

"I'd forgotten it was Wednesday," said Mandy, "and my turn for Mother and Toddlers. I had to go out for biscuits. Carry on without me," she called rather unnecessarily to the others, because they already were.

She led me towards the kitchen. "Was I expecting you this morning?" she asked. "I'm in such a muddle."

"Are you?"

I smiled. "Camilla wants me to help out at the do on Friday night. She said you'd tell me all about it." I smiled again and waited, hopefully.

"On Friday?" A frown creased her normally wrinkle free forehead. She seated herself on a high kitchen stool, unthinkingly crossing her legs and arching her back so as to display her voluptuous figure to its best advantage. She was the kind of woman every man I knew would drool over.

She reached for a bulldog clip full of papers and riffled through them vacantly. "I'll never be any good with paperwork," she muttered, dropping the bundle amid the clutter on the worktop. It knocked over a plastic beaker of milk, and fell among foil pie dishes, smears of raw pastry, and bits of a plastic racing car in the process of being glued back together.

"Shit," said Mandy, reaching for a cloth. "Oh, *I've* got it, you're Heather and you're going to help out at the Pringle wedding on Saturday. Right. There are two hundred frozen vol-au-vent cases in the freezer. You can take them now, and – "

"No. Camilla said I was to help with the Folly Farm do on Friday."

Mandy's nicely drawn eyebrows knitted in bafflement.

"There's nothing to do for Friday. Only smoked salmon canapés, and I do them."

I got out my notebook, smiling in a businesslike way. "Don't you worry. I'll sort out the details." I raised my voice above wails from the front room. "Look, I know the Folly Farm parties are a bit special – who lays on the entertainment?"

A hint of suspicion tinged Mandy's bafflement.

"I think I'd better check this with Camilla," she said, and reached for the wall phone. "Not now, Andrew," she added, to the toddler, who had just wandered into the room. "Mummy's busy."

I watched in horror as she dialled Camilla's number. Once she got through I'd be sunk. Her finger hovered over the last digit, and then remarkably, she replaced the receiver.

"I forgot," she said. "Camilla went to collect the new hot cupboard this morning. She'll be back after lunch."

"Oh dear, and I'm busy this afternoon," I said. "Look, why don't you just give me the name of whoever is in charge of the – er – floorshow, and I'll get out of your way. I mustn't keep you from your guests."

Mandy began disentangling the kettle lead from that of the food processor.

"Look," she said. "I've got a lot to do. I've got a hundred mince pies to finish off, a sandwich lunch to make up, all those women out there – " She looked desperate. "This is the first time I've had the Mother and Toddler group here. What will they think of me? Will you please go now and come back later. *I* organise the entertainment at Folly Farm, and I can't imagine what Camilla was thinking of, telling you – "

She wrenched the kettle lead free and her bosom reverberated with shock, like the hills of San Francisco during the Big One.

"You've – er – got quite a few talents other than cooking," I suggested, with a sudden flash of insight. "You do a bit more than organise the entertainments, don't you? I think you're part of them. Don't you ever feel you're being exploited?"

"*Exploited?*" By chance I'd not only hit a nerve but I'd hit the right one. "Come on! Christ, if you can't use your body to get on, what can you use? I mean, if I had good leg muscles and a head for heights, no one would think twice about me using them to become a skiing champion, would they? I've never understood you feminists rabbiting on about exploitation." She began opening cupboards and looking for things. "Oh *God*, I can't find *anything*. Will you please go away and come back later? Where's the damn coffee?"

I pointed towards the jar, hidden behind a giant sized Fairy Liquid. "Catering's quite respectable," I said. "But topless waitressing isn't. Was this Camilla's idea to boost your sales or your prices or something?"

"Mummy – " said Andrew, holding up what looked like a teddy bear's leg.

"No!" snapped Mandy. "Not now!" She turned him round, then propelled him bodily from the kitchen. "Who *are* you? You're not Heather about the vol-au-vents, are you? Go on, get out of my house, I've got nothing to say to you – whoever you are."

I said, "All right. It's OK. If you won't tell me about the Folly Farm parties I'll go into the next room and have a chat with your friends about them." And then I averted my face so she wouldn't see how horrified I was at what I'd just said.

"Look," I went on, when she hadn't answered. "I know what it must be like, trying to pay the mortgage on this place and bring up a child. You're divorced, aren't you, like Camilla? I imagine you've had to do some things you're not proud of, and – "

"Christ! You think I'm on the game!" exclaimed Mandy, angrily.

"I didn't say that. I don't know what some of your other customers might think, though. The wedding you're doing on Saturday – the Pringles, for example. What would they think?"

Mandy gasped. "My God, you work for one of our competitors, don't you? How did you get on to this? The Folly Farm parties are a special favour for a special client. Are you with Wendy's Pantry? Honestly, it's a one off, a special arrangement. We were doing a stag party one evening at a private club, and a stripper was supposed to jump out of a birthday cake. She didn't turn up, and this guy offered me fifty quid if I'd do it." She gave a little giggle. "I'd never done anything like it before, but – well – I'd had a couple of glasses of champagne – "

"So you did."

"Yes, why not? It was exciting. If you've got a good body why shouldn't you be proud of it? Suddenly there were all these men looking at *me* – just at me. They weren't looking at me and wondering if I'd washed their dirty socks or put enough salt in their sandwiches – they were just *admiring* me. It was great." She looked starry eyed at the memory. "And afterwards this man approached Camilla and said he wanted to arrange a stag do at Folly Farm – "

"Victor Taylor?"

"Yes. He said he wanted a few girls like me, and a couple of porno films for the guys to watch. He wanted Camilla to arrange everything. Well, you know how it is in this business. We were in debt up to our eyes. He offered to give us an interest-free loan and provide us with a couple of cars – the finance company had just taken ours back. Christ, what could we do? And anyway, it's only a bit of fun. We're not going to offer the same thing to anyone else. We're not cutting in on anybody's business," she added, earnestly.

A head peered round the kitchen door. "Sorry, Mandy, love, but we're *parched*, and Andrew's screaming his head off. Can I say you're doing the coffee?"

Mandy looked desperate. She began grabbing cups and plates at random. "I'll be *two minutes*," she exclaimed, adding to me, "now, you listen. I know all about bloody Wendy's Pantry. Camilla's brother-in-law works for Ratend Pest Control and he told her all about the state of Wendy's kitchen. If you think – "

I was suddenly extremely glad I hadn't gone into catering.

"I'm not from Wendy's Pantry. I'm from the *Tipping Herald*."

Mandy turned pale. She closed her eyes. "Oh my God!" she muttered.

Earlier, I'd spent half an hour in the *Herald*'s archives, and had come up with a photograph taken at the laying of the foundation stone for the new District Hospital. I showed it to Mandy.

"Do you know any of these people?" I asked.

She glanced at it. "No," she replied, sullenly.

I stared meaningfully in the direction of the mayhem from the living-room. "Yes, you do. Take another look."

She hesitated, then pointed at Maurice Prestage, Dudley Kravitz, one of Dudley Kravitz's associates, and, to my surprise, a prominent local councillor.

"These men have all attended parties at Folly Farm?" I queried.

"Yes. And they're private parties in a private house. It's got nothing to do with anyone else. Oh God, Camilla will *kill* me."

I raised my eyebrows. "Will she? Do you know this woman?" I produced the photograph of Rosemary Tindall, which Mandy obviously recognised immediately.

"She's the one who was found dead in the woods the other day."

"Yes. And did you know what she had in her handbag? One of your business cards. She worked for Victor Taylor, and she wrote a letter to the *Herald* about these parties of yours. That's how I got on to you."

I waited for this to sink in, then decided to try something else. "Rosemary had made a note in her shorthand book – Folly Farm, 9th November. Does that date mean anything to you?"

She stared at me. "Mr Taylor had a party that evening – "

I smiled. "I thought so. That was the night Rosemary died. Do you remember anything unusual happening during the evening? Was Mr Taylor called away to deal with an unexpected visitor?"

She thought about it. "I don't think so. Why? What

are you suggesting? You can't seriously be suggesting – "
Mandy's eyes bulged. Her toddler rushed into the room and
she grabbed him and clasped him to her knees. Some instinct
told me the time had come to quit while I was ahead.

"Thank you very much for your help," I said. "I shall
probably be in touch again." I put the photographs away
and turned to leave.

I was on the front step when Mandy caught up with me.

"Look," she hissed, in a stage whisper. "All this, believe
me – it was nothing more than making a few middle-aged
men very happy. It was just harmless fun."

I raised my eyebrows.

"Really? Try telling that to Rosemary Tindall."

16

I could hear my phone ringing as I climbed the stairs. I ran to pick it up before it stopped, and my ear recoiled from an outburst of raucous laughter.

"Hallo, darling," said Pete. "Just ringing to let you know you'll have to do without the pleasure of my company next week. I've got to go up to the Midlands."

"Oh. But I thought we were going to make a big effort on the decorating this weekend. That means I'm going to be stuck doing it all by myself next week."

"Can't be helped," he replied, jauntily, not sounding at all sorry. The laughter reached another crescendo. I waited for it to die down.

"Will you be gone all week?"

"I'll let you know. But I thought I'd better tell you about it now so you won't turn round later and say I didn't. All right? Have you got it?"

I sighed deeply. "Well, I suppose you can't help it." I thought about all those cans of paint currently weighting down the boot of the Mini. "Pete – about Friday. It's on."

"What is?"

"This thing at Folly Farm. You said you'd come with me."

"Did I? Not so much tonic, darling, thank you. Oh, so I did. Right, I'll make a note in my diary to bring home a camera and some fast film. You organise the soup and the thick socks."

"What for?"

"What do you mean, what for? Because it'll be bloody cold out there, that's what for. Shit, I've left my diary in my other jacket. Cheers."

"What's going on over there?"

"Someone's birthday, I think. I don't know the guy actually. Any excuse – you know."

"Yes," I agreed, sourly. "But you won't forget about Friday, will you? You're wonderful, Pete – I couldn't do this without you."

He sounded embarrassed. "Ah well," he said, "it's nice to know I can do something SuperKeith can't. Love you."

I was still mulling over his reference to SuperKeith when my phone rang again.

"It's me," said Keith. "You're never there when I ring."

"What do you want?" I asked, primly.

"Oh, come on, don't be like that. Look, I'm sorry about the other night. I suppose you didn't really mean to humiliate me. You just didn't think." And then he made it worse by adding, "As usual."

I closed my eyes and prevented myself from responding.

"Look," said Keith. "I meant what I said the other night. I really think we can work things out. Can't we give it one last try? Don't you think you owe me at least another attempt to talk things over after all the time I put in with you?"

He really had a way with words, but somehow even this didn't stop him from getting to me.

"I don't know if there's any point," I said, resignedly. "I'll think about it. Give me a ring next week."

"Oh yes, and will you be permanently washing your hair? Or maybe you're permanently washing lover-boy's hair?"

"Keith, stop it," I said. "I've said we'll talk next week and we will. I promise – I'll give you a ring early next week."

After I'd put the phone down I got out my handbag mirror and looked in it. I practised saying the word "no" over and over again, noting how it rounded my lips and tightened my cheeks. It even made me look a year or two younger. Perhaps one day I'd actually learn how to say it at the right moment.

By Friday, right on cue for the weekend, my cold had got a lot worse. I huddled over my desk at lunchtime drinking hot monosodium glutamate and water that had come out of a packet labelled soup. Mr Heslop emerged from his office, chewing manfully on an alfalfa sprout sandwich.

"Chris," he said, beaming effusively. "How's the cold?"

"Pretty awful, actually." I reached for a tissue.

He wagged his finger at me. "You should try sprouting your own vegetables. I'm telling you, all the raw energy packed into something like this – well, compared with dead flesh and chemicals – anyway, I mustn't lecture you. Look, I wonder if you could do me a favour." He held up a folded sheet of paper. "One of my nephews has got a speaking part in the school panto, and I promised I'd review it. Only unfortunately I've been invited to some dreadful dinner at the Clocktower Hotel. It'll be an awful bore, but what can one do? Mustn't let the wife down. Anyway, this is much more up your street really. You'll probably enjoy it." He dropped the paper in front of me.

"Certainly," I said, forcing a smile. "When is it?"

"Tonight. Thanks awfully." He nodded, and turned to go.

I gasped. "No, I can't – not tonight! Any other night I'd be glad to, but not tonight – "

"Another night wouldn't be any good. What have you got on?"

"Well, it's – you know – something."

"Cancel it. There's a good girl." He gave me a light pat on the head. "I know you're much too nice to let a little boy down."

"But Mr Heslop!" I protested, leaping to my feet. "Think of all that rich food – dead flesh and chemicals – " I was desperate. "What about your stomach?"

He walked off, pretending not to hear.

It was the middle of the afternoon before I managed to get hold of Pete.

"Thank heavens," I said. "You'll never guess. Something awful's happened."

"Don't tell me," he said. "God's cancelled Christmas!" And I could tell by the two double s's he inserted in Christmas that he'd spent several hours in the pub.

"It's about tonight," I said. "Mr Heslop's asked me to cover a school panto and I couldn't think up an excuse. You're going to have to go to Folly Farm by yourself. Do you mind?"

There was a silence that seemed to go on for ever.

"Hallo?" I queried.

"Christ. I forgot. Sorry. Oh, Jesus."

"What do you mean you forgot? I reminded you yesterday about the camera. Weren't you listening? You can't have forgotten. You said – "

"Come on, we discussed this *ages* ago. It's not in my diary, darling. I swear by that diary – if it isn't in the diary then it doesn't exist for me. I've said I'm sorry."

"Oh *God*!" I screamed, loudly enough to turn heads. "How could you do this? You promised!"

"But I've promised someone else now. I was about to phone you anyway. I'm meeting a couple of the guys tonight and I might not get back at all. We've been working on this story for weeks, about reject food finding its way on to the shelves of a well known supermarket – we're going out for a curry to celebrate our success. I could've sworn you said this Folly Farm thing was *next* Friday. You should've made me check my diary in front of you."

"Oh, *Pete*!" I exclaimed despairingly. Had I not been so angry with myself for failing to say no to Mr Heslop I would certainly have said a lot more. As it was I reached for another tissue and blew my nose indecorously.

Pete said. "OK. Let's think our way out of this one. *I* can't go, *you've* got a panto to attend. A school panto, you said? Have you ever been to a school panto before?"

"Of course I have."

"Good. So you get hold of a programme, ring the school, check out a few details on the kids and teachers involved. It'll take you five minutes. You can write it up when you feel like it. There's no need to watch the bloody thing."

I thought about this. "That's cheating."

"Yes. You got a better idea?"

I wrote down his suggestions. "I haven't got a camera," I said sulkily.

"That's no problem. Nick one of Ernst's. And listen, as well as the pictures, keep a note of car numbers tonight, will you. I've got a friend who's got a friend who's got access to the police computer."

I groaned. "How am I supposed to spend hours sitting in a car without looking conspicuous?"

"Oh, do what all reporters do. Just lounge about, picking your nose."

I counted to five. "If that's what all reporters do, anyone who sees me will instantly know I'm a reporter."

He gave this a moment's consideration. "Only if you do it with a blue plastic pen top. Just use your finger, then they'll probably think you're with Special Branch."

"Thank you, Pete, very much. And when will I see you?"

He hesitated. "Actually, let's say tomorrow morning. I'll find a floor somewhere. Tell you what, I'll give you Joe's number. Hang on." After a lot of rustling he came back with a number. "But this is just for emergencies, darling," he said. "If you call up at three in the morning don't expect a kind word from anyone."

I went downstairs, shivering, to argue with Ernst about the loan of a camera.

The powerful glare of headlamps on full beam lit up the scaly trunks of trees and moved on, leaving the trees to waltz round one another in its passage. I crouched low over the steering wheel, my camera at the ready, but the car – actually a dark blue Bedford van – carried on down Polepit Lane towards the quarry. I had already seen it pass twice before. I let my muscles relax. It was something past eight – my only contact with time in the darkness was the hourly bleep from my watch – and I was freezing. I'd parked the car a safe distance from the street lamp, and taken a roll of film of arrivals at the farm, definitely recognising Dudley Kravitz and Maurice Prestage, and I was beginning to wonder if it was worth hanging around any longer. The major excitement of the evening had been occasioned by Victor Taylor's arrival, because as his car found its way into my viewfinder I had mistaken it first for Mark Williams' Renault, then for a Porsche. I couldn't quite get Jennifer Saunders' story out of my head. A few moments ago Victor Taylor had reappeared on foot at the top of the lane leading to the farm, and had shut the gate to Polepit Lane. I *guessed* that meant he was expecting no more guests, but I decided to wait just a few more minutes to be on the safe side.

I reached into the glove compartment for my soup. It

really was too bad of Pete. I adjusted my rear view mirror and practised saying "no" into it, even though I couldn't see myself properly. If only I'd said "no" to Pete five months ago on the floor of his flat, when he'd looked so beautiful and so irresistible . . . It wasn't as if I'd been swept off my feet by a total stranger; I'd known exactly what his weaknesses were – although perhaps I hadn't recognised them as weaknesses. I practised a few more "no's" into the mirror. Five months ago if I'd asked Pete to spend an evening with me sitting in a car beside a lonely road he wouldn't have forgotten about it. Condensation streamed down the windscreen, and steam clouded the mirror. I rubbed it with my sleeve and said "No, no, no" into it, very slowly and deliberately.

Suddenly the passenger door of the Mini opened.

"Well, well, fancy seeing you here," said a voice.

"Oh my God!" Tomato soup leapt from the cup and landed hotly and wetly on my thigh. "Oh, God!"

"What a welcome!" remarked Wayne, settling his long legs into the footwell as best he could. "And what, may I ask, is a nice girl like you doing in a place like this?"

"Oh, God," I said again. "You nearly gave me a heart attack. Couldn't you have knocked, or something?" He seemed to be laughing. "Well, we've got reason to believe – "

"Hang on, that's my line. Go on, what are you up to?"

"Just – watching someone."

"Not the Parry-Davies' at Wintershall House, I trust? Acquaintances of the Super, they are."

I said nothing.

"*I'm* here because of the Parry-Davies'," said Wayne. "They've got a collection of priceless Victorian chamberpots, or some such rubbish, and there's a gang of antique thieves doing the rounds. It doesn't do for acquaintances of the Super to get themselves robbed. You're not moonlighting as an antiques thief, are you?"

I found a bundle of soggy tissues and blew my nose.

"I thought you'd got an overtime ban," I remarked.

He shrugged. "The wife went out, and I couldn't think of anything better to do." He peered at me inquisitively. "I don't know what you're up to, love, but you ought to have locked your doors. There's some very funny people about."

I shivered. "I know. I didn't think. By the way, there's a blue Bedford van which went down to the quarry a few minutes ago and didn't come back. I've seen it twice. Perhaps it belongs to your antiques thieves."

"Oh? I'll have to take a look at it." He didn't seem in any particular hurry. "How long have you been here? You look frozen. Can I try and warm you up?"

I made a sort of embarrassed noise and stared at the condensation trails on the window.

Wayne cleared his throat, sounding even more embarrassed.

"I've been meaning to call you," he said. "About the Tindall case. This is strictly off the record, but I think after all your efforts you deserve to be the first to know."

"What?"

"Well – " He paused for dramatic effect. "We think we'll soon be able to make an arrest."

"*Who?*" I demanded, astonished.

He rubbed his hands and blew on them. "Jesus, it is parky, isn't it? Well, you remember I told you we got the owner of the Granada to give us a list of people who'd been in his car?" I nodded. "Right, well, we tracked down some of them and eliminated them but there were quite a few prints we couldn't identify. So somebody in forensics had a brainstorm. He fed every single print we found on that car into the computer, and – Bingo! We came up with one that matched the prints of a known criminal – a known criminal with a history of violence against women, I might add."

"Oh." I was stunned. "Who?"

Wayne rubbed his hands again. "You'll love this, you really will. It was the owner of the car, *the owner*. Smooth-talking bastard," he added, bitterly. "He committed his offence twenty years ago, and he'd changed his name, otherwise we'd've got on to him sooner, but fingerprints don't lie. Your fingerprints will always find you out."

My mouth fell open. Steam from the soup was dissolving the condensation on the windscreen in a slow tide of water.

He laughed. "You look like you've just seen a ghost.

This guy was convicted of criminal assault on a woman, and remanded for psychiatric testing. What do you make of that? You see, when we first hauled him in he was so respectable looking, and so plausible with his story of having his car nicked from the Eldon Lodge car park that we fell for it. He'd got no previous under his present name, and anyway, there were witnesses who'd seen him check into the hotel at a time we knew Mrs Tindall was still alive. Or *thought* we knew she was still alive. And then you came along and pointed out that our neighbourhood watch lady wasn't actually a very reliable witness, and it set us thinking about a number of things."

I was still speechless. I managed to say, "What?"

"Well, what if in fact this guy killed her *before* he checked into the hotel? Discount Mrs Stubbs' evidence and all options are open. And there's the car itself. If as we'd assumed it was borrowed for a few hours from the car park whoever borrowed it wouldn't have had time to give it a thorough clean-up. But the owner? Christ, he had the car a whole *week*. He had it valeted."

"But, but – you're now saying you suspect the owner of the Granada because there *isn't* any evidence he ever had the victim in his car! That's *ridiculous*!"

"It may sound ridiculous to you, love, but believe me, it has a logic all its own."

I wanted to say, look, I know Mr Redfern and he's awfully nice and whatever he did twenty years ago, he couldn't possibly have – but somehow I didn't think it would do any good. Instead I said, "But you've got witnesses to the fact that he stayed in his hotel room all evening."

"Correction. We've got one witness. And I'm not happy about her. We hauled her in earlier this week and she's still sticking to her story, but I've got a feeling she's lying about something. Probably she slipped out back for a quick snog with the barman, and doesn't dare admit she left her post vacant."

I frowned. " 'Snog's' a very old fashioned word," I remarked. "Anyway, why don't you just question the Granada owner again? I'm sure he'll be able to account fully for his movements for the whole day."

"Oh, I'm sure he will, too," agreed Wayne, sarcastically. "He's a cunning bastard. That's why I don't want to pull him in until we've got something on him. These middle-class pillocks with their talk of false arrest – " I could feel his scowl through the darkness. "Anyway, we'd like you to publish another appeal if you would. We want help from anyone who saw any incident – no matter how unimportant it might seem – involving a maroon Granada, *and*/or a woman answering Mrs Tindall's description at any time on Tuesday 10th November." He shook his head. "It's pathetic, really, just how little we still know about Mrs Tindall's last hours."

I hesitated. "I suppose you still won't consider the possibility that Mrs Tindall was really killed on the Monday night?"

He laughed, and didn't even bother to answer.

I said. "There's something I was supposed to tell you. A message from a witness who lives at Cottis Wood, and who doesn't want to speak to you herself. Apparently this woman – Jennifer Saunders – insists she saw a black sports car of some sort parked near the murder scene on Tuesday night. I'd've told you before, but she also insists there was no Granada parked out there."

"And everyone else is lying? Yes. Paranoia. I know Jennifer Saunders all right. She's a very bad shoplifter. It's always someone else, according to her, and all the witnesses and especially the police are liars. She's an outpatient at the Manning Green Institute. If you ask me she ought to be an inpatient somewhere, but there you are. That's community care for you."

Silence fell, broken only by the sigh of wind outside. I had the feeling Wayne was preparing to say something, when suddenly a car appeared, screeching to a halt inches before the gate leading down to Folly Farm. The car door opened and a man in a dark suit got out to open the gate. Instinctively I reached for my camera, and Wayne muttered "Bugger me!" and raked his hand across the windscreen.

"Ssh! Don't! They'll see us!" I begged, lunging towards him.

He stared at me. He opened his mouth and leaned towards

me. Before I'd worked out what he was up to his mouth had closed over mine and his designer stubble was tickling my lips and chin. I tried to resist, but the kiss was enthusiastic and unavoidable.

Afterwards, I remained wooden and immobile. I'd just been kissed by a man who was still learning how to harden his conkers with vinegar when I'd moved on to human biology lessons behind the bike sheds.

"What did you do that for?" I demanded.

"To give us cover, of course! Don't you ever go to the movies?"

I threw my head back and laughed.

"Oh, come on, it wasn't that funny," protested Wayne, hurt. "I've fancied you ever since I saw you in that wine bar." Hesitantly, he placed a hand on my thigh. His searching fingers found the warm wetness of the tomato soup. Surprised, he lifted his hand to the light and studied the sticky red stain.

"*Jesus!*" he exclaimed in horror, proving that even men who are liberated enough to let women pay for their lunches haven't quite come to terms with all aspects of femininity.

I laughed. "It's only tomato soup. Here." I handed him a tissue.

"Bloody hell! What *are* you up to?"

"I told you. Watching someone. Can't I do that? It's a free country, isn't it?"

"Course it isn't! Who told you that?"

I stared out of the window at the tail lights of the car disappearing in the direction of the farm.

Wayne sighed. "All right. I can take a hint. I'll be off after my antique thieves." He opened the car door. "I suppose – I don't suppose you'd fancy going out for a meal sometime? I know this great Chinese, or we could go somewhere really flash, whatever you like."

I smiled. "Thank you, but I'm involved with someone else at the moment."

"Oh, that's all right. I don't mind being your bit on the side."

I looked him straight in the eye. "No," I said.

I watched him walk away in the darkness, towards the

quarry. "No," I said again, to my reflection in the mirror, and I sat in the Mini all by myself, chuckling.

It was half past eleven when I finally got home, and the house was in darkness. From upstairs I could hear Julie's soft, irregular snores. I smiled fondly, and went into the kitchen to make myself a hot drink. I didn't like the idea of going upstairs to a bed that didn't have a warm, male body in it, but at least I could smother myself in moisturiser and not worry about what I looked like in the morning. Everything has an up-side. Carefully I placed the camera, exposed film, and a list of barely decipherable car numbers on the top shelf of a cupboard and closed the door on them. All things considered, I hadn't done a bad job.

I went upstairs and undressed. As I switched off the light the red glow of the clock caught my eye: 12.02. I didn't know it then, but I'd just begun what I sincerely hope will turn out to have been the worst seven days of my life.

17

Julie looked at me severely.

"I don't know, Mum," she said. "Gallivanting out at all hours with a cold like that – what would you say to me if I did that?"

"I'd say you jolly well deserved to feel rotten the next day," I said, between shivers.

"Precisely!" She was delighted. "Haven't we got any Coldrex? I'll go out to the chemist, shall I?" She stared in dismay at the rain hurling itself against the kitchen window.

"No, don't worry. You've just washed your hair. You can't go out in this."

"Ah! Brilliant idea!" she exclaimed. "Let's see if we can catch Pete at his friend's place. Knowing him, I'll bet he's still sleeping off last night." We exchanged glances. She just thought it was funny. "Well, he can pop into a chemist on his way home. Where did you put the number?"

"It's in my bag. You'd better let me do it. He might be cross," I said, without making a move.

"Don't be silly. He's never cross with you. He thinks the sun shines out of your – ears." She hugged me and kissed me on the head. "Go on, Mum. You look awful."

I sighed. I'd woken up feeling very angry with Pete, and I didn't want to ask him for help. Still, as it probably was his fault I had a head full of cavity wall insulation this morning –

I stood shivering in the hall as I dialled the number. The phone gave three double rings and then stopped.

"Hallo – " I began.

"Hi," said a warm female voice. "I'm Josie, and I'm sorry I'm not able to take your call right now. If you'd care to leave your name and number after the tone, I'll get back to you as soon as I can. Catch you later!"

At first I was just puzzled as to how "Joe" had turned into Josie, and why she'd got her answerphone on at this time of the morning when she and Pete must be at home and in bed – and then a draught of cold air pierced through the cavity wall insulation. I stared at the phone, and at the awful brown squares on the hall wallpaper. I didn't feel particularly angry, or at least not any angrier than I had been already. I didn't feel anything much. Of course, I might be jumping to quite the wrong conclusion, but it was a conclusion which had a sort of inevitable logic to it. And anyway, what did it matter? A cold ball of anger filled my stomach like a lead weight. This was just the last straw. I didn't really blame Pete for being unfaithful, I blamed him for letting me down, I blamed him for not turning into the husband I'd thought he would, and I blamed him for making me break up my family when I didn't really want to. I *hated* him for making me fall deeply and irrevocably in love with him when I was old enough to know better, for letting me tell him on the phone only the other day that I thought he was wonderful, and for the fact that some part of me even now still believed that this was true. And worst of all – and this was what was doing for my brain cells what Jane Fonda's Workout Programme is supposed to do for your body – I'd absolutely no idea what I was going to do about it.

Pete arrived home mid-morning, thrust a bunch of red roses into my hands and treated me to his best and most beguiling smile.

"Sorry, darling," he said. "I am, really. I'll make it up to you."

I let him kiss my cheek, and then realised with disgust that I was sniffing him for perfume. "I hope you slept all right on your floor," I said, pointedly.

"Oh, don't worry. I did a bit better than that. I got a sofa. How did you get on last night? Christ, you must have been frozen. I hope it was worth it."

I swallowed. "Well, I won't know that, will I, until the pictures are developed. I got a list of car numbers as well."

"Good. Let's just hope they don't turn out to be on contract hire or we'll really be in the shit. Give it to me on Monday and I'll pass it on for you."

I smiled. "When are you off to the Midlands?"

"Tuesday. But I'll get this guy to mail you the printout as soon as he's got it. Are you all right? You seem a bit – tense."

The smile had cemented itself to my lips. "I'm fine. Actually I'm a bit worried about John. I ran into DS Horton last night and he says they're thinking of pulling him in again."

"Christ. Why?"

"Well, for one thing – John's got a criminal record for an assault on a woman. It happened twenty years ago and he's changed his name since, but they found out through his fingerprints."

"You're joking!" He stared at me. "You're not joking. Oh, well, twenty years ago – we all did some stupid things when we were young. I certainly did. Twenty years ago he'd've been – thirty. Oh." He bit his lip. "No, I don't believe it. He probably spent an evening with some poor woman and bored her comatose. He's nearly done that to me a couple of times. What Helen sees in him I'll never know."

"No, not when she could have had you, I suppose," I said sourly, and then hurried on. "Anyway, I think we ought to warn him. He ought to tell them his real reason for staying at the Eldon Lodge, and then they might believe him. He came to Hudderston again just recently, you know, presumably to visit Joyce." I had a sudden vision of him sitting in the car outside Cottis Wood with the length of copper piping in his hand. I shivered. "Don't you think we should warn him?"

He grimaced. "Yes. Yes, I suppose we should. It might save a lot of embarrassment later." He put his arms round me and kissed my neck, and I managed not to melt. "I'll go and do it now."

He went out to the hall and rang his old telephone number in Maidstone. I listened to him chatting awkwardly with one of his sons about Arsenal Football Club.

"John, I thought I ought to warn you," he said, finally. "Chris has been keeping in close touch with the police about this wretched murder . . . Yes . . . Well, they haven't been able to come up with any new suspects and I'm afraid that means *you're* the only one they've got for target practice . . . That's what I thought, too . . . Thing is, they'll be doing quite a lot of digging into your past, not to mention the present . . . Well, just that if you were able to beef up your alibi a bit, fill in a few gaps . . . I don't mean anything, John, I'm just playing Devil's advocate . . . Right . . . All right, and give mine to the lovely Helen . . . Yes, we'll be in touch again about Christmas."

I had to hand it to Pete – he could be very tactful when the occasion demanded.

I got through the weekend by resorting to an awful lot of unnecessary dusting, and alternately and strategically brandishing Coldrex and Feminax tablets. What good are hormones if you can't make use of them occasionally? I was quite determined to avoid an emotional confrontation with Pete – any kind of confrontation, in fact. I was going to work this out for myself, and by myself, and if I could just keep the lid on things until Tuesday I'd have almost a whole week to do just that.

By Monday morning, it looked as though I was going to make it.

Mr Heslop gave me a friendly smile as I placed the panto review on his desk.

"Oh, don't go!" He gestured towards a chair. "I'll just glance through this. I'm sure you've done an excellent job." He went slowly over the piece, nodding appreciatively. He raised his eyebrows once or twice, as though pleasantly surprised and impressed.

"Well, well. I should think you're feeling quite pleased with what you've produced here. A quite remarkable job."

I felt a twinge of guilt. "One does one's best," I muttered, embarrassed.

"Does one, does one?" He leaned across his desk, and suddenly he'd stopped smiling. "And exactly whereabouts in the school hall were you when the roof collapsed killing four of the parents and maiming half a dozen seven-year-olds?"

I gave a horrified gasp. "*What?*"

He leaned back and studied me impassively.

"Oh my God!" I cried. "I didn't know! I didn't – "

He folded his arms. "No, you didn't, did you? You weren't bloody well there." He was really enjoying this. "I know, because fortunately I was. In the end, I decided that my duty really lay with the promise I'd made to a little boy, a little boy who'd worked extremely hard along with a lot of other little boys and girls to put on a production for a lot of lazy, ungrateful slobs like you."

I let out a moan.

"Actually, the wife went down with flu, but that's neither here nor there. I hope you've got a very good explanation for this."

"You mean – you mean the roof didn't actually collapse?"

He didn't bother to answer.

I gave a sigh of relief. "Oh, God, I'm really sorry, but you see, I was following up this hunch I've got about Victor Taylor being involved in Rosemary Tindall's murder. Pete promised he'd – "

"Ah. Yes. I rather assumed he'd be at the back of this. And that's the only reason I'm not actually going to fire you on the spot."

I trembled. My lower lip had already started doing that by itself. This seemed to be my week for last straws.

"Well." His tone changed. He was obviously horrified at the prospect of my bursting into tears. "I don't think I need to say too much more on the subject. It was a sorry day for this paper when you fell under his influence. And for you, in my opinion."

For once, I wholeheartedly agreed with him.

"Mr Heslop," I began, timidly. "The police have asked us to publish another appeal for information to the public in the Tindall case."

"Do it," said Mr Heslop, "and then consider yourself off the case. Permanently and irrevocably. Do I make myself clear? In the unlikely event that those idiots over at Hudderston Central ever get their act together and charge someone, I shall be putting someone else on the story. Do I make myself clear?"

"Yes, Mr Heslop," I murmured, and I crept ignominiously back to my desk, brushing a wretched mascara-stained tear from my cheek.

(There was a small and insignificant postscript to this humiliating event. When the *Herald* appeared on Friday it carried a report on the panto, attributed to Mr Heslop. It was a good two inch piece, full of correct names and ages, and the school rang us to thank us. I recognised every comma of it, because it was exactly as I'd written it.)

We were sitting in front of the television that evening, watching a film. Or at least, Pete was watching it. I was just staring at a collection of coloured dots that didn't really look like much, and Julie was upstairs doing her homework. I had tried to keep the lid on my emotions but that little scene with Mr Heslop today had been too much for me. Suddenly the contents of the pressure vessel that was my head topped 252°F and my safety valve blew.

"I just hope," a voice began from my lips, "that your friend Josie has been HIV tested."

There was silence. Pete's eyes remained fixed on the screen and he looked vaguely perplexed. For a moment I wondered if I'd said H*G*V tested instead of H*I*V.

The silence continued. It slowly dawned on me that this was not the silence of a man shocked by an insightful comment, but the silence of a man watching the motor bike sequence in another pre-Christmas showing of *The Great Escape*.

"What?" he asked.

"Your friend Josie," my voice went on. "You slept with her, and I'm not sure I want you sleeping with *me* until I know what you've caught."

He stared at me, and then laughed. "That's quite good. If I ever get round to writing my novel about love and marriage in the eighties, I must put that in. You're not serious, are you?"

"*Serious*! Of course I'm serious! How can you ask that? Don't you care at all? We've only been living together for one month – you couldn't even make it through *one month* without – without – "

He got up and switched the television off. I got up and switched it back on. "Julie will hear," I hissed, trying not to cry. "How could you do this to me?"

"I haven't," said Pete, trying to put his arms round me. "Jo's an old friend. I knew her years before I knew you, she's engaged to a friend of mine, and – "

"Oh, so that makes it all right, does it? It makes it all right, your screwing old friends, does it? Anyway, I don't care about that. I don't care what you do. You can go through the entire female population of London, if you want to. I really don't care! You just don't know the trouble you've got me into."

He paled. "What do you mean? I can't have. I've always been very careful. Are you sure?"

I stamped my foot, angrily. "I'm not talking about that." I swallowed a sob. Not so long ago I'd fantasised about being ten years younger and having his baby. "I'm not pregnant! Is that all you can think of? Don't you know what you've done to me? I had everything I ever wanted – I had a beautiful house, I had two nice children. *You* made me give it all up. *You* lied to me. You said you loved me and you wanted to marry me – "

"I do love you. Christ, what's got into you?"

"Nothing's got into me, except that I've seen how stupid I was!"

"Have you?" He stared at me, assessing me. "Wait a minute, I've got it. I should've known. You saw SuperKeith the other night, didn't you?"

I had no reason to feel guilty. "No, I didn't."

"Yes, you did. I thought so at the time, but I didn't say so. I didn't think you'd do that to me. I thought I knew you better. Well, well. So what's he been promising you? He wants you back, doesn't he? What's the bribe – bigger and better fitted wardrobes? Wall to wall shelving in the toilet? Jesus Christ!"

"You leave Keith out of this! He's got nothing to do with it!"

"Oh, yes, he has. He's got everything to do with it. You're a fool, you know. He doesn't want you back because he loves you – he wants you back because you're one of his possessions." He gave a derisive snort. "Did you think I didn't notice he's stamped his bloody postcode over everything? It's a wonder I haven't found it on you. Or maybe I just haven't looked in the right places. Christ, is that why you always make me turn out the light?"

I took a step towards him and slapped him hard and dramatically round the face. It was a stupid thing to do. It just made me feel bad as I watched the red handmark forming on his cheek.

"I *hate* you," I said. "I *hate* you and I wish you'd go up to Birmingham and never come back!"

He nodded. "OK. That's great. Do what you like. Go back to him. Spend the rest of your life handing him spanners and folding his underpants. I suppose that's really what you're best at." He hesitated, waiting for me to say something. I didn't. "Yes, you go back to him and play at Happy Families. See if you still enjoy it now you know the rules are crap."

He picked up his glass and strode to the door. He'd gone very white, and just for a moment I almost weakened. I wanted to put my arms round him and say I was sorry, and that I still loved him, that I hadn't meant any of it. But I didn't. I just didn't know myself well enough any more to be sure I'd mean it.

18

I swallowed a Coldrex tablet with my morning coffee and my finger dialled Keith's office number on automatic pilot.

"Hattons, may I help you?" asked the girl, efficiently. It was like walking into a time warp.

"Keith Martin, please. It's his wife."

"Won't keep you, Mrs Martin."

"Hallo – Martin," said Keith.

"Hallo," I said. "It's me. How are you?"

"Fine. You sound as if you've got a cold."

"I have. Look, do you still want to meet and talk?"

"Of course I do. When can you make it? Tonight?"

"No." I'd been crying all night and blowing my nose all morning. "Let's make it tomorrow."

"OK." He hesitated. "I'd like to show you my place. I think you'd like it. Can you come round about eight?"

"Yes. I'll see you then."

"I'll look forward to it."

Ernst delivered the Folly Farm photographs to me in a plain brown wrapper, and accompanied by a sarcastic sneer.

"Worst case of DTs I've ever seen," he remarked.

I didn't even bother to look at them. Mr Heslop had told me I was off the Tindall story, and at that moment I couldn't have cared less who Victor Taylor invited to entertainments at his farm, or what they got up to.

My phone rang.

"Pete?" I queried, in spite of myself.

"Hallo?" It was a woman.

"Chris Martin. Can I help you?"

"You said you'd go to the police for me, but I don't think you can have done because there's been nothing on the radio. You haven't, have you? The police might go after the wrong man."

"Ah. This is Jennifer Saunders, isn't it? Look, Miss Saunders, I did tell the police, but the fact is what you said doesn't fit in with the other evidence. I spoke to one of the officers in charge and I'm afraid he thinks you're – " The word "bonkers" presented itself. I resisted it. "A little mixed up."

"Oh." There was a long silence. "Look, if you come and see me again I might tell you something else. It's important. Could you come this morning?"

I shifted the phone impatiently to my other hand.

"Look, I'm afraid I've got a lot on at the moment, and anyway I'm not working on the Tindall story any longer. Hang on, I'll give you DS Horton's number at Hudderston Central and you can have a chat with him." I gave her the number, and rang off. I didn't feel at all guilty. I'd got my own problems, and there was no reason why I should add Jennifer Saunders to them.

Julie was unnaturally quiet as she teased my hair into shape.

"Does Pete know?" she asked suddenly.

"Does he know what?"

"About you meeting Dad."

"Of course he does. Why shouldn't he? Look – you're making my hair much too bushy. I can't go out like that. I'm not exactly a teenager any more, you know."

She sighed, pulled a face at my reflection in the mirror, then said meaningfully. "No. You're not."

"What's that supposed to mean?"

"Well – you're not, are you? I mean, this feminism stuff's all right for people *my* age, but – well – if you want to know, Stephanie's mum says you're jolly lucky to have found a boyfriend at all at your age. She says she's got lots of friends whose husbands have left them and who'll be on their own for the rest of their lives. You shouldn't go looking gift horses in the mouth."

"Oh, did she, indeed!" I blushed angrily. Stephanie's mother had done me the favour of looking after Julie for a weekend, and now felt free to pass judgement on my life. "Well, she's got no right, telling you her opinions. I've a good mind to pick up that phone and – "

"Oh, no!" Julie looked horrified. "She's ever so nice. She didn't say it to me. It was just when I told Stephanie you'd decided not to marry Pete, Stephanie told her mum and she was so surprised. And as a matter of fact I agree with her," she added, defiantly. "I think it's really dumb of you, not wanting to marry Pete. I think you've really – really changed, just lately."

"I haven't," I protested, wishing I could bring myself to tell her the truth.

"Yes, you have," she said, and added with an adult smile I'd never seen before. "And I just hope you like yourself."

Keith's doorbell was illuminated by one of those small glowing halos. I pressed it and stood back, straightening the creases in my trousers.

As he opened the door, a wave of garlic and expensive aftershave swept over me.

"Come in." He led me into a large room with an enormous picture window overlooking the lights of Tipping. I stood still, watching distant cars illuminate the blackness of the by-pass, the wink of an aircraft among the stars.

"Oh," I said, surprised. "It's very nice."

He pulled the blinds across the window, and gestured towards a table I instantly recognised because I'd spent twenty years polishing it. He made some remark concerning the table, but I didn't hear it because I'd spotted Richard's metalwork collage – made during his first year at secondary school – hanging on the wall, and a very tasteful dried flower arrangement standing in the fireplace. The dried flower arrangement wasn't at all Keith-like.

"Sorry – what?" I asked, as he stared at me, waiting for an answer.

"Do you mind rosé wine with chicken?" he repeated, impatiently. "I've already opened it actually. You're late."

"With chicken?" Now I noticed that he was carrying a pristine oven glove neatly folded over his right arm, and that the table was set for two. I didn't have the heart to tell him I'd already eaten.

"That'll be fine," I said, wondering if the waistband of my trousers would be able to cope.

I sat at the table and waited while he fussed over the chicken. "Here you are," he said, half dropping a plate in front of me and staring at it in consternation. "Is that all right?" He sat down, contemplating his own meal. He hacked off a piece of chicken, put it in his mouth, and said with a shake of the head, "God, how are we going to get out of this mess?"

"What do you mean? What mess?"

"Well, you've thought about what I said, haven't you? Isn't that why you're here? Come on, don't let's waste any more time playing silly games. You made a mistake – admit it."

I wasn't ready to admit it.

He sawed angrily at the chicken. "I don't know why you had to get yourself mixed up with a jerk like that," he said. "I really don't. If you fancied a fling, why didn't you go for someone harmless like Howard – or Ken Scrivenor? You must have known they always fancied you."

"What? Are you saying you wouldn't have minded my sleeping with one of your friends?"

"Oh, of course I'd've minded. But it wouldn't have got out of hand, would it? It would've been more normal. We could have *contained* it," he said, as though speaking of a minor nuclear incident. "This is the thing. Now the whole business has run its course but we've still got *him* to contend with. Have you said anything to him yet?"

I felt both irritated and relieved by Keith's assumption that our reconciliation was a *fait accompli*.

"I haven't really – said anything definite."

He gave a superior smile. "Don't you worry. I'll soon sort him out for you. Little creep. God, what did you see in him! I bet he hasn't been near an exercise bench in years."

"There's more to life than physical fitness," I said, edgily.

"Oh, yes, of course." He filled my wine glass to the brim. "And I've been thinking about that. You know – this all started because you got that job on the *Herald* and I didn't want you to. Well, of course it turned out I was right, but so what?" He spread his hands magnanimously. "It's all in the past now. You're at the *Herald*, you're happy there, you don't want to leave – I bet you're on quite a decent salary now. Who am I to stand in your way?"

"You mean, you don't object to my working at the *Herald* any more?"

He smiled. "If it's what you want, Chris, why should I? There, I can admit *my* mistakes. Listen, I've been working things out." He pushed his plate to one side and produced a sheet of paper. "I got this flat cheap – it was a steal. Even with the house price slump on I'll still make a profit on it. And as for that dump of yours – well, you must have got *that* at a knockdown price, surely!"

I pretended to have trouble swallowing a chip. We hadn't got it at a knockdown price at all.

"So," went on Keith. "We sell the two properties, pay off lover-boy. And I know this super house that's going to be going cheap. I mean really cheap. Chap's wife's left him and he's taking a job in the States." He rubbed his hands together, gleefully. "Nothing like a bit of inside knowledge. It's at Mountview – you know, where you always wanted to live."

I thought about Mountview, the wide, quiet street, the panoramic view over the river and the Recreation Ground.

"This is all a bit of a rush," I said.

"I bet you Richard would come back home," said Keith. "He's not happy in that fleapit. I think he'd jump at the chance. It would be a much shorter journey for you to work. Think of the saving on petrol! We might even – "

"Keith," I put my knife and fork together on the plate. "I'm sorry. This is very nice, but I just can't eat any more."

He jumped up quickly and put his arm round me. "I know," he said. "You never could eat when you were feeling emotional. Remember our engagement do? I'm not really hungry, either. Let's just sit down and have a good long talk."

He ushered me over to the sofa, plumping up cushions for me, then went and fiddled about with his stack of stereo equipment.

"Right." He sat down and sighed. "Do you know, I feel suddenly *years* younger – I can't believe it. I reckon all this may actually have done us good." He put his arm round me and gave me a squeeze. "I *had* started to take you for granted. It's an awful thing to admit, but there were times when if I'd closed my eyes I could hardly have told anyone what you looked like." He looked me up and down. "That wouldn't be true now, though."

I smiled, helplessly.

"You're not saying very much," he remarked. "Ah. There. Listen to that. What do you think?"

The opening notes of Paul McCartney's "Yesterday" hung quivering in the air. Actually, I thought it was a bit over the top, but it brought a lump to my throat all the same, and I said, huskily, "It's very nice."

"No, no, I don't mean the song. The *hum*. Listen." He cocked his head to one side. "It's the speakers. You took the ones that went with the amplifier, and these aren't compatible. I shouldn't have let you have them."

"They were mine," I protested, mildly. "We've already been through this."

"Oh well, who cares?" He stretched out his legs and flexed his ankles. "This is just like years ago, when we were kids, and you used to come round to my place when my Mum and Dad were out."

Instinctively I crossed my legs, just as I used to when Keith's Mum and Dad were out.

He laughed. "You were the best girl I ever took out. I'll never forget the thrill I got walking past the Odeon with you – the look on their faces in the queue! They were all so jealous."

"What? That's not what you said to me at the time. You said you could only fit me in every other weekend when your Number One girl went to visit her Gran."

Keith grinned. "Tactics. And they worked too, didn't they? Remember the first time I borrowed that sleeping bag and took you into the woods behind the station? God, you put up a fight!" He leaned my head on his shoulder. A whiff of the foot odour from that sleeping bag seemed to manifest itself from nowhere. Oddly, it had an aphrodisiac effect on me.

"You were the first, Chris – and the best," said Keith,

kissing the top of my head. I turned to protest again that that was definitely not what he'd told me at the time, and he caught my mouth in a sudden and unexpected kiss. It was the nicest, tenderest kiss he'd ever given me.

"You still taste the same," I said, letting him pull me on to his knee. He ran his hands up and down my body gently.

For a while, neither of us spoke. We cuddled each other, each aware that this was a very significant, not to say climactic, moment. Keith slipped his hand under my sweater, and with fingers that were a lot gentler than I remembered, began tracing the line of my rib cage. I felt guilty about all those times I'd pushed him away in the darkness, complaining that he was too rough. He bit my ear, giving me goose pimples. Blood began flooding to my cheeks, but I wasn't yet sure whether what I was feeling was passion, or an intense, almost unbearable sadness. I let him undo my bra.

"I just want to look at you," he whispered. "Can I?"

It must be passion. "All right," I said, cautiously. He pulled my sweater off over my head, and I let my arms fall to my sides. Slowly, assisted by the deep breaths rising from within me, my bra straps trickled their way down my shoulders, and the garment landed in Keith's lap.

He gave the sort of grunt vacuum cleaners make when you turn them off, and launched himself upon me. Suddenly, I wasn't quite so sure that what I'd felt was passion, but I didn't want to spoil things. I let him kiss my shoulders and breasts, and dapple my skin with the red impressions of his moustache stubble. I let him bite my left nipple and I gasped as if I liked it. Perhaps I even did like it. But when he undid my trousers and began massaging the flabby part of my stomach, something started to feel decidedly wrong. I gasped again, as though with pleasure, and this time I recognised it as a gasp I'd heard coming out of myself before, whenever I didn't want to spoil things I wasn't really enjoying. I tensed. He wasn't making me feel good about myself. In Pete's hands my body became the most beautiful, lithe and sensuous body in the world; in Pete's hands I loved myself; in Pete's hands –

"Keith, don't." I dropped the words on to him like stones,

222

retrieving his hand from the top of my pants. "I don't want to do this."

"Oh, come on, yes you do. Don't start playing games again, for Christ's sake." He made another dive at my groin.

"No!" I shouted, climbing awkwardly off his knee, "I don't want to. You're rushing me."

He closed his eyes and gave an exasperated sigh.

"Sorry," I said, touching his arm. "I did try, but it's too soon. I'm awfully sorry – I just need a bit more time."

"*Time!*" Keith seemed to explode. I watched in horrified fascination as the impassioned flush drained from his cheeks. I didn't know what I'd said to make him so angry. "Time! You need time? Don't talk to me about needing time! Fifteen years – *fifteen years* I waited for you to get over your post-natal depression after Julie was born! That's how much time I gave you! What were you doing – going for a listing in the *Guinness Book of Records*? I put up with you and your bloody fake orgasms and your headaches for fifteen years – I take you back after you've been unfaithful – and you tell me you *need time*?" He was beside himself with anger. I was stunned. I'd copied my fake orgasms from Jane Fonda in *Klute* and I thought they were brilliant.

"What do you mean?" I asked, "What do you mean about post-natal depression?"

"Well, that's what you women call it, isn't it, after you've had the baby you wanted and you go off sex? Howard said Elaine was the same, only she got over it after six months. *Fifteen years*, I waited, fifteen years – and when you finally got over it, what happened?" He picked up my sweater and threw it at me. "Who was the recipient of fifteen years' worth of pent-up passion? Not me, oh no, that would have been too much to hope for – it was that bloody Romeo on the *Tipping* bloody *Herald*!"

I was still seething over his reference to Howard's verdict on my lack of interest in sex. "Are you saying you discussed our private affairs with Howard? Is that what you're saying? How could you do that?" I demanded, thinking of all those lasagnes Howard had consumed at my dining table while thoughtfully chewing over my performance in Keith's bed.

"Oh, it was just men's talk," he muttered, dismissively.

Then I started work on the rest of it. "And I didn't have post-natal depression for fifteen years!" I shouted. "No one has post-natal depression for fifteen years. If you want to know the truth – " And it came to me, as I spoke, in a great shaft of light just like the adverts for all those household cleaners that are supposed to miraculously illuminate your dark corners. "If you want to know the truth, the only thing that was the matter with me for fifteen years was that I'd had enough of you!"

I pulled on my sweater, stuffed my bra in my pocket, and began hunting for my coat. For the first time since I could remember, I didn't feel guilty about Keith.

Keith's temper had an annoying habit of evaporating when someone shouted back at him.

"Look," he said, following me into the kitchen. "This is silly. This isn't the way to make a fresh start. Come back and sit down and let's talk about it. How are we going to put things right if you won't talk about them?"

I stared at him incredulously. That had been my line for years.

"Maybe I did rush you," he began in a conciliatory tone. Then he pointed to the sheet of paper on the dining table, where he'd made his calculations for our future. "What about all this? Aren't you even interested?"

I hesitated. I thought about Barrington Avenue, about Mountview, about twenty years of days and nights – "No," I said, finally, and a great weight lifted from my shoulders.

"Right," said Keith, grimly. "That's it! You've had it. I'm divorcing you. Sod you, you bitch!"

"Good!" I screamed, opening his front door.

As I ran down the stairs, he shouted after me. "And I want those bloody speakers back! They're mine!"

I turned my key in the lock, pushed open the front door, and stared at the brown geometric patterns on the wallpaper. They stared back at me, their angles opening out in a welcoming sort of gesture. Home. After all this time – suddenly I was home. It didn't seem the right moment to make this discovery, but at last I knew where I wanted to be. I sank down on to the stairs, exhausted. And then it came to me – it was apparently my day for having shafts of light shone into the recesses of my soul; if after only a month of living with me Pete was having an affair with another woman, perhaps it was *my* fault. I listened to the silence of the house, and thought how I'd nagged Pete about that dripping tap and the bathroom wallpaper – Perhaps Julie was right; perhaps I'd changed into something I didn't like.

I climbed painfully to my feet and went upstairs to bed. Tomorrow I'd have to work out what I was going to do about all this.

19

It was only eight a.m., but Julie's door was wide open and she was heaping clothes into a small suitcase in preparation for the school disco that evening. I'd had half a mind to veto her plan to spend the night at Stephanie's house, after what Stephanie's Mum had said about me, but convenience and compromise had won out. I shook my head at Julie in just the way she expected and went downstairs to the kitchen.

I switched on the radio absently as I fumbled with the kettle.

"*And in local news this hour*," said the voice of the Three Counties presenter, "*the big story this morning is still the revelation in this week's* Hudderston Advertiser *concerning local businessman Victor Taylor.*"

I gasped and ran round the kitchen table, knocking over a bottle of milk. I turned the volume control to maximum.

"*. . . alleges that Victor Taylor used the services of what she describes as 'reluctant vice girls' to influence a leading local property development company to award him substantial contracts. Other prominent local figures are implicated in the story, and we'll be talking to Fiona Lomax herself later on in the programme. Meanwhile, over now to our reporter Linda Craven, who's had the good fortune to meet Father Christmas at –* "

The words echoed round the kitchen, bouncing off wall cupboards and reverberating through my head. Fiona Lomax – of course – the elegant redhead who'd visited Folly Farm pretending to be a prospective purchaser –

I bought a copy of the *Hudderston Advertiser* on my way to work. Under the headline "Town Rocked by Vice Scandal" was the following story.

"Local people who may have wondered how Taylor Group have risen in less than three years from being a small-time

226

operation with a reputation for overcharging, to a big-time contractor employed on major local developments, need look no further than Folly Farm. Folly Farm is the property of Victor Taylor, head of Taylor Group, and it is in this secluded location that Mr Taylor – the well-known supporter of local charities and a prospective Tory party candidate – has given what even this newspaper cannot fail to describe as 'saucy sex romps' for members of the business fraternity. In a switch from exploiting his customers, to exploiting the desperate financial needs of single mothers trying to keep their heads above water in Thatcherite Britain . . ."

Mr Heslop was sitting at my desk, looking murderous, and gripping a copy of the *Hudderston Advertiser*.

"And what have you got to say about this?" he demanded, through clenched teeth. "This is the story I told you to hand over to someone who could cope with it. Do I have to check out your every move?"

"Mr Heslop, listen!" I pleaded, throwing off my coat and shopping bag. "I was in the middle of it – I couldn't – Look, you remember the night of the school panto? Well, that's what I was doing, taking photos outside Folly Farm. Look!" I found the packet of photographs Ernst had given me, ripped it open, and spread the contents across my desk.

"Oh," I said, peering closer at the photographs. They were of shadowy, blurred heads framed inside what I knew to be car windows. Some of them showed beams of light bouncing artistically off car roofs, and one or two were quite striking silhouettes. None of them was identifiable. "I got a complete list of car numbers as well," I said, boldly, "and I'm having them checked through the police computer."

Mr Heslop picked up one of the photographs. "Photography isn't my best thing, either," he remarked, "but as a general rule if you can't see a subject properly through the viewfinder then pressing the shutter isn't going to help matters much."

"Oh, but I could – "

"Have you any idea how much this is going to cost us in sales lost to the *Advertiser*?" he demanded. "My God, isn't our advertising revenue low enough for you already?"

I reached further into the bottom drawer of my desk

and produced my file on Rosemary Tindall. I pulled out the cut-up newspaper pages I'd retrieved from outside the bungalow.

"Look," I said. "Rosemary must have written *two* notes, one to us, one to the *Advertiser*. No wonder Fiona Lomax tried to put me off questioning Taylor staff! She was already working on the story and she was afraid we'd get on to it. I think they must have had someone there the other night – that Bedford van in the quarry – " I began laying out the sheets, in an attempt to count the number of holes in them. "The *Advertiser* obviously followed up their letter, but what I don't understand is – "

"Don't be bloody silly!" thundered Mr Heslop, snatching my sheets of newspaper and screwing them up. "You've wasted enough time already!" He rose from my desk. "When I've worked out what I'm going to do about you, I'll want to see you in my office. My God!"

He went off, muttering, to have a glucose tablet. I put my coat back on. I was already in so much trouble it wouldn't matter, and I'd got to know. My phone rang. I started to walk away from it, but it might have been a personal call.

"I – just – can't – stand it," said Jennifer Saunders, in a taut, stricken voice. "If he does it again it'll be my fault. You said he was going to."

"I did?"

"In your paper." There was a rustling sound. "It's got your name on it. 'Police are making a further appeal for witnesses because they fear the killer may strike again,' you said."

"Yes, but that's just – you know." To make people read newspapers.

"Oh please, oh please, I can't go to the police! You don't *understand*! I don't know what to do!"

I looked at my watch. "All right, all right," I said, groaning inwardly. "I'm on my way over to Hudderston anyway. I'll come and see you on my way back. I should be there by ten thirty – and don't go to any trouble, Miss Saunders, because I won't have time to stop."

Fiona Lomax was seated in her cream leather reclining chair, wearing a casually draped silk scarf and a smug smile.

"Chris! How nice to see you. Must say, I was half expecting a visit." She leaned forward. The scarf settled elegantly across her folded arms but did not fall off.

"It's about the Victor Taylor story," I said, tensely.

"Of course. I think you did jolly well to get on to it at all, even if rather belatedly."

I frowned. "Why do you say that?"

"Well, of course, *we* had a tip off, an anonymous letter. The writer of the letter, whoever she was, obviously felt – and with some reason, in my opinion – that the *Tipping Herald* wouldn't respond to such an approach. Poor old Bill. I'm afraid he's not really up to the cut and thrust of life even of a town like Tipping." She leaned back, doing everything but wipe the cream from her (electrolysis removed) whiskers.

I smiled. "I take it, then, that you don't know the identity of your informant?"

"No." She paused. "Why? Do you?"

"Oh, yes. As a matter of fact, we did get a letter, but that's not important. As you say, for various reasons we didn't follow it up at the time." I paused, dramatically. "The sender of the letter was Rosemary Tindall."

"Rosemary – " Fiona looked blank. She twitched suddenly, and the scarf slid off. "Oh God! Rosemary Tindall! The woman who – God, what a coincidence! Well, no wonder she didn't keep our meeting. And I thought it was my fault. I rang the number myself, you see, and I did my best to put her off. One always suspects a hoax, of course." She stared thoughtfully out at her view of Hudderston rooftops. "She said she'd found out that her boss was entertaining people he hoped to influence into giving him business." Fiona laughed. "Well, of course, that's hardly news, is it? Wimbledon Centre Court tickets, theatre boxes – all part of the game these days. Anyway, then she went on about girls and parties at a farm, and it began to sound interesting. She promised to meet me the following Wednesday to talk about it – although I must say, she seemed to have strong reservations about the whole thing." She shrugged. "Which is why I wasn't particularly surprised when she didn't show up. All I'd managed to get out of her was the address of the farm, and a date. Well, the rest is history, as they say." Her smug smile was back.

I shook my head. "I don't think it was a coincidence that Rosemary was murdered. I think she was murdered to stop her meeting you."

Fiona looked baffled, and slightly annoyed. "For goodness sake, she was killed by some kind of psychopath. She was killed because she was a *woman* – we've had this conversation before."

It was stuffy in Fiona's office. I tugged uncomfortably at my coat collar. "Did you keep watch on Folly Farm on the night of Monday, 9th November? Because if you did I think you must have seen Rosemary call there. I think you *did* put her off when you spoke to her on the phone. I think she went to the farm herself, probably to confront Victor Taylor, and I think he killed her."

Fiona couldn't make up her mind whether or not to take me seriously. She ran her eye over me, frowning, and finally said, "Right. Let's take a look. I had a couple of people there that night, running up overtime bills – " She propelled her chair noiselessly across the room and unlocked a filing cabinet. Then she produced a small stack of photographs and laid them out on the desk as though dealing a pack of cards. I studied them. They showed the tarmacked parking area outside Folly Farm, and men dismounting from cars. The photos were well lit by a high powered security light.

She smiled. "We got into the farm the back way, through the old quarry," she remarked. "There weren't any dogs."

I gritted my teeth. If Pete had been with me –

"Anyway," went on Fiona. "I don't see Mrs Tindall amongst them. Sorry."

"Are you sure? I mean, perhaps your people went away for a while?"

She shrugged. "You can never totally rely on anyone. Anyway, what difference does it make? Mrs Tindall died the following evening, the Tuesday. That's about the only thing the police do know, surely. I'm doing a piece next week about police ineptitude – "

I shook my head impatiently. "Look, I don't know the exact details, and it would take too long to explain – " Fiona glanced away rather guiltily from the wall clock. "But I've got good reason to believe that whoever killed

Rosemary did it on the Monday night, and then went to a great deal of trouble to try and make it look like one of the Face Murders. I've looked very thoroughly into her personal life, and, believe me, the person with the strongest motive for killing Rosemary Tindall is Victor Taylor."

Fiona rearranged her scarf and folded her arms purposefully. "Look, Chris," she began, patronisingly. "All credit for sticking to this thing in the face of opposition. All credit, too, for getting cracking on the Taylor story, even though you didn't quite make it in time." She chuckled to herself. "In fact I think I owe you a vote of thanks. You'd really put the fear of God into Mandy Woods, and she came across with a very nice statement. Also she apparently received an offer from a modelling agency at just the right moment." Fiona sighed and shook her head. "A case of a woman suddenly finding her true vocation, I do believe. Anyway, Chris, all credit to you, and jolly well done, but I think the time has come to close our files on the Tindall story, don't you? And I am, actually, very busy this morning."

Right on cue, her phone rang. Groaning aloud, I rose to leave. "Good morning," said Fiona, into her telephone.

I collected my umbrella from Fiona's wastepaper basket.

"One moment. Chris," I turned. Fiona was smiling at me. "Chris, I've just thought of something. I think I should tell you – you know, to save your face." Her smile broadened. "You seemed to be implying that Rosemary's killer murdered her on Monday, and went back on Tuesday to shoot her in the head and make it look like one of the Face Murders. Well, I'm afraid, that rather lets Victor Taylor off the hook. You see, on Tuesday evening, at the time your murderer was in Cottis Wood firing his gun into Rosemary Tindall, Victor Taylor was attending a charity concert at Hudderston Civic Hall. Sitting next to me."

Fiona Lomax had just administered the *coup de grâce* to my Victor Taylor as murderer theory. I thanked her, and left.

I sat at traffic lights. I was in the wrong lane on the Hudderston one-way system, nothing was moving in any direction, and the lights kept changing. Red – red amber – green – amber: I – told – you – so. Rosemary Tindall had been killed by a psychopathic killer, a stranger, a person unknown to her – and everyone but me had understood this. I – told – you – so. The car in front of me crept into a space and I followed, hopefully operating my right indicator. I'd been through every single aspect of Rosemary's life, I'd wasted time and energy and nearly given myself pneumonia – and all for nothing. I – told – you – so. I was going nowhere; I had never stood a chance of getting anywhere.

It was eleven fifteen when I finally got to Cottis Wood. I splashed across the muddy road, holding my coat over my head because it was raining and the last thing I needed on top of everything else was a ruined hairdo. Jennifer's front door was slightly ajar, but I rang the bell anyway, glancing down with disgust at my muddied shoes. A cold gust of wind drove the rain against my legs, and I huddled closer to the door. "Oh, come *on*," I muttered. The sooner I got back to the office and made my peace with Mr Heslop, the better. Rain clattered down Jennifer's front window in an unrelenting torrent, and sizzled in the gutter like chips in a fryer. There was another water noise, too, a steady dripping sound, which, as the wind died down, seemed to increase in volume. To my surprise, I realised that this was coming from *inside* the house.

"Miss Saunders?" I called, and pushed at the door. It moved a few inches, then stopped. I pushed harder, calling out again, and the door gave another six inches before jamming against something with a jarring finality. I stepped over the threshold and looked down. Wedged between the door and the doorpost was what looked like an arm. I blinked, hoping to clarify the image. It was definitely an arm – a white, outstretched arm smeared unpleasantly with red. I suppose I knew then what I was going to find. I squeezed round the door. The small hallway was filled with steam. Water dripped relentlessly through a bulge in the ceiling, forming a dark pool on the worn carpet. Jennifer Saunders was completely naked. Her eyes gazed unseeingly towards the bulging ceiling, and through the gap in her front teeth I could see the still pinkness of her tongue. Fighting down a desire to scream, I tried to do the right thing. I turned over her wrist to look for a pulse, and it was then that I discovered the source of all that blood.

Jennifer Saunders was quite unmistakably dead.

Overhead, there was a sudden creaking sound and great lumps of plaster fell in a disrespectful avalanche on to Jennifer's stomach. I could feel my breakfast coffee rise up in my throat. Upstairs, the tap was still running. I climbed the stairs, avoiding the bloodstained banister, and found the bathroom. I wished I hadn't. A great arc of dark blood had been thrown against the tiled bath splashback, like an accusing question mark, and the water spilling on to the floor and through the floorboards was tinted red. Later, standing in the bathroom making meticulous notes, a detective sergeant would remark with a hint of admiration, "Well, at least she made a good job of it," and retrieve a bread knife from the bottom of the bath.

I turned off the hot tap. On the wet floor lay a muddled pile of faded underwear and a pair of pink slippers. As I stepped over the slippers I noticed a piece of paper sticking out of one of them. I picked it up. It was a faded black and white photograph of a couple sitting on a park bench. On the back was a date: June 15th, 1968. I took a closer look at the couple. The girl resembled Jennifer Saunders – a young, pretty Jennifer Saunders with thick dark hair and a full set of teeth – and the boy was tall and good-looking and obviously in love with her. He had his face turned away from the camera to look at her. For a moment I thought there was something familiar about him, but it was only the familiarity of a young face surrounded by long hair, the sort of face there were hundreds of in the sixties.

I dropped the photograph and ran downstairs. I knew Jennifer had a phone, but I wanted to get out of there. I stepped over the body, squeezed round the door, and escaped into the road. The last thing I remember, after hammering at the door of No. 1 Cottis Villas, is a lavender coloured doormat inscribed "Welcome" coming slowly up to meet me.

20

"It's a little known fact," said Mr Heslop, cleaning his glasses with his handkerchief. "But the majority of suicides don't leave notes. I think the suicide is supposed to say it all."

"But I don't understand why she did it. What had Rosemary Tindall's murder got to do with her? She told me about the car she thought she'd seen, and I told the police. How can she have imagined it was her fault if they didn't believe her? Oh God, I wasn't very nice to her," I added, haunted by my last words to Jennifer Saunders.

He shook his head sympathetically. "I've put a call through to the Manning Green Institute. We'll try and get a quote from someone who was working on her case. Of course, I doubt that they'll want to comment, in which case we'll have to do a piece on how Government cuts are forcing sick people out into the community prematurely. Put it behind you, Chris. You're only supposed to write about what happens, not take responsibility for it."

Gillian put her head round the door.

"Awfully sorry," she said, "but there's a woman in Reception."

Mr Heslop looked irritated at the mere sight of Gillian. "What woman?" he asked, testily.

"She won't say. She's asking for Chris. Sorry."

Mr Heslop waved her away.

"There are going to have to be a few changes made around here," he muttered. "Er – as far as the other business goes, we'll say no more about it for the moment. Go and sort out this woman, and then go and have some lunch. Try that new vegetarian place round the corner. A nice big wodge of wholemeal pastry will settle your stomach down a treat."

"Thank you, Mr Heslop," I muttered, trying not to think about the nice big wodge of wholemeal pastry.

Seated in Reception, next to our new rubber plant with the variegated leaves, was Joyce from the Eldon Lodge Hotel. She looked up as I approached, and donned a sulky expression.

"It's you," she said, disappointedly.

"Yes. You asked for me."

"I didn't know you were Chris Martin," said Joyce. "You came to the hotel with that other fellow. I didn't know you worked for the *Herald*."

"Well, what can I do for you?" I asked, brightly, trying to close my eyes to images of Jennifer Saunders.

Joyce looked uncertain. She began fiddling with one of the leaves on the rubber plant.

"I'm still not sure," she said. "I still haven't made up my mind about things." She glanced down at the leaf and scratched it with her fingernails, then looked up at me shiftily from beneath her eyelashes. "I didn't know it would be you, see. I mean, I only took the other fellow's money because he offered it. And I haven't got it any more. It's hard to make ends meet, and I hadn't had a new dress for ages." Her face brightened. "Is the other fellow here? Maybe I should tell him."

"No, he isn't. Look, is this something to do with the Cottis Wood murder? Is there something you want to add to what you said already?"

"Yes. I saw your appeal in the paper. See, the police questioned me last week, and I almost told them then." Suddenly she ripped the leaf apart along its spine. "I was scared, see. I mean, I know I've been stupid. Can't you pass on information without revealing your source?"

I felt a twinge of alarm. "What are you talking about?"

"Well, about that night. You know, the night of the murder. I said Mr Redfern was in his room all evening." She hesitated, staring at the milky sap oozing on to her hands from the leaf. I was horrified; I happened to have seen the receipt for the plant. "He told me to say that," she added.

"What do you mean – he told you to say he was in his room? Why should he do a thing like that?"

She dragged one thigh bulkily over the other in an effort

235

to cross her legs. "Well, he always did. I mean I knew he was up to something but I thought – well, cheating on his wife. Lots of 'em do it. He used to give me money and buy me drinks, and he was ever so nice. He said if anyone ever came asking for him I was to say he'd been in his room all evening and wasn't to be disturbed. He never said anything about the police! I never meant to lie to the police, but they didn't tell me what they were investigating. I didn't think," she added, pleadingly.

"Wait a minute. You're saying Mr Redfern *didn't* stay in his room that evening? He went out? What time was that?"

"About eight o'clock."

"Did he say where he was going?"

Joyce said nothing.

"I'm not going to pay you anything, you know. If you're making this up it won't do you a bit of good."

She looked disappointed, but she shrugged. "I'm not making it up. I'm scared, see. Look." She reached into her pocket and produced an envelope containing money, and a piece of paper torn from a notepad.

"He put this through my door," she said, handing me the paper. "He knows where I live."

I took the paper from her. Scrawled on it was the message, "Joyce. I won't forget. J."

"You could've written it yourself," I said, handing it back to her. I was shaken, but I knew better than to believe Joyce. I didn't think she'd recognise the truth if it leapt up out of a hole in the pavement and bit her.

"I didn't make it up!" she exclaimed, round eyed. "I wish the other fellow was here."

Actually, so did I. "All right." I sat down next to her. "You are now saying that Mr Redfern came regularly to your hotel, went out for the evening, and told you to tell anyone who came asking about him that he'd been in his room all evening, doing paperwork, is that right?"

"Yes. Something like that."

"You let my colleague and me believe you were having an affair with him. Are you now saying that's not true?"

She made a face. "I never slept with him. It's not my fault what you thought."

"All right. You say he went out about eight on the night of the murder. How can he have, if his car had been stolen?"

She shook her head. "I think he made that up." She reddened. "The police will go spare, won't they? They'll put me away! I didn't think!"

I stared out through the foyer at the Christmas lights winking in the window of the department store opposite.

"Look, it doesn't mean he's the murderer," I said. "It doesn't mean anything of the kind. You were probably right – he's probably been seeing another woman. That's what Pete thought," I added, half to myself. "In fact it was probably Pete he expected to come enquiring about him at the hotel. After all, if Helen were to suspect he was up to anything in Hudderston, then she probably would – " I was trying to put the pieces together but they wouldn't quite fit.

Joyce was staring at me. "He was weird," she said, suddenly. "He used to come back from wherever he'd been and buy me a drink in the bar. I liked that, 'cos most people in hotels treat you like shit. Anyway, he'd be all agitated and funny – talking to himself, sort of, and not to me. Do you know what I mean? He kept on about having no choice, and how he was a fool. He said he wished he could stop listening to the voice in his head."

"The voice in his head? I don't believe you! You're making this up! *Honestly!*"

Joyce shrugged. She uncrossed her legs, swung them up and down and studied her feet.

"I'm not," she said, stubbornly, giving me another long, under the eyelashes look. She glanced at the clock behind the Receptionist's desk. "I've got to go. I'll be late at Johnsons'."

She rose to her feet, and I followed her towards the door.

"Oh, yes," she said, turning. "About that night. There was something else I specially noticed in the bar. About Mr Redfern's feet."

"What about his feet?"

"Well, his shoes, and his trouserlegs. His trousers were all splashed with water, and his shoes – " She pointed down at my feet. "His shoes were all covered in a thick sort of mud. Just like yours are now."

I chewed the blue bit off the end of my biro and crushed it tentatively between my molars. My gums twinged comfortingly. In front of me, the telephone number of Zircon Water Softeners sat innocently on my notepad, waiting for me to dial it. There had to be a reasonable explanation. I only had to ring the number to find out what it was.

Mr Heslop returned from lunch and regarded me thoughtfully. He was about to speak when I lifted the receiver and began dialling John's number. Shrugging, he departed to his office.

"John," I said, when the girl had put me through. "It's Chris."

He didn't answer, and I knew in that instant that he knew exactly why I was calling.

"Chris," he said.

"I've just had a visit from Joyce," I began. "Joyce at the Eldon Lodge."

"Yes."

He wasn't going to make this easy.

"Well, why did you do it for Christ's sake?" I asked, desperately. "Why? I just don't understand."

"Let me shut my door, Chris," he said. There was a brief silence. I could hear him crossing and recrossing his room.

"Have you told the police yet?" he asked. "Or Pete? Have you told Pete?"

"Not yet." I waited. This was impossible. "Why don't you tell them yourself? I'm sure it would be the best thing?"

"Why would it be? Look." He sounded exasperated. "It won't help, will it? It won't put the past right. Think about it, what it'll do to Helen. Whatever you may think I love her very much."

"John," I said. "You knew you couldn't get away with it. You knew they'd get on to you. It was just a matter of time – you knew that, didn't you?"

238

"Oh God, yes. I knew that when Pete rang the other night."

"Well, then – "

He groaned. "I don't know what to say to you. You must think I'm a pretty awful person." I said nothing. "Look, I'd like to explain the whole thing to you, Chris. Please, before you tell anyone else. If we're going to be related – "

I shuddered at the thought, dropping the phone.

"Are you still there?" asked John. "Let me come and talk to you about it. I can explain everything."

Still plausible to the end, I thought. I took a deep breath. "I don't understand you, and I don't want to understand you," I said. "You disgust me. The only thing I'll do for you is keep my mouth shut until tomorrow. And I'm not doing that for you – I'm doing it for Helen. Give yourself up!" Without giving him time to answer I slammed down the phone and held it there, willing it to weld itself to its rest.

It was three o'clock in the afternoon. I had just lifted my hand from the receiver when the thing rang again, setting every nerve in my body jangling. I didn't want to answer it. I didn't want to listen to John's tales of an abused childhood, or whatever else he was going to come up with. But it wouldn't stop ringing so I lifted it and put it to my ear without speaking.

"Hallo? Hallo? Is anyone there?" The voice was Carol's.

"Oh, Carol," I said, relieved.

"Got you at last," she said. "I tried to ring this morning. You'll never believe it but it's finally come to me. Am I too late?"

"Sorry – what for?"

"Mr Demarco. I finally remembered where I saw the name. It was on one of the cheques – you know, the ones Mark sends out for signature. I expect he must be one of our sub-contractors, or something. Don't know how Rosemary would have met him, though."

"One of your sub-contractors?"

"Yes. Well, not mine – Taylors'. I keep forgetting I've left. Taylors use quite a lot of sub-contractors these days, specially on big contracts. It's funny he isn't in the phone book.

239

Anyway, there it is. By the way," she added, with heavy emphasis. "Isn't it exciting – that story in the *Advertiser*? Mr Victor must be hopping mad. I suppose that must have been the wrongdoing Rosemary was on about. Do you suppose she wrote to the *Advertiser* about it, too, and they managed to ferret it out? Wasn't it clever of them?"

I covered my face with my free hand. "Yes, it was."

"Well, honestly, fancy Mr Victor doing a thing like that! You wouldn't believe it, would you? You know what my Steven says – *he* says – "

I wasn't in the least interested in what Steven said or thought, but I listened to it anyway and made appropriate noises. Afterwards, I rang one of Pete's colleagues and told him I'd simply got to speak to Pete, that it was a matter of life and death. The colleague seemed to think this was extremely funny, but he said he'd do his best.

Of course the correct and sensible thing to do at this point was to dial the number of Hudderston Central Police Station and ask for either DI Carver or DS Horton. I might have got a "scoop" out of it; they might have let me ride down to Maidstone with them in the Panda car, to be in at the arrest. But I didn't think of that. I didn't want to be in at the arrest; I wanted to be as far away as possible.

Gillian was making a nuisance of herself in the newsroom with a stepladder and a box full of gold tinsel. In order to avoid having to give advice on where she might best stick her drawing pins, I busied myself tidying up the Tindall file. On Monday I'd have to hand it over to whoever was assigned to cover the dramatic story of the arrest of Rosemary's murderer. I decided I'd impress Mr Heslop by having the file completed. I rang Mark Williams at Taylors.

Taylors' phone rang for a very long time, and was finally answered, to my surprise, by Mark himself. He sounded hoarse.

"We've got no further statement to make," he snapped.

"Please wait," I begged. "I'm not ringing about the *Advertiser* story. This is personal. As you know I spent a lot of time on the Rosemary Tindall murder, and the police are about to make an arrest. I just want to know – to tie up all the loose ends – this Mr Demarco. You said you didn't know him, but I understand that in fact he's one of your firm's sub-contractors."

"One of our sub-contractors," repeated Mark, flatly.

"Yes. Carol saw his name on a cheque." In the background I could hear another phone ringing, and someone shouting. "All I want is his new address so I can add it to my file."

There was a long silence.

"Hallo?" I queried. "Are you still there?"

He cleared his throat. "It's the middle of a Friday afternoon," he said. "I'm busy. I've got a lot of work to do. What time do you go home?"

"Oh! About five."

Mark Williams muttered something that was incomprehensible and probably unpleasant, and cut me off.

I stayed in the office until five twenty, hoping Pete would ring. I kept myself busy doing all the things I'd been avoiding doing over the past few weeks – anything to prevent myself having to think about John, and Rosemary, and Helen. Just before leaving I had one last go at getting hold of Pete.

"He should be half way down the M6," said the colleague. "Didn't he ring you, love? I gave him your message."

"No, he didn't."

"Not my fault, love. It is Friday. I'll leave a message on the night desk, if you like. He was probably put off by the life and death bit."

"Yes," I agreed, sharply. "He probably was."

I replaced the receiver and stood up. The newsroom was empty, and its distant corners filled with dark shadows. For a moment I thought one of the shadows moved, and that was when I remembered Joyce. Joyce, whose evidence could put John in prison; Joyce, who, in half an hour – I checked my watch – would be starting her shift at the Eldon Lodge. God, why hadn't I thought of this before? John knew her address, he knew what time she started and finished work –

I ran down the stairs to the car park, my heels echoing hugely up the stairwell. In the basement, the central heating boiler rumbled dyspeptically into the empty building, and the door to the street slammed shut in the wake of one of the tele-sales girls. I stepped out into the darkness just in time to see her disappear with an armful of Christmas shopping and her white boots catching the light. My car key gripped comfortingly in my hand, I began to run across the car park. Somewhere close by I heard the whine of a reluctant starter motor, and an engine throbbed into life. Joyce would be hurrying along towards the Eldon Lodge Hotel, probably thinking about her little boy and her money problems, not listening to footsteps closing up behind her . . . The car that had started a few moments ago was swishing gracefully through the puddles and potholes that pockmarked the tarmac, and I knew it was getting close. But I was thinking about Joyce and about John, and the length of piping he carried in his car. I may have thought at the last moment, when it was too late to do anything about it, that it was odd the car didn't have its lights on, but I didn't even think of running until the driver had pulled across my path with his door open.

21

I shook my head and stars spewed out into the blackness, mingling with red shafts of pain. I groaned and opened my eyes, with difficulty identifying the familiar shapes of a gear lever and handbrake, viewed from beneath. As I blinked at the gear lever, a hand covered in short black hairs descended on it and rammed it into a new position.

"What're you doing?" I asked, not recognising the hand, but thinking somehow that this must be Keith. "This is stupid. I think you've broken my wisdom tooth."

The hand disappeared from view. Lights were scudding wildly but rhythmically across the interior of the car, street lights, I guessed, and I could see a dark stain spreading across the fabric of the seat my head was resting on.

"I'm bleeding!" I could feel the wetness in my hair with my fingers, and that set the adrenalin flowing as well. I began to struggle out of the footwell. I wasn't scared, I was furious at Keith's behaviour. "This is just about the stupidest thing you've ever done," I muttered, and then I stopped, because I'd got far enough out of the footwell to see that this wasn't Keith. This was someone else, someone –

He lifted his hand again, and this time he was holding a length of pipe. Suddenly we were in darkness. I cringed back down into the footwell, moaning, waiting for the blow.

"You stay down," said the voice I'd been half expecting to hear again on the telephone this afternoon. "You stay down or I'll make you stay down."

I gave a gasp of surprise and breathed in the faint scent of wintergreen.

"Why are you doing this?" I asked. "I don't understand why you're doing this to me."

It was Mark Williams' turn to be shocked.

"You don't know? You don't know?" he repeated, and

for a moment I thought he was going to stop the car. Then his hand came down again on the gear lever and he accelerated jerkily. "Oh, but you'd have worked it out – even *you* would have worked it out in time. *I'm* Demarco, that's why."

"*You're* Demarco? How can you be?"

He laughed derisively. "Oh dear, it's so simple. I've been writing cheques from Taylors to myself. It's called embezzlement. The Fraud Squad don't like it very much."

"Oh." Oh, of course. That subdivided house of Mrs Kaussmann's, where mail sat waiting unforwarded for previous tenants to call and collect it. A perfect address for someone who'd never existed. "But why did you do it? I thought your wife had a private income."

"My wife?" He laughed. "My wife," he repeated, as though the word was a particularly unpleasant expletive. "She thinks she owns me. Thirty years I've put in with her. Do you think her father would have let me walk away from her with any of his money? I was only taking what I was entitled to, from a bastard who wouldn't pay me what I was worth. How did you get hold of the name Demarco anyway?"

"Rosemary had your bank statement in her purse."

The car swerved violently to the left.

"Silly bitch," Mark Williams remarked, venomously. "The stupid, stupid bitch."

"Why did you give it to her?"

"To show her I was serious about leaving my wife. I told her I was putting the money away for our future together – as if I wanted to swap one silly bitch for another."

"I see," I said. "So when you ended the affair with Rosemary she threatened to turn you over to the authorities."

He took his eyes off the road for long enough to give me a stare loaded with malice. "Of course she didn't. She loved me. She thought God wanted us to be together, and his mysterious ways allow for embezzlement, apparently, his wonders to perform," he added, sarcastically.

The car slowed down. We were in traffic. I began to wonder if I could get the door open without him noticing. I edged across the seat towards it.

"So why did you kill her?"

He laughed again. "What does it matter? I killed her because she was a stupid bitch who didn't know a good thing when it looked her in the face. Victor Taylor – well, you know all about Victor and his ways of winning friends and influencing people. *I* found out about that when he added a couple of Metros to our car leasing contract and I knew no one on the firm was driving them. I thought this Douglas woman might be his mistress."

Central locking, I thought suddenly, with a sinking heart. This car was bound to have central locking.

"Rosemary did some PA work for Victor and found out about the little soirées he had at the farm. We pieced it together. It was perfect. I said to Rosemary – we've got the bastard! He wants to be an MP – one day we'll really screw him! And do you know what? She wouldn't have it. Embezzlement was OK, but people enjoying themselves – no. And it was just about then that Petra put her oar in between us and we had to cool it." He executed a sudden emergency stop and swore under his breath. I hit the top of my head on the bottom of the glove compartment and bit my tongue.

"So Rosemary thought things out by herself and decided the time had come to do her Christian duty," said Mark, bitterly. "She came round to see me and told me about it. I didn't mean to kill her, but she wouldn't listen. She said she was going to leave Taylors and work for the Church, but she'd got to put things right with her conscience first."

"So you *did* see her on the Monday night!" I interrupted, disgusted by the taste of my own blood.

"Yes. How did you know? She thought Petra would be out with her lunatic friends and knocked on my study window – luckily Petra was pissed out of her head because sodding Jerry hadn't turned up – " We had stopped at what seemed to be a busy junction. Mark tensed, leaning over me threateningly. "I stood on the patio and tried to reason with her – "

I decided that leaping up screaming wouldn't do me any good.

"She said she was trying to make up her mind whether to go to the papers with a copy of the car hire document. I said to her, do what you like, leave your husband, go into a nunnery – anything – but *don't* do anything about Victor and his little game."

"Why did you want to protect Victor Taylor?"

He made an impatient noise. "I didn't want to protect Victor Taylor! I couldn't give a toss about him. But she'd've got me into trouble as well! We'd've had the Inland Revenue and the Fraud Squad down on us like a ton of bricks – VAT, everything. I told her that. And do you know what the silly bitch said?" The car jerked forward suddenly. "She said if I went to prison she'd wait for me. She said no matter what happened she would always be there for me." He laughed, and seemed to be expecting a sympathetic response. He didn't get one. "So that's when I hit her, with one of Daniel's bloody exhaust pipes, I think – "

We made another left turn, plunging into total darkness.

Mark Williams' voice kept coming out of the blackness. He had a voice like cold water on a cold night. "I didn't panic," he said. "I knew I could think it out calmly and logically. Petra was semi-conscious from pills and booze, so I left her and took Rosemary's body to the woods. First I tried to cover it with branches, but then I had the idea of making it look like one of the Face Murders. Petra's little terrorist friends had very kindly left a couple of shotguns in our garage."

"So you went into Taylors the next morning and told Gail Rosemary was sick. You knew her husband was away – "

He changed gear clumsily. Maybe he was getting nervous.

"I slipped back to the woods the next evening with the gun. Petra had sent me out for more gin for her beloved – I was only gone fifteen minutes, not long enough to dent my alibi. But nobody even asked me for one. Except you."

I frowned. "It must have taken you a little while to steal the car from the hotel car park."

"Oh, that! That was the best part. I never touched that car. It was already parked in the layby when I arrived, and it was still there when I left. That was a real gift from the Gods. The police have wasted so much time on that damn Granada – " He laughed. "If it wasn't for that bloody woman

246

at the *Advertiser* I'd be completely in the clear. I thought I'd got away with it. But then anyway – there'd still be you."

The car coasted slowly to a halt, its wheels squelching in mud. A twig cracked, he switched off the engine, and then there was silence.

"Right," he said. "Get up."

I looked up. From somewhere, a faint glow illuminated the trunks of trees.

I didn't move. He said "Get up", again, and reached towards the back seat of the car. When he turned back he was carrying what television had taught me to recognise as a shotgun.

"Get up and get out of the car," he said, his voice rising an octave.

"I can't – I won't – "

"You will. You'd better!" He jabbed me in the neck with the gun, reaching for the doorhandle. The car door opened and I half fell out of it into the mud. He followed me across the passenger seat.

"Keep – on – going." His voice sounded taut and flat, like an overstretched rubber band on the point of breaking. I got up, clinging to the warm bonnet of the car, and trying to remember what the layby looked like in daylight, whether there was anything – a branch, a brick, anything – that I could get hold of –

Mark Williams jabbed me in the back with the gun, propelling me towards the gate. In the light from No. 1 Cottis Villas, I could make out the rusted bolt, the broken remains of a padlock. I turned round.

"You can't do this," I said. "You can't shoot me here. This isn't how the Face Murderer disposes of his victims. I won't go."

By way of answer, he drew the gun backwards and jabbed it at me. He was carrying it awkwardly against his hip with his left hand – his right held the ugly shape of the length of piping. I'd been right: he planned to do to me what he'd done to Rosemary. The hairs on the back of my neck began to rise. No matter what happened, I couldn't turn my back on him now. I couldn't walk into the woods, a lamb to the slaughter, and wait for my skull to splinter into my brain.

Mark Williams brandished the piping menacingly.

"Move, you bitch, move!"

"No!" I screamed, and energised by the scream, lunged forward and grabbed at the barrel of the shotgun. With both hands I twisted at it, desperate to wrest it from his grip before he could point it into my stomach. For the first time in my life I could feel every inch of my intestines, every part-digested morsel of food they contained, every pulsing nerve in my spine. And this wasn't going to work. I hadn't enough strength to pit against his arm, even his left arm, and we both knew it. We struggled round in a tortured circle, and with each step I lost ground. Like a red hot poker the gun muzzle nudged hard into my hip bone. If he'd pulled the trigger then he could have blown the lower half of me into the middle of the road, but he didn't; I suppose he knew he still had the advantage, and decided to stick to his original plan. He raised the pipe in readiness to smash it down on my skull. I screamed, releasing the gun barrel and ducking hopelessly, just as his right arm reached its zenith. I didn't mean to, but I caught him off balance. Suddenly he'd skidded and reeled backwards against the gate. I heard him grunt, and the gun must have slipped from his grasp while he groped to save himself. It landed heavily on the soft verge near my foot.

Blood pounded in my head, blurring my vision. Mark Williams was struggling to his feet. I dived towards the gun, found the smoothness of the wooden butt amongst the wet grass, and grabbed it. Somewhere I'd read that if you fire a shotgun at someone at close range you're bound to hit something: an arm, a knee, an eye. I wouldn't get another chance. I aimed it towards the figure rising up out of the darkness, and fired.

I rolled over on to my right side, and instantly regretted it, because there was a lump the size of a quail's egg just above my ear. The clock glowed reluctantly in competition with sunlight filtering through the worn curtain: 10.04 – a.m., presumably. I sat up in bed, confused and dry-mouthed from the valium the police doctor had given me. Pete's pillow was plump and undented. I got up. I'd had this dream about phones ringing, but that was probably all it was. I went to the bathroom and had a long, hot shower, leaving the door open, just in case. While I dressed I glanced casually downstairs towards the phone, as though doing so might make it ring, but it just sat there, refusing to oblige.

On the doormat next to my mud encrusted shoes lay two long, white envelopes. One of them was addressed to me and marked "Private and Confidential", and the other was also addressed to me, but in unfamiliar masculine handwriting. Puzzled, I opened it. It contained a computer printout of car registration numbers together with names and addresses, and attached to it was a note: "Hope this will help. Tell Pete we are now all square. Regards, Hal". I tucked it into my handbag together with my solicitor's letter. Next to the phone sat the message pad with Joe/Jo's phone number scrawled on it. It gazed at me mutinously, like a spot that had got to be picked. Taking a deep breath, I lifted the receiver and began dialling Joe/Jo's number. I wanted Pete back, and if I'd got to fight some glamorous American with perfect teeth and ear to ear lip gloss to get him, then so be it. I glanced at my chipped fingernails and buffed them on my jeans pocket.

"Hi," said Josie's voice, sounding throatier than on her answerphone.

"I'd like to speak to Pete, please," I said, stiffly.

"Pete who?"

"Pete Schiavo."

"Oh, *sure*, I know him!" Her accent was reminiscent of Californian sunshine, flat, tanned stomachs, and surfing movies. It did not endear her to me. "He's not here, though. Who's that?"

"Chris."

"Oh, Chris, *sure*! I've heard a lot about you. Pete's just crazy about you, that's all we ever hear about. What makes you think he's here right now?"

"Well – he's not *here*, and he gave me your number."

"Oh, right, well, I haven't seen him since last Friday. He spent the night here – on my couch," she added – rather pointedly, I thought. "Jees, I hope he's OK. I can't imagine where he'd be if he's not with you."

"Can't you?"

"No, I can't. But I wouldn't worry, Chris. I've known Pete on and off for ten years, and believe me, he always turns up again. Probably on the floor of some bar somewhere!" she suggested, laughing. People always think it's funny when other people's partners end up on the floors of bars. "Say, we must all get together some time. I'd really like that. You have a house in the country, don't you? Maybe a party of us could come down and we could all go horseriding or something. What do you say?"

"Well, Tipping's not exactly – " If she'd lived in the UK for ten years and still thought that beyond the GLC area fox hunts and genteel country houses stretched from horizon to horizon, there wasn't much point in arguing. "All right, some time, perhaps."

My front doorbell rang.

"Sorry to bother you, Jo," I said, fervently hoping I'd ruined her breakfast.

The tall figure on the doorstep turned out to belong to John Redfern. He looked at me, looked at his watch, and said, "Sorry, I suppose you were sleeping in. You didn't hear the phone."

So it had been him on the phone.

"Where's Pete? What happened to your face? Oh." He looked embarrassed.

"It's not what you think," I protested, but he was looking at his watch again and clearly had something else on his mind.

"Look, can I take you out for a coffee? I know what you said on the phone – and I will tell Helen, honestly. I'm going to do the right thing. Chris, I've driven all the way from Maidstone and I've got half an hour. Won't you hear me out?"

"Well – " I stared at the wretched phone. I'd no idea, of course, what he was talking about. "All right."

He took me to a nearby café and we ordered coffee and pancakes. He was tense and edgy, and his hand shook as he rearranged the cruets and the menu on the table top.

"I will tell her," he said. "It's just a question of finding the right time." He hesitated. "How much time do you think I've got before the police – "

250

"Actually, John," I said. "The police know now who killed Rosemary Tindall. I don't think they'll be interested in you any more."

"Oh." He stared at me uncertainly, then let out a relieved chuckle. "Of course, this doesn't change anything, but — wow, thank Christ! Maybe — maybe we won't actually have to involve the police at all — " he added, pleadingly.

I dropped my gaze to my coffee. The radio began playing John Lennon's "So this is Christmas", a song I have always disliked.

"Look, I know how it must seem to you, but let me explain how it happened," began John. "The irony is that *I'm* really the injured party. *I'm* the one who was abused. I did time for her, you know. She chucked a brick through some woman's window and it hit her — I said I'd done it to get her off the hook — I've got a criminal record! Can't you understand why I did a runner and changed my name? I just wanted to escape from an appalling situation!"

I nodded, trying to look cautiously sympathetic instead of baffled.

"Of course, I should have divorced her — but, well, time passed. She could have been dead for all I knew. In between the bouts of aggression, when she was normal, she sometimes talked of suicide."

"Suicide?" I interrupted.

"Yes. I mean, not that I wanted her to do that or anything. It all started after her abortion, and believe me, that was *not* my idea. It was her career. She'd just landed a job with a top advertising agency and when she found she was pregnant she panicked. She never seemed to recover from it emotionally. That was when these bouts of aggression started and everything began to go downhill. Some sort of hormone imbalance — PMT. Well, I expect she told you." He shook his head. "The tragedy of it is, of course, that these days she'd've got a sympathetic hearing from the medical profession. Then? Well — do you know they even gave her electric shock treatment?"

"Jennifer Saunders!" I whispered, round-eyed.

He nodded absently. "I got involved with Helen without meaning to. You know how these things are. Eventually it just got too late to turn round and say, 'Hey, by the way, I've got a wife in a nuthouse somewhere I'm still married to – ', and anyway, like I said, she could have been dead." He sighed. "God, it's been like a nightmare. You wouldn't believe what happened. Helen and I got married, and not two months later Jenny got in touch. She'd had somebody trace me through the Sally Army. Well, what could I do? She was cured, so she said, but she was wrecked and institutionalised – I've been popping over to see her whenever I could."

John Lennon made way for the weather bulletin.

"And to make matters worse," continued John, "about a year after Jenny got herself nicely installed in that cottage near the Manning Green Institute, *Pete* came back from the Gulf and got himself a job on the *Tipping Herald*. It was like a disaster waiting to happen! I found this awful grotty hotel I thought no one I knew was likely to use and made friends with the little receptionist there."

"She thinks you're the Face Murderer," I remarked, failing to mention that I'd also come to this conclusion. "She's all ready to sell her story to the highest bidder. She says you talked about voices in the head."

He raised his eyebrows, then laughed. "I think I may have mentioned the voice of conscience a few times. That last time I came to visit Jenny, the night of the murder, the awful thing was I *saw* the murderer's car there – well, I presume it was the murderer's car. But I couldn't do anything about it because I'd already made up this dumb story about my car being stolen – and Jenny wouldn't have anything to do with the police. That's why I put her on to you."

The radio time signal bleeped loudly.

"John," I said, gravely. "I'm afraid there's something I've got to tell you." I touched his hand across the table. "Jennifer's dead. She killed herself yesterday morning."

His hand twitched under mine. The newsreader began talking about the latest negotiations in a long-running pay dispute.

"Oh," said John.

"*The top local news story this hour*," announced the radio, "*concerns the dramatic abduction last evening of a local news-paper reporter . . .*"

"Of course, it doesn't change anything," said John. "I've still got to come clean with Helen."

"*. . . just heard within the last few minutes that a man has been arrested after he attempted to seek medical attention for a minor gunshot wound.*"

Minor? There went my chance for an Annie Oakley award . . .

"*It's also understood this man may face charges in connection with the murder of another woman last month.*"

"I'm sorry you and Pete are having problems," said John, stirring his coffee. "It's nice to see things work out for people. I think everyone's entitled to a second bite at the cherry – don't you?"

I smiled weakly.

John looked at his watch. "Better get you back," he said. "The sooner I get home and find the right moment – "

Somehow, I just knew he never would.

The garage door was open and I could see the rear of Pete's MGB protruding from it. I dashed up the front path, ignoring the milk bottles just as everyone else had done that morning.

He was in the hall, one hand on the phone.

"Chris," he whispered, relieved, and took a step towards me. He touched a finger to my bruised cheek. "That looks like it hurts. Listen – I don't know what to say."

I took his hand from my cheek and gazed at it, studying the pattern of lines on his palm. It was a very young looking hand, one that had never been hit by hammers or immersed in bleach solutions.

"Do I owe you an apology?" I asked, without looking up.

"Shouldn't think so." The phone rang. He picked it up, disconnected the call, and dropped the receiver on to the hall table. Then he laughed nervously. "According to Helen and her solicitor, I'm immature, irresponsible, and impossible to live with. I shouldn't think anyone needs to apologise to me."

"No, you're not."

"Aren't I?"

"No. I'm sorry, Pete."

The phone began to emit angry clicking noises. Pete lifted it, opened the hall table drawer, pushed the phone into it, and slammed the drawer shut.

"What's the matter with the phone?" I asked.

"Idiots ringing up to interview you. Fiona rang, and Three Counties. I told them all to get stuffed – apart from Fiona, that is. She scares the shit out of me. Look, Chris, about Josie – Honestly, nothing happened. She's not my type, and even if she was, I'm totally committed to you. I love you – you're my last hope – I wouldn't risk screwing things up between us just for a night of not particularly satisfying passion. Especially not when I know the extent of your investigative powers, darling," he added, with a smile.

I smiled back. "All right, I believe you. But I wish you'd got in touch with me yesterday. Didn't you get my phone message?"

He grimaced. "Didn't you see what happened to the car? Some idiot motorcyclist drove into the side of me on a roundabout – I had to get the damn thing towed home this morning. I tried to ring you half a dozen times, but – "

I stared at him in horror. "Oh, God, had you been drinking? Your licence – "

"If I'd been drinking I'd've been going too fast for the bastard to get near me! No, I hadn't. And about the drinking – I'll cut down. Really I will. I'm not going to stop completely because I'm not an alcoholic, but I will cut down. What are you laughing at?"

"Nothing. You're sweet."

"That's not what you said last week."

"I know. I'm really sorry."

We went into the living-room, holding hands.

"Nobody's ever called me sweet before," said Pete. He pulled me round to face him. "Tell me honestly. Where do we stand with SuperKeith? Have we seen the back of him yet, or is he still hovering in the shadows with his Black and Decker and the latest Texas Homecare catalogue?"

I winced. "We've seen the last of SuperKeith," I said, and let my breath out in a long sigh.

He kissed me chastely on the lips. "Good. Tell me – was it a close run thing? No, on second thoughts, I think I'd rather not know. Look, I'm sorry, Chris, honestly, about the other night. It was unforgiveable, so I'm not going to ask you to forgive me. But can we start all over again?"

"Yes," I said, "I think we'd better."

He kissed me again, a bit less chastely, and departed to the kitchen to make coffee. When he'd gone I extracted my solicitor's letter from my handbag and opened it. It said they were pleased to inform me that Mr Keith Martin's solicitor had now replied to their various letters, and, subject to the vagaries of the legal system, I should be a free woman by next spring. A free woman? I smiled at a reflection of myself, dimly superimposed on to a framed photograph of Richard and Julie and Richard's tenth birthday cake. I don't think so. Not really.

ANNETTE ROOME

A REAL SHOT IN THE ARM

Chris Martin – housewife – was dead from the neck up until she joined the staff at the *Tipping Herald* and dead from the neck down until Pete Schiavo touched her.

The corpse she discovers on her first assignment, hanging from a fire escape, doesn't look to *her* like suicide – heroin addicts don't OD and then string themselves up. And what's the connection with the proposed property development in the most run-down part of town? Every one of her novice steps to find the truth leads Chris further into a web of police corruption, blackmail and civic disobedience.

Strange though, that it took death to drag her out of domestic desolation and back-smack her into life again, like a murderous midwife.

'One of the best crime novels I've read for a long time'
B M Gill

'A terrific debut for a wholly sympathetic, wryly witty sleuthess'
The Times

'Narrated with splendid comic disenchantment . . . this is an exhilarating debut'
The Sunday Times

HODDER AND STOUGHTON PAPERBACKS